Harper laughed, a surprisingly deep, husky laugh

Eddie realized it was the first time he'd heard her laugh, the sound grating pleasantly along his nerve endings.

But having her laugh at him wasn't funny.

"What?" he growled.

She shook her head. "It's just...you keep surprising me."

He studied her through narrowed eyes, figured she was telling the truth. He was edgy and amped up, worried about his son, and he hadn't reacted to a woman this strongly in longer than he could remember.

Couldn't remember the last time a woman had captured his thoughts. Had slipped into his dreams.

He edged closer, gratified and relieved when she didn't back up, just smiled at him. "You like surprises?" he asked, his voice gruff.

Her grin widened. "Love them."

"Good," he said.

Then he leaned in to kiss her.

Dear Reader,

I'm having such fun writing the stories in the In Shady Grove series. When I initially came up with the idea for the first book in the series, *Talk of the Town* (April 2013), I knew very little about the secondary characters. Now, having finished three In Shady Grove stories and starting a fourth, I'm constantly discovering new insights into the people who call Shady Grove home.

For instance, while I knew that Eddie Montesano, the middle son of the Montesano clan, was quiet and a bit shy, I had no idea he was so stubborn! Or that when he does speak, he usually manages to say the right thing.

I also knew that single mother Harper Kavanagh was a teacher and a recent widow. She was supposed to be sweet and perhaps a bit naive. Instead, she stormed onto the scene ready to take on the world—but afraid of moving on too quickly after the loss of her beloved husband. It was a conflict I hadn't planned on, but one that so moved me and seemed so real, I had no choice but to write it.

Yes, Eddie and Harper were full of surprises, taking me in different directions than I'd planned. I wouldn't want it any other way. After all, I may have drifted off the road I'd mapped out, but the destination remained the same: Happy Ever After.

Next year brings three more In Shady Grove stories—I hope you'll look for them! Keep an eye on my website, www.bethandrews.net, for publication details. Or drop me a line at beth@bethandrews.net. I'd love to hear from you.

Happy reading!

Beth Andrews

BETH ANDREWS

—

Caught Up in You

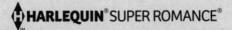

Recycling programs
for this product may
not exist in your area.

ISBN-13: 978-0-373-60814-0

CAUGHT UP IN YOU

Printed in U.S.A.

ABOUT THE AUTHOR

While writing *Caught Up in You,* Romance Writers of America RITA® Award winner Beth Andrews survived her older daughter's graduation, her younger daughter's driving lessons and her son's causing her grocery bill to double during his summer home from college. In her free time, Beth can be found at the grocery store. Learn more about Beth and her books by visiting her website, www.bethandrews.net.

Books by Andrews

HARLEQUIN SUPERROMANCE

*The Truth about the Sullivans
**In Shady Grove

Other titles by this author available in ebook format.

For my sister Karen.

CHAPTER ONE

EDDIE MONTESANO SQUIRMED on his seat like a fish on a hook and sighed. Hell, a few minutes in his son's classroom and he'd somehow regressed to the second-grader he'd been twenty-five years ago, uncomfortable on the hard chair, anxious to get away from the rigid rules and expectations.

Terrified the teacher would call on him to answer a math problem she'd written on the chalkboard. Or worse, ask him to read aloud from their reading book. It'd been torture, speaking in front of so many people—even if they had been his classmates. Humiliating to have them all witness his struggles sounding out simple words.

He hadn't been able to sit still then, either. He'd always been moving—tapping his fingers, shaking his leg or wiggling his ass. He'd been lectured, plenty of times, about not fidgeting, but it hadn't done any good. He'd had too much energy, like a live current zipped through him, making his thoughts race, pushing him to move, move, move.

Though he'd taught himself to be more self-contained, to focus on one task at a time, he'd still much rather be doing than sitting. Especially when sitting made him feel like that restless, nervous kid again.

He stretched out his legs. His left knee whacked the bottom of the desk, the steel toe of his work boot hit the chair across from him, shoved it out a few inches.

What was with this setup? The desks were in groups of four so that half the class faced the blackboard, the other half the teacher's desk. It didn't make any sense to him. The kids were staring at each other, two by two. Seemed like a distraction.

Then again, the teacher was a woman, and a lot of things women did made no sense to him.

He checked the time. Eight minutes until his meeting with Mrs. Kavanagh, Max's teacher. Not that Eddie was in a hurry to see her again, but he would like to know what was behind this whole parent/teacher thing. Max had assured Eddie he wasn't in trouble, and Eddie hadn't received any calls from the principal so far this year about Max's behavior.

But the note Mrs. Kavanagh had sent home requesting a meeting had been vague enough that Eddie wondered if he'd gotten the whole story from his son.

Max had a habit of keeping his thoughts to himself. Especially if he'd done something wrong. And while Eddie agreed it was better, safer, to keep your thoughts in your head, he wished his son would just admit when he'd messed up so Eddie could tackle the problem, fix it and move on.

He glanced around the room. Shelves filled with row after row of neatly lined-up books took up the entire wall behind the teacher's desk. A white wooden rocking chair was tucked into the corner in front of a circular rug next to the chalkboard. Artwork, graded papers, a huge calendar and equally large schedule covered the walls, along with bright banners and posters—most sporting a cartoon or picture of a baby animal—encouraging the kids to read, imagine and go for the gold. Assuring them they were a team, books were treasures waiting to be discovered and that with hard work, anything was possible.

A nice sentiment, that last one. Complete bullshit, but nice.

He was all for doing one's best, putting in full effort and sticking with a job until it was done. But believing that if you worked hard enough, long enough, you'd achieve your goals no matter what, was setting these kids up for disappointment.

And possibly years of therapy.

Eddie had worked his ass off to save his marriage and look where it got him. Divorced, raising his son on his own and constantly trying to be everything to Max. Hoping he was doing enough. Being enough.

Worrying that most days he didn't even come close.

But he'd keep trying, doing his best to make up for failing at his marriage and not being able to keep Max's mother in their lives. And not because he was staring at a poster of a kitten at the end of a rope—literally—telling him to Never Give Up.

He'd do anything for his kid.

"This is the drawing I told you about," Max said, shoving a picture in Eddie's face.

Eddie leaned back, the hard edge of the metal chair digging into his shoulder blades as he took the paper. He raised his eyebrows. It was good. Damn good.

His kid never ceased to amaze him.

"It's Pops's pumpkin patch," Max said. He pointed at the cottage in the background. "See? That's his house."

"It looks just like it." Right down to the curtains in the windows and brick walkway winding its way from the back door to the garden.

Green vines tangled around fat, bright orange pumpkins. Beyond the cottage, trees in all their autumn glory of copper, red and auburn covered the rolling hills. And standing to the left, a hoe in one hand, his other hand tucked behind his back, was Big Leo Montesano. Max had perfectly captured Eddie's grandfather, from the top of the straw hat on Pops's balding head to the tips of the black rubber boots he wore when gardening.

"It's great, bud," Eddie said.

Shifting from foot to foot, Max beamed. "Mrs. Hewitt said it was the best one out of the whole second grade."

"Mrs. Hewitt?"

"She's the art teacher." Now Max hunched his shoulders. Chewed on his thumbnail. "I forgot I'm not supposed to tell anyone that."

"You're not supposed to tell anyone she's the art teacher? Is she some sort of spy?"

Max frowned as if Eddie was the one not making sense. "I'm not supposed to tell anyone she said my picture was the best."

Eddie's heart swelled. Christ, but he loved his kid. Max was tall for his age and stocky, with Eddie's hazel eyes and dark hair, and Lena's light coloring and nose. Shy around everyone but family, when he opened up, he was funny and entertaining as hell. Max went full throttle from the time he woke until he hit his bed and slept like the dead, recharging for another nonstop day.

He was Eddie's greatest joy. The best thing he'd ever done.

"We'll keep it between us." Eddie mussed Max's hair, making a mental note to get him to the barber sometime this week. "But I bet she's right."

Max stopped gnawing on his nail long enough to send Eddie a small, proud smile. "She is."

Eddie grinned. That was his boy. "How about we make a frame for this and give it to Pops."

"Yeah. He'll love it. He loves all my pictures. But we can't take it now. Not 'til Mrs. Hewitt says so."

"Okay. Maybe you should put it back, then."

Max did some sort of galloping walk over to the wide windowsill where the rest of his classmates' drawings were laid out. Afternoon sun streamed through the glass, raising the temperature in the room a good ten degrees. Sweat formed on Eddie's upper lip, along his hairline. Reaching behind him, he grabbed the sweatshirt at his shoulder blades and tugged it upward. Only to realize he was stuck, his lower back pressed against the chair holding the shirt in place. He scooted forward and rammed his stomach into the edge of the desk. He grunted. Banged his elbow when he tried to straighten.

"Shit," he muttered, his funny bone tingling painfully.

Someone cleared their throat, the sound delicate, feminine and, if he wasn't mistaken, subtly chastising.

The back of his neck heated with embarrassment. Standing, Eddie shoved the chair back. It toppled over. He sighed. Some days a man just couldn't win.

He yanked the sweatshirt off, avoided looking at the door while he tugged his T-shirt down, then righted the chair. Smoothing his hair—and realizing Max wasn't the only one who needed a trim—he turned. Scanned the curvy blonde in the doorway.

Harper Sutter—now Harper Kavanagh—didn't look much like the perky cheerleader she'd been in high school. Then she'd been petite with light brown hair that fell to the middle of her back. Now her hair was several shades lighter and at least six inches shorter, her face, hips and breasts fuller.

His gaze flicked to her chest.

Much fuller.

A tickle formed in the back of his throat. Interest—basic and purely physical—stirred. Ignoring it, he shoved his hands into his pockets, focused on her face. Same high, pronounced cheekbones and gray eyes that turned down slightly at the corners. Same full, heart-shaped lips.

He'd had a few fantasies—brief, insignificant fantasies—about her mouth.

Then again, he'd been seventeen. Sexy dreams had pretty much been a nightly experience.

Those lips curved into a bright smile. She switched her coffee cup to her left hand and offered him her right one. "Hello, Eddie. It's so nice to see you."

With a nod, he shook her hand. Though he'd known her since kindergarten, he'd never touched her before. Her palm was warm against his. Soft.

Awareness bolted through him. He acknowledged it was partly due to the remnants of the teenage fantasies playing in his head. Accepted it as a man's instinctual response to an attractive woman.

Acknowledged it, accepted it. Then let it—and her hand—go.

"I hope I didn't keep you waiting," she said.

"You didn't."

He wasn't sure if she'd meant it as a real concern or a reprimand for his being early. He gave a mental shrug. Didn't matter to him either way. He'd had a break at work so he'd taken off. No sense finding something to do for a few minutes so he could arrive precisely at four o'clock.

"Max," Harper said, sounding surprised when Max sidled up to Eddie, pressed against his side. "Still stuck here?"

Max lifted a shoulder.

She wrinkled her nose. "That's a drag. I can't wait to leave at the end of the day. Hey, would you do me a favor?" Before Max could even blink, she continued in her rapid-fire speech. "Could you walk—and by *walk* I mean that slow movement of putting one foot in front of the other that is not running, hopping or skipping—to the office to check if I have any mail?"

Seemed she knew Max well. He didn't do anything slowly. Except talk.

While Max headed toward the door, Harper gestured for Eddie to follow her as she crossed the room. His gaze fell to the sway of her hips. She had on tan pants and a long sweater the color of rust that molded to her ass. A wide brown belt accentuated the indentation of her waist and he wondered, briefly, what it would be like to set his hands there.

He stumbled, bumped into a desk.

She glanced over her shoulder at him.

His face burning, he stared resolutely at a spot somewhere above her head. Maybe he hadn't fully let that earlier awareness go.

"I appreciate you taking the time to meet with

me." She set her cup on the desk. "Although, I have to admit, I was hoping to speak with you alone."

"I didn't have time to find a sitter."

Hadn't taken the time to find one. Not when it wasn't necessary. He only asked for help with his kid when there was no other solution. Absolutely, positively no other solution.

"It's not a problem," she assured him. "But would you mind if I gave him something to keep him occupied while we talk?"

Eddie shrugged.

"I'll take that as a yes," she said cheerily, then gestured to the chair across from her desk. "Can I get you anything? There's coffee in the break room or—"

"Is Max in trouble?" Eddie loved his kid more than life itself, but that didn't mean he thought Max could do no wrong. Everyone made mistakes. Best if you owned up to them, learned from them and, most importantly, never repeated the same one twice.

Max was having a hard time with that last part.

"Trouble? No, he's not in trouble," she said slowly enough that he didn't believe her. "I thought we should touch base on a couple of things, that's all."

After sitting, she organized a pile of papers. He could practically see her organizing her thoughts, as well. Her desk was covered; papers and math workbooks were stacked in neat piles, a plastic bin sat empty at the corner. A stapler, tape dispenser and hole punch lined up with the edge of the desk.

Pencils, pens and markers were jumbled together in a wooden holder declaring that Teachers Have Class.

She was as tidy and put together as her desk, her hair smooth, her nails trimmed and painted a light pink.

He rubbed the frayed knees of his jeans. Wondered if he should have gone home, shaved first, but that would have been stupid, going all the way across town to comb his hair and rid himself of his day-old—okay, three-day-old—beard. He had no one to impress here. Nothing to prove. His kid was well dressed, well mannered and, other than a few scrapes in the playground last year, well behaved.

And well loved.

If Harper didn't see that, she wasn't as smart as her rank in their high school graduating class had indicated.

"No mail?" Harper asked as Max returned.

He shook his head.

"Thanks for checking. Would you like to play a game on the iPad while your dad and I talk?"

"Okay," he said quietly, his gaze flicking to his teacher's face before lowering again.

"Great." She took an iPad from her desk drawer, handed it and headphones to him. "Why don't you sit in the beanbag chair?"

He hurried to the corner and toed off his sneakers. Sitting cross-legged, he put on the headphones and, as easily as that, was cut off from the world, lost in whatever educational game Harper had on that tablet.

Those things were like magic.

"I was thrilled to see Max's name on my class list at the beginning of the year," Harper said, sounding as if she really meant it. "I had your niece and she was a pure delight."

Because Bree always worried about doing the right thing, loved to read and never got a grade lower than an A. Sort of like the woman before him. In school Harper had been one of the brainiacs. Popular with both students and teachers, she'd been incredibly smart and impossibly friendly.

It wasn't natural to be that nice all the time.

No surprise Harper thought highly of Bree. He didn't hold his niece's sweetness or intelligence against her. He loved her like crazy.

He just didn't want his son compared to her.

"Bree's a good girl," he said.

"She is. She must be in what…? Fifth grade now?"

"Sixth."

"Middle school? It doesn't seem possible. How's she liking it?"

"Fine." And what any of this had to do with Harper's reason for calling him to meet with her, he had no idea. Women. Why couldn't they just say what was on their mind? It would save everyone a hell of a lot of time and trouble.

"I'm glad she's doing well. It can be a big transition for some kids, that leap from elementary to middle school."

She looked as if she expected him to respond to that but since he had nothing to add, he kept quiet.

"Well," she said, "anyway, thank you for coming in today. I was sorry we didn't get a chance to talk at the open house."

He narrowed his eyes slightly. Straightened in his uncomfortable seat. Was that a reprimand? If it was, why couldn't she lay into him instead of making him guess whether or not she was pissed? "I was working."

When he wasn't working, he spent time with his kid, not running off to meetings and socializing. He wasn't going to apologize for it.

"Are you still at Bradford House?" Harper asked.

He nodded. Everyone wanted to know about Bradford House. Some were interested in the renovations Montesano Construction was doing at one of the oldest homes in Shady Grove, Pennsylvania. They wanted a description of every room, or an invitation to see the soon-to-be fully operational bed-and-breakfast themselves without actually paying to stay there.

Or they brought up Bradford House's owner, Neil Pettit, a hometown boy who was now one of the NHL's elite players. They wanted the latest gossip, insider information about Neil's reasons for buying the Victorian, his sister Fay's suicide attempt and his reconciliation with Eddie's younger sister, Maddie, a few months back.

Eddie drummed his fingers on his thigh. Waited for Harper to start with the inevitable questions or probing comments, ones designed to get answers to topics that were none of her business.

"It's so great that Neil and Maddie are together after all these years of living separate lives."

See?

He grunted.

She remained undeterred and, unfortunately, talk-ative. "It's so romantic." She leaned forward as if they were two good buddies sharing happy secrets and fun times. "High school sweethearts falling in love again."

Romantic. Christ.

Funny how so many people agreed with Harper. Guess they conveniently forgot how Neil took off after getting a sixteen-year-old Maddie pregnant. That he'd been in their daughter's life only part-time until recently.

Most people except Eddie and his two brothers. Hard to let something like that go, especially when it happened to your baby sister and niece. Eddie, James and Leo might forgive what Neil did—mainly because Maddie wanted them to. But forget? Not in this lifetime.

"I think it's wonderful Bradford House is being renovated. It's always been one of my favorite houses in Shady Grove," Harper continued. "I was by there last week. That wraparound porch you added is gorgeous."

"I didn't add it," Eddie said. He'd been working on a bathroom remodel across town when the exterior work had been done at Bradford House.

Her smile dimmed, going from supernova bright to regular shining-star glowing. "I meant *you* as in Montesano Construction."

He lifted his right shoulder.

"Okay," Harper said, drawing the word out. "Guess that's enough shop talk. No, no—" she held out her hand as if to stop him from speaking, though his mouth remained tightly closed "—really, I know you could go on and on and on about your work but let's stick to the subject at hand, shall we?"

Scratching his cheek—he really did need a shave—he narrowed his eyes. She was messing with him. He wouldn't have thought she had it in her, not when she looked all innocent and sincere.

"Max is a very sweet boy," Harper said as if she hadn't been yanking Eddie's chain. "He excels in art, has a real talent for it. Not that I'm an expert or anything but I know what I like." She smiled at her own lame joke, didn't seem to mind that Eddie didn't.

"I really enjoy having Max in my room. He's kind and thoughtful but a bit of a loner. If we could get him to open up more, to come out of his shell—"

"Being shy isn't a character flaw that needs overcoming," Eddie said quietly.

Max was fine the way he was, and if he wanted to

stay in his shell, so be it. As a kid, Eddie had been told to talk more, be more outgoing and friendlier. All he'd ever wanted was to be left in peace with his thoughts.

"No, of course it's not." Harper sounded confused, looked flustered and embarrassed. "I only meant it might be good for him to make a few friends."

Max had friends. Max had *a* friend, Eddie amended. Joey Malone, a kid he'd met in first grade. They were in different classes this year but still hung out.

"That why you wanted to see me?" Eddie asked. "To discuss Max's social life?"

She opened her mouth only to snap it shut and shake her head, as if getting rid of whatever she'd been about to say. "Actually, I want to discuss Max's progress so far this year. The first marking period ends in two weeks." She slid a yellow paper from the pile on her desk and held it out to him. "Maybe once you see his progress report, you'll understand why I'm concerned."

Eddie forced himself to take the paper. The diamonds in her wedding rings caught the afternoon sunlight so that it dappled across the top of her desk.

He rubbed his thumb around the base of his left ring finger. It'd been years since he'd worn his own wedding band, but he could still feel the weight of it. As the foundation of his marriage had become weaker, the gold ring signifying the vows he'd taken—the vows he'd given—had grown tighter. Heavier with the weight of his failure.

But then, Harper hadn't failed at marriage—she'd probably never failed at anything in her entire life. Her marriage hadn't ended due to lack of effort or love, but because her husband had been in the wrong place at the wrong time, an innocent bystander killed during a convenience store robbery in Pittsburgh last year. She still wore her ring.

Eddie had taken his off the moment Lena had shut the door when she'd walked out on their marriage. When she'd walked out on their son.

He'd never put one on again.

Bracing himself, he read Max's progress report. Exhaled heavily. One D. Four Fs.

"As you can see, Max is struggling in all subjects." Her voice was laced with compassion. She watched him with understanding.

He wished she'd knock it off. He didn't need her pity. Didn't want her kindness.

"What do we do?" Eddie asked.

She nodded as if that was the right thing to ask, the correct response. Great. Give him a gold star for being a concerned parent.

"Max has some issues focusing which, I believe, could be one of the factors affecting his schoolwork."

"I'll talk to him," Eddie said. "Tell him to pay more attention in class."

"That would be helpful, but I'm afraid it might not be enough. What I would like is your permission to have Dr. Crosby—one of the school district's psychologists—observe Max's behavior."

"Observe?" Like an animal in a test lab? Poked and prodded and singled out from his classmates.

"It's only to see if she agrees with my assessment."

"Your assessment." Yeah, he sounded like a parrot, repeating everything she said, but he couldn't figure out what the hell she was getting at. "You said he's not paying attention in class."

"Yes, but I'm concerned that lack of focus—along with other symptoms—could be signs of a bigger issue."

Eddie stiffened to the point he worried one errant breeze would break him into a million pieces. "What symptoms?"

"I'd rather not get too far ahead of ourselves until after Dr. Crosby—"

"What. Symptoms."

The only sign she gave that his low, dangerous tone bugged her was a small, resigned sigh. "Max has a hard time sitting still—"

"He's a boy. He has a lot of energy."

Her lips thinned but her tone remained calm. "He frequently fails to finish his schoolwork, even when given ample time to do so, and he often works carelessly. He shifts from one unfinished activity to another, has difficulty following through on instructions, working on his own and waiting for his turn in tasks, games and group situations. He's also easily distracted, often loses or misplaces items necessary to complete tasks—such as his pencil or workbook."

"He's seven." Eddie bit out the words, her list of the ways his son was lacking blowing through him, swirling around his head in endless repetition. "Kids misplace things and aren't always patient."

"True. And that may very well be the case here. But as Max's teacher, I feel it's in his best interest to have Dr. Crosby come in and give her opinion. If you'll just sign this—" she slid a paper in front of him "—we can get started."

Eddie glanced from the permission slip to the pen she held out and then to his son's grades, the black letters stark on the pale yellow background. He should sign the damn paper and let Harper do what she felt necessary, what she thought best. She was the teacher, the person entrusted with his son's care and education for the next eight months.

"What bigger issue could it be?" Eddie asked.

"I'd rather not speculate—"

"I'd rather you did."

She slowly lowered the pen. For the first time, she seemed reluctant to speak—must be a new sensation for her. "Max's behavior could…possibly…be symptoms of Attention Deficit Hyperactivity Disorder. But I'm not qualified to make any diagnoses," she added quickly. "Which is why I'd like Dr. Crosby's help."

"ADD," Eddie said, still trying to wrap his mind

around the fact there could be something wrong with his son. "Don't they put kids on drugs for that?"

"Medication is one option, but there are also modifications that can be made in the classroom. Instructional strategies and practices that can be implemented to help children with ADHD learn."

"So if Max has ADH—" he emphasized the H as she had "—D, and you use those strategies, his grades will improve?"

"Possibly."

The second *possibly* she'd given him in under a minute. When it came to his kid, Eddie preferred *definitely.* "What else is there?"

"There are other options." She averted her gaze as she moved the stapler to the left only to put it back exactly where it had been. "But let's not worry about any of that until we get through these first steps."

He had a child, was solely responsible for the well-being of another person. For making sure his son was healthy and happy and whole. It was his job to worry. And to get straight answers out of smiley, sunshiny teachers who were blowing smoke up his ass.

"What options?"

Her smile turned to steel. "Options we'll discuss after Dr. Crosby has made her observation."

Nudging the paper forward, she held out the pen again.

Eddie's fingers tightened, crumpling the edges of the progress report. Frustration coursed through him, hot and edgy. But worse than that was the fear. The terrifying thought that if Max was diagnosed with ADHD, he'd spend the rest of his life wearing that label. His peers would judge him, would think he was deficient in some way. He'd be put into a box, one he'd never be able to escape from.

Eddie wanted to slap the pen from Harper's hand. Wipe his arm across the top of her desk, knocking aside the wooden holder so that pens and pencils scattered over the floor. He wanted to tell her in no uncertain terms what she could do with her observation, her opinion and her sympathetic expression.

He looked at his son. Max was perfect, just the way he was. And Harper wanted some psychologist with more education than common sense to tell him there was something wrong with him? So Max would think he wasn't smart enough? Capable enough? Good enough?

There was only one response to that, one he was more than happy to give as he faced Harper.

"No."

CHAPTER TWO

HARPER KEPT THE pleasant, understanding smile on her face. But it cost her. Boy, did it cost her.

Because Eddie Montesano, with his dark scowl, broad shoulders and cool hazel eyes, was getting on her last nerve. She'd spent the day surrounded by seven-and eight-year-olds who were alternately loud, whiny, cranky, happy, hilarious and fabulous. And most of them had better manners than this man.

"I'm sorry," she said, though she had nothing to apologize for. Honestly, the man should be the one begging her forgiveness. "No?"

"I'm not signing that."

Her hand dropped to the desk with a thud. "Maybe I didn't make myself clear—"

"You did."

"Well, good. That's good," she said cheerily.

She would remain cheery, polite, in control and, above all else, professional. Friendly. She'd watch her tongue and choose every word carefully. She had a habit—some said a bad one—of speaking her mind. Which was fine in her personal life, but in her professional one? Not so good.

At least not according to Sam McNamara, Shady Grove Elementary School's principal.

She twisted her engagement ring. "Maybe you don't understand how important it is—"

"I'm not an idiot."

Something in his gruff tone, in his hard expression, gave her pause. Made her think she'd somehow insulted him. "I never thought—"

"We're done."

He stood. The man actually stood. And he'd dismissed her, as if he had the right to end this meeting. Stunned, she stared for a moment, her mouth slack, her mind reeling. She'd done everything right, the way it was supposed to be done. She'd talked to Max's first-grade teacher, had checked his file to get more insight into his schoolwork the past two years. Then she'd met with both Julie Giron, the school's guidance counselor, and Sam about her concerns, had gotten their go-ahead to bring up those concerns with Max's father.

The only way she'd veered away from the usual protocol in situations like this was by meeting with Eddie alone instead of with Julie and Sam. She'd thought Eddie would appreciate her discussing Max's situation with him one-to-one.

That was the last time she tried to be nice to someone just because they'd known each other since the first day of kindergarten and had relatives dating each other—his brother, her cousin.

Hurrying around her desk, she stepped in front of

him and smiled. Okay, it was more a baring of teeth, but surely she couldn't be faulted for one tiny slipup.

"Eddie, I'm not sure what the problem is," she said, all faux conciliatory and apologetic. She checked on Max, who was still engrossed in his game. "I certainly didn't mean to offend you in any way."

She waited. And what did she get for her patience? Nothing. Not even one of his nods or shrugs.

Easy to see where Max got his reserve from.

"It's important that we assess what issues Max is having so he can overcome them and reach his highest potential."

"Why? So you can bump up the school's test scores?"

"This has nothing to do with standardized testing." The bane of teachers everywhere. Luckily for her, they didn't start testing kids until third grade. "It has to do with helping Max."

Her only priority.

Eddie shifted closer, bringing with him the scent of sawdust. "Maybe this isn't Max's fault."

"I'm sorry. I'm having trouble following you." Hard to believe seeing as how he used as few words as possible to get his point across, but there you had it.

"If you did your job—did it better—Max wouldn't be having problems."

Her vision assumed a definite red tint, her fingers curled around the stapler.

She heard him, of course. He stood right before

her, close enough for her to see the starburst of gold around his pupils, to notice that his right front tooth slightly overlapped the left. She even understood what he'd said as his meaning had been crystal clear. But his voice was like a roar in her head. A whooshing wave that swept away all her good intentions and drowned any hope she had of remaining professional.

And it was all Eddie Montesano's fault. She'd tried to be polite. To not let her growing frustration with him show. But did he appreciate her efforts or the great strength of willpower it'd taken her not to simply lift the stapler and hit him upside the head with it? Did he consider what was best for his son or care that all she wanted was to figure out how they could work together to help Max?

No, no and triple no. He blamed her, *accused* her of not doing her job.

Oh, yeah, all bets were officially off.

"Max," she called loudly, setting the stapler on her desk and peeling her fingers off it. She tucked her hands behind her back—just to be on the safe side.

When Max looked up and took the headphones off, she forced her tone to remain light. Easy. No simple task when she was two seconds away from kicking his father in the shin. "Your dad and I will be in the hallway. Please wait here."

Eddie grabbed the sweatshirt and tugged it on. "I have nothing to say."

"That's a shock," she muttered. "It'll only take a

few minutes," she assured him from between gritted teeth when his head became visible again.

He glanced at Max, who watched them with wide eyes, obviously picking up on the tension in the room. Finally, Eddie brushed past her.

Fuming so hard she lifted her hands to her ears to make sure steam wasn't billowing from them, she followed him out into the hallway. She shoved her sleeves up to her elbows. She was sweating. She was actually sweating she was so angry. Her skin over-heated, her blood boiled. She shut the door with a quiet click, wishing she could slam it with a resounding bang, open it and slam it shut again.

"If you have a problem with me teaching your son," she said, proud of the composure that kept her tone calm, her temper in check despite the trembling of her fingers, "you may certainly take it up with the principal. But for the record, all I want is for my kids to do well. To succeed."

"*Your* kids?"

That composure cracked enough to have her lifting her chin, straightening her spine. "I'm with those children—your child—for close to eight hours a day, one hundred and eighty days of the year. I feel a connection to them, so yes, they're my kids. In a certain context."

More than a connection, she felt a responsibility toward them. It was up to her to help them reach their highest potential.

She crossed her arms. "How about we clear the

air so we can move forward and both do what's best for Max. What, exactly, is your problem with me?"

Surprise and, if she wasn't mistaken, respect flashed in his eyes before they shuttered again.

"No problem."

Her left eye twitched. She pressed the tips of her fingers against it. "No need to hold back." She certainly didn't like to keep her opinions, her thoughts to herself. Not when she could share them with the world. "I can't fix the problem if I don't know what it is."

Eddie wiped his palm down his mouth. His jaw tight, his shoulders rigid, he gave a short nod. "You're judging Max based on our history."

Finally they were getting somewhere. "Max's and your history? Because I'm not all that familiar with it. I mean, I know you're divorced and that Max's mother lives in Chicago—"

"Our—" he gestured between them "—history."

She raised her eyebrows. "I hadn't realized we—" she mimicked his gesture "—had a history."

Sure, they'd gone to school together but they hadn't run with the same crowd. Actually, she couldn't remember Eddie running with any crowd. Then again, she hadn't paid much attention to him. Boys like Eddie Montesano had never been her type, though a small segment of her girlfriends had found him appealing.

She had no idea why.

Okay, so he wasn't exactly a troll, and yes, he had

the whole not-quite-tall, dark and handsome thing going for him with a wide chest and flat stomach. His hair was thick and brushed back from his high forehead to fall in wavy disarray. He had heavy eyebrows, a sharp, square jawline covered in dark stubble and a Roman nose with a prominent bridge.

All in all, a pretty package. But Harper had always preferred guys who were more charming, less brooding. Outgoing instead of introverted. Lighter in coloring and personality.

Men like Beau, her blond, blue-eyed husband, who'd swept her off her feet with his humor, charm and joy for life.

Her throat tightened, and she swallowed a pang of grief. Averted her gaze so Eddie didn't see the pain she knew must be in her eyes. She missed Beau so much. Every day without him was a step in a new direction, toward a future without the man she'd promised to love for the rest of her life.

She wasn't sure which was worse. The days she couldn't stop thinking about him. Or the more recent days when she realized she hadn't thought of him at all.

She cleared her throat, concentrated on the glowering man in front of her. "Did I do something to offend you in high school?"

"You tutored me. In English," he added when she just stared.

"I remember, but what does my tutoring you a

hundred years ago have to do with anything in the here and now?"

His jaw worked as if he was grinding his teeth into dust. "You think there's something wrong with Max because I had issues in school."

She hadn't known it was possible, but he'd managed to shock her into silence for a second time. It had to be some sort of record.

"First of all, there is nothing, not one blessed thing *wrong* with Max," she said, her voice vibrating as indignation on behalf of that sweet boy swept through her. "He's having some issues that I feel need addressing. What I'm suggesting is that we figure out what those issues are so we can devise a strategy to help him succeed. And for your information, my evaluation of each student is based on his or her individual efforts. I take into account their past grades, test scores and how they're currently doing in my class. And for you to suggest that I look at Max and think, 'Oh, well, there's the son of someone I helped understand *King Lear* junior year so he must have some…*issues,*'" she said, doing a fair impersonation of his gravelly voice on that last word, "is not only one of the most ridiculous things I've ever heard, it's also one of the most insulting."

There. She'd given him a piece of her mind said in her best do-not-mess-with-me-I-am-a-teacher tone, the one that had cowed many others.

That those *others* happened to be under the age of ten didn't matter.

"It was *The Grapes of Wrath*," he said, not the least bit intimidated, darn him. "Sophomore year."

She rolled her eyes then immediately squeezed them shut. God. Bad enough he had her acting unprofessionally, now she was reverting to the teenager she'd been when they'd spent a few hours studying Steinbeck's classic novel. Next thing she knew, she'd be telling him, as clearly and succinctly as possible, exactly how big of an ass he was being.

Inhaling deeply, she held it for the count of five. She could do this. She dealt with children all day, had weathered more than her fair share of tantrums, meltdowns and bad behavior.

"All I want," she said, "is to help Max. Surely you want the same thing."

"If Max needs help, I'll give it to him."

"In the interest of doing what's best for Max, I'm sure we can come to some sort of compromise." Though she hadn't been able to charm him in the least so far, she tried another smile. Hey, she may be banging her head against his obstinacy but that didn't mean she had to give up. "Seeing as how we're old friends and all."

"We weren't friends."

Her smile slid away. Then again, giving up had its merits. Such as saving her from one heck of a headache. "What would you call it? Acquaintances? School chums? Oh, how about tutor and tutee?"

"Is that a real word?"

She had no idea. "The bottom line is that I'm concerned about Max."

"I appreciate your concern," he said in a tone that made it clear he couldn't care less about her concern, her opinions or her standing as his son's teacher. "But I don't want Max observed by some psychologist or singled out in any way. Like I said, I'll talk to him. Get him to pay more attention, to not fidget as much."

"I don't think it'll be that easy. And as Max's teacher, I feel it's my responsibility to tell you I disagree with your decision and wish you would reconsider."

"You don't have to be his teacher."

His threat, implicit but oh, so clear, slid along her spine, had her narrowing her eyes. No one threatened her. No one. "You'd pull Max from my class?"

He shrugged as if that said it all—which, she supposed, it did.

She stared at his broad back as he opened the door and called into the classroom, "Time to go, Max."

"You're not serious," she said when he faced her. Then again, he looked as if he was never anything but serious. Serious. Stubborn. Annoying.

And most of all, just plain wrong.

When he twitched, as if moving to lift his shoulder, she held up a hand. "For God's sake," she snapped, "use your words and not one of those shrugs you're so fond of."

If possible, his frown became even darker. "I'll do

whatever's best for Max," he said as his son joined them. "And I'll do it on my own."

This isn't what's best for him, she wanted to yell. But Max shot worried glances between them, so she kept her thoughts to herself. Continued keeping them to herself as Eddie and his son walked away.

EDDIE PUSHED OPEN the school's front doors, stepped into the sunshine and descended the wide, concrete steps, Max next to him. At the bottom, they turned left and headed toward the parking lot.

He breathed in the fresh air, but it did little to ease the tension tightening his neck, causing a headache to brew behind his temples. Worse than the pain? He couldn't shake the image of Harper's mouth, of those pink, heart-shaped lips moving as she'd talked.

And talked and talked and talked some more.

There were much better things she could do with that mouth.

All I want is to help Max. Surely you want the same thing.

Of course he did. That was all he'd ever wanted. All he cared about.

And damn her for questioning him like that, for making it seem as if his resistance to her concerns was something other than his protective instincts.

She wanted to stick Max with a label, one he'd have for the rest of his life. One that would screw up his self-esteem, make him question his own abilities. No way would Eddie ever let that happen.

No way would he let his son go through what he'd gone through.

He'd handle it, he assured himself, in a calm, rational way.

Though Harper might disagree about the rational part.

Didn't matter. He had to do what he felt was right.

Eddie would work with Max, talk to him about how important it was to pay close attention in class. He'd go over every bit of Max's homework, make sure it got completed to the best of Max's capabilities. In a few weeks, his grades would improve and Harper would realize she'd been wrong. That she'd overreacted about the fidgeting, short attention span and impatience—which were all normal traits shared by a great many seven-year-old boys.

His son was no different from anyone else.

"Dad?" Max asked, breathless as they reached the parking lot.

Realizing Max was jogging to keep pace with his long, angry strides, Eddie slowed. "Hmm?"

"Am I in trouble?"

Eddie stopped. "No. Why?"

Max stared at the ground, kicked a pebble. "'Cause Mrs. Kavanagh wanted to talk to you."

"It was a parent/teacher conference. So she could tell me how you're doing."

"I haven't been fighting," Max blurted, his cheeks turning red. "Not even a little. Not even when Aaron took my turn on the monkey bars today. I walked away, like you told me."

"That's good." Though he should probably add something about standing your ground when you know you're in the right, not letting people push you around and learning how to talk things through. To compromise.

Use your words.

Easy for Harper to say. She had more than her fair share of words while Eddie was always searching for the right ones.

"Does Mrs. Kavanagh like me?" Max asked.

"Yeah. She likes you a lot." That much had been clear. "Do you…" He grabbed the back of his neck, massaged the ache there. "Do you like her?"

Max nodded so hard, his hair flopped into his eyes. "She's nice. And funny. And she doesn't yell even when someone's being really bad."

Eddie dropped his hand. "That's…great."

Yeah, freaking terrific. It would be so much easier switching Max to another class if he'd disliked Harper or, at the very least, didn't give a damn about her one way or the other. Not that Eddie was set on that course of action. She'd said herself she needed his permission for Max to be observed by the shrink. As long as she didn't push him, Eddie wouldn't have a reason to pull Max from her class.

"Come on," he said. "We have to stop at Bradford House and see how Heath did with the kitchen cabinets."

"Can I get a snack before practice?"

Damn. That was right. It was Tuesday. Max had hockey practice. Eddie would never stop being grateful Mark Benton had stepped up and offered to coach before Eddie could get stuck with the job.

He glanced at his watch. Why were there never enough hours in the day? "Sure, but we need to get moving."

He clasped his son's small, warm and slightly sticky hand. There would be a time, not too far in the future, when Max would grimace and shrink away when Eddie offered his hand.

But not today.

Today, his son held on instead of running ahead. Today, his son still needed him.

They climbed into the truck.

"Want to know what else I like about Mrs. Kavanagh?" Max asked as he buckled his seat belt.

Not in the least.

"Sure," Eddie said with a sigh.

"She's pretty," Max whispered, a blush coloring his fair skin. "And she smells good."

Eddie turned on the ignition, slammed his foot onto the clutch and jammed the truck into first gear. He'd noticed both those things, too.

He wished like hell he hadn't.

"HE HAD THE NERVE…the utter…utter…"

Harper tipped her head back and stared at the ceiling of Dr. Joan Crosby's office in hope the word she was searching for would somehow magically appear in the air.

"Gall?" Joan asked from behind her neat desk.

Harper whirled on the older woman. Jabbed a finger in her direction. "Yes! The utter *gall* to threaten to take Max out of my class."

She still couldn't believe it. Pacing to burn off some of her temper before she picked up her daughter from day care, her quick, short strides took her to the far edge of the room and back in seconds. An easy enough task given the size of the office and the fact that there was nothing in there that wasn't completely necessary. A desk and chair, three other chairs—two facing the desk, the third off to the side—and floor-to-ceiling shelves lined with books. A small, round table with two kid-sized chairs sat in the far corner along with a plastic bin Harper knew held drawing paper, crayons and colored pencils.

Joan didn't believe in wasting space, materials, time or words.

Harper grabbed a handful of M&M's—her third such handful—from a ceramic bowl on the desk and tossed several into her mouth. They didn't help. She ate some more.

Stick with something long enough, and you were bound to get the results you wanted.

Naive? Perhaps. But it kept her happy and optimistic in the face of adversity. After Beau had been taken from her so suddenly, Harper had wanted nothing more than to curl into a ball and die herself. She couldn't, of course. She had people who counted on her, who needed her to be strong. Her daughter, Cassidy, for one.

Joan, Beau's mother, for another.

So, yes, she lived a life of clichés. Chin up. Search out the good in life. The sun will come out tomorrow and all that jazz. Looking on the bright side had kept her sane during the past ten months. Believing in some greener pasture, in better days, helped to push her through each hour, every minute without her husband.

Convinced her things would get better.

Each day got a little easier. She no longer cried herself to sleep or felt as if there was a weight on her chest, one making it unbearable to breathe. She was living again, could see real hope for the future, could even imagine herself moving on. Dating. Possibly falling in love again.

Eventually. When the time was right. In another year or so when the idea of being with someone new didn't seem out of the realm of possibility. When it wouldn't feel like a betrayal of her husband, of what they'd shared.

Someday she would move on. Fully. Without regrets or guilt. She had to. Even when you lost the man you loved with all your heart, life went on, day after day.

It was funny that way.

She ate a red M&M followed quickly by a blue one. She froze in the act of reaching for another handful, her fingers twitching, and glared at Joan. "What are you, a sadist?"

Her mother-in-law considered that, as if the question deserved real thought. "I don't believe so."

"Then why are you letting me eat these? You know I'm trying to lose this extra baby weight." Baby weight she carried on her hips and thighs despite delivering said baby two and a half years ago.

Guess not everything worked out the way you wanted, no matter how hard or long you stuck with it.

"I was afraid to suggest you slow down," Joan said. "Or take the bowl lest you chomped my hand off at the wrist."

"Ha ha." Harper flopped onto the chair as Joan reached for the candy. "Wait," Harper cried, leaping back up. She took two more. "Last ones. I swear."

She'd make up for the extra calories by getting on the treadmill tonight.

Feeling better, if not entirely virtuous about her choice, she sucked on the first M&M to make it last as long as possible.

Joan tucked the bowl into a side drawer then clasped her hands together on top of the desk. "Now that you've settled down, why don't you tell me what's got you so upset?"

Harper slid the second chocolate into her mouth. Perhaps she'd chosen the wrong person to vent to. Why did she have to have a psychologist for a mother-in-law? And vice versa?

But they'd known each other a few years before Joan had introduced her only child to Harper. Even though Beau no longer tied them together, they were still family. More than that, they were each other's connection to the man—the husband, the son—they'd both lost. During the worst grief imaginable, they'd stuck together, had been there for each other.

That would never change.

Through it all, their relationship had grown and evolved into friendship, one Harper cherished. It was that friend she needed now.

She'd just have to put up with the therapist butting in with her two cents every once in a while.

"I'm upset because he wouldn't even listen to reason." Wouldn't listen to her. "I explained that Max needed help, that he was dangerously behind in all subject areas, and the first step toward getting to the bottom of Max's problems was for you to observe him, but Eddie…brushed all my reasons aside."

Like she was some annoying gnat come to burrow in that mop of hair on his head.

"Uh-huh. Is that all?"

Harper gaped. "Didn't you hear me? He threatened to take Max from my class." The more she thought of it, the more upset she got. She started pacing again. "Not once, in all my years of teaching—"

"Sweetie," Joan said not unkindly, "you don't get to use *in all my years of teaching* until you've been here at least twenty years."

"Well, in the ten years I've taught I've never had any parent ask to remove their child from my class. I'm the most requested teacher in second grade."

Joan arched a perfect eyebrow. "Bragging, dear?"

Harper's cheeks heated. Too bad the candy was put away. The best cure for the blues, bad temper and embarrassment was chocolate. It fixed what ailed you.

"I'm stating a fact." She chewed on the inside of her lip. "Maybe I should have told him that. Then he could have realized what a mistake it would be for him to take Max away from me."

"I'd like to make sure I have this straight." Joan steepled her fingers under her chin, her reading glasses on top of her graying blond curls. "Mr. Montesano is reluctant to discuss the possible reasons behind Max's struggles in school and became defensive when you stated your opinions."

"Very defensive. And then he got *offensive*."

Joan hummed in a way that made Harper feel as if she was being analyzed. Which, let's be honest, she completely was. "And how did that make you feel?"

Harper's lips twitched. "Please. I'm trying to keep a good mad going here."

"And you're doing an admirable job. But it might

be better for your stress levels if you collect your thoughts and think of a solution to the problem."

"I'd rather stay mad," she grumbled.

"But mad doesn't solve anything."

True. She sighed. Stared at the framed photos on Joan's desk—one of Harper and Beau on their wedding day, another of Beau holding their daughter, Cassidy, on his birthday last year.

Ten days later, Beau was gone.

"Eddie accused me of not doing my job."

"Ah…"

"Oh, no. No."

"What?"

"I know what you're up to with that *ah*. You think you've got it all figured out, that there's some deep-seated issue here causing me to be so upset. Probably something to do with my dog running away when I was four or my not getting enough love as a child."

"Your parents adore you."

"Exactly." And, being an only child, she didn't have to share that adoration with anyone else. "So there's nothing to *ah* about here."

"Hmm…"

With a groan, Harper flopped into the chair. "That's even worse."

"Seems to me," Joan said in the same slow, thoughtful tone she employed when speaking with students, "the problem isn't Mr. Montesano's reaction—or at least, not only his reaction. It's your reaction to that reaction."

"He started it."

Joan smiled. "Surprisingly, that's not the first time I've heard those words uttered from someone sitting in that chair."

Considering Joan's usual clients were the under-twelve set, Harper wasn't sure whether to be horrified or amused. "You're right. I shouldn't have let him get me so upset."

"Have you considered the reason why you reacted the way you did?"

"I'm going to blame it on my never getting over Sparky running away and leave it at that."

Unfortunately, Joan never left anything alone. Tenaciousness must have come with her Ph.D. "You've dealt with numerous parents on matters both big and small throughout the years without letting them upset you. It seems to me, the difference this time isn't that Mr. Montesano was resistant to your help, but that he bruised your pride."

Though the words were said gently, without reprimand or judgment, Harper flinched. "You think this is about my ego?"

"What do you think?"

"I think it's annoying the way you answer a question with another question."

Joan simply waited. As if she knew it was only a matter of time before Harper broke. She was right.

About everything.

Harper slouched farther into her seat, wished she could disappear into the fabric. "Maybe he poked at my pride a little." Staring at her left hand, she slid her engagement ring and wedding band up and down her finger. Up and down. "What do I do now?"

"I think the best way to proceed is to give Mr. Montesano time to process your discussion, your concerns. After report cards are sent out next month, call him in for another meeting. Sam and I can sit in on it if you'd like."

Harper wondered if that last bit was a reprimand for skirting the rules and meeting with Eddie on her own. "That would probably be for the best. Thanks."

Having Joan and the principal there might be enough to persuade Eddie that she knew what she was talking about. Or it could get her in a boatload of trouble if she couldn't keep her mouth shut.

Like today.

Her mouth. From the time she'd said her first word at eight months old it'd been getting her into trouble.

She pressed her fingertips against her temples. She'd snapped at Eddie, had told him not to shrug at her again. Her stomach got queasy, embarrassment coated her throat. He had every right to complain about her to her superiors.

She wrinkled her nose. Maybe not *every* right. He had been incredibly stubborn and unreasonable. But that didn't mean he wouldn't complain about their little meeting. She may as well have handed him the phone numbers of the principal, superintendent and president of the school board, and told him to have at it asking for her resignation. Or, more realistically, asking Max to be moved to another class.

Worse, instead of getting him to see he was hurting Max by ignoring her suggestions, she'd pushed him into digging in his heels even deeper.

She'd messed up. Royally. Now she had to make it right. Tonight she'd write up some ideas for strategies she could implement in her class, ways to help Max focus and succeed.

After all, she didn't need to meet with Eddie or get his permission to try different teaching methods. To do what was best for one of the students in her class. He wasn't the damn boss of her.

Joan shut off her computer and got her purse from the desk drawer. "Would you and Cass like to come for dinner? Steve's making chicken pot pie."

"We'd love to, but it's Uncle Will's birthday so we're eating at Aunt Irene's."

Since Beau died, she and Cass never had a shortage of dinner invitations. It was as though her loved ones thought if they didn't feed her and her daughter, they'd starve.

Not that she didn't appreciate the support. She did. Really. It was just sometimes all she wanted after a long day was to pick up Cassidy from day care, go home, put on sweatpants and play with her baby.

But she tried to make sure Cass saw Joan and Steve—Beau's stepfather—a few times a week. It was important that her daughter have a connection to her paternal grandparents.

Keeping everyone happy—and convincing them she and Cassidy really were fine—was exhausting sometimes.

"Can we get a rain check?" she asked.

Joan came around the desk and walked with her to the door. "Of course," she said, shutting off the lights. "How about tomorrow night?"

"That sounds great." At least it would save her having to throw together something for dinner. "Thanks. For everything."

"That's what family is for. Try not to worry about Max. I've seen this before, parents who are reluctant to admit there's a problem. They usually come around and I'm sure Mr. Montesano will be no different."

"I'm sure you're right."

Even if she wasn't, it didn't matter. Because Harper wasn't about to let Eddie take Max away from her. She couldn't. Max needed her.

And to help a child she'd gladly do battle against any opponent—including grumpy, taciturn Eddie Montesano.

CHAPTER THREE

WITH MAROON 5'S "Payphone" playing over the radio in Bradford House's kitchen, Eddie crouched in front of the rough plumbing for the sink. He measured the distance from the floor to the hot water pipe, wrote the figure on a piece of scrap paper and repeated the action with the cold water pipe and drain. Then he measured them all again.

Measure twice, cut once. Good advice that had been drilled into his head since he started working for his father at the age of fifteen. Advice he heeded on the job literally—and in life figuratively.

Be careful, cautious, and you were less likely to make a mistake.

Behind him, the door opened. "If you're not going to keep your phone on," a familiar voice said as Eddie wrote down the last of the measurements, "why do you bother to have one?"

Straightening, Eddie stuck the carpenter pencil in his back pocket and laid the paper on top of the cherry cabinet he'd built for the sink base. "Who says it's not on?"

"Me." James Montesano, Eddie's older brother,

waved his own phone in the air. "And the fact that I've been calling you for the past hour."

Eddie pulled out his phone and turned it on, then slid it into his pocket. "I had a meeting."

He'd rather keep it off. He hated the damn thing. Had no desire to talk to most people face-to-face, why would he want the torture of trying to keep up a conversation over the phone? Or worse, send and receive text messages like some teenager? The only reason he even had one was in case of an emergency.

And if something had happened to his son, if he'd gotten hurt or sick at hockey practice, James would have told Eddie that immediately instead of laying into him about his lack of cell-phone manners. Besides, their mother was the secondary emergency contact for Max and she would have simply picked Max up if he'd needed her.

"Hand me the hole saw," Eddie said, marking the measurements on the back of the sink base.

James sighed. "Aren't you going to ask why I've been calling you for the past hour?"

"I figure you'll tell me when you're ready." No sense rushing a man when he had something on his mind. Eddie hated being pushed to speak before he was ready. "You going to give me the saw or not?"

"I've been calling," James said as his phone buzzed, "because I'm tired of acting as your message service."

"Customers wouldn't bug you so often if you didn't answer each call and respond to every text message."

As if to prove him right, James checked the number of the incoming call. "Shit," he muttered before answering it with a cheerful, "Meg, hi. How are you?"

Though their father, Frank, was the head of Montesano Construction, had built the business from the ground up thirty-five years ago, James was the one who kept the company running smoothly today. His anal tendencies, love for organization and rules and unnatural fondness for his smartphone made him the perfect man for the job.

Thank God. Eddie could handle coming up with the work schedules, and both he and Maddie wrote up estimates for potential jobs. But Eddie would rather shoot himself in the bare foot with a nail gun than have to deal with customers changing their minds, whining about costs and bitching about jobs taking too long.

And if Maddie, with her sharp tongue and take-no-prisoners attitude, was in charge of customer service?

Montesano Construction would be out of business in two months. Three, tops.

Better to keep things the way they were. Even if that meant putting up with James's nagging, bossiness and him ceasing all conversation to stroke his phone.

Not that Eddie actually minded that last one. At least it got James to shut up for a few minutes.

Saving himself the time and trouble of asking for the hole saw again—no sense when James was absorbed in conversation—Eddie crossed to the corner cabinet and got the damn thing himself.

While he'd been at the parent/teacher thing, Heath had finished installing the two lower cabinets to the left of the sink base. Eddie could let the sink wait until tomorrow, but with Max at hockey practice, he had two hours on his hands. A good opportunity to make up for the time he'd missed.

Time he never should have missed, he thought, his irritation once again spiking when he remembered his conversation with Harper. He should have been working instead of listening to her try to convince him to go against his instincts.

The ones screaming at him to protect his son.

He cut through the back of the sink base, the loud whine of the saw and scent of sawdust filling the air. When he had three perfect circles, he tossed the scraps aside, set the tool on the floor out of the way and went to the front of the cabinet. Grabbing the corners, he wiggled the base into position then stepped back.

They still had a long way to go—three more lower cabinets along this wall needed installing as did a dozen upper cabinets, and he was putting the finishing touches on the large center island at the workshop. But the floor had been laid, the walls prepped and painted, the appliances were on order and the lighting fixtures were being delivered in two days.

"That woman is one hundred pages of crazy in a fifty-page book," James grumbled, putting away his phone.

"That's why God invented voice mail."

"You should know, seeing as how most calls I make to you go straight to it. Mine and everyone else who dials that number." James crossed his arms, braced his legs wide. Eddie knew that stance. It was the one James adopted when he was getting ready to do battle. "Including, apparently, your ex-wife."

And there was the reason for it.

Eddie stilled. "What?"

"Lena phoned me. Told me she's been trying to get ahold of you for the past five days but you haven't answered any of her calls or returned them. I told her you and Max were both fine and that I'd relay her message."

"What message?"

"To call her. What do you think she wants?"

He didn't know. And that was the problem. The reason he'd been avoiding her calls.

"Thanks," he said. "I'll tell her not to bug you."

"She didn't bug me and I don't mind that she called. Especially when she was obviously upset and worried something had happened to Max."

"You told her Max was fine."

She had no reason to worry. No right to. Not when she was the one who walked away from their son.

"She seemed relieved," James said. "What's going on? She still bugging you about more time with Max?"

"Nothing's going on." Nothing except his ex-wife changing the rules they'd lived by for the past five years. "I've got it handled."

About four months ago, Lena had started calling several times a week instead of every other weekend. At first, Eddie hadn't thought much of it, but then she'd started talking about spending more time with Max, how she wanted to be a bigger part of his life.

That was when the fear had set in. Ever since their divorce, ever since she'd willingly granted Eddie full custody, she'd never wanted to be more than a partial influence in their child's life. Twice-yearly visits—always in Shady Grove—had been enough for her all this time. It should continue to be enough.

Or at least that's what he'd thought until she'd admitted the reason for her change of heart.

Cancer.

Lena had been diagnosed with ovarian cancer in January. Per her wishes, Eddie hadn't told anyone, not even his family. Not Max. Lena was fine now, her prognosis excellent after a hysterectomy and chemo treatments.

No sense worrying Max needlessly. No point in letting him know it'd taken a near-death experience to make his mother want back in his life.

Eddie had agreed to let Lena see Max anytime she wanted. It was the right thing to do.

But that didn't mean Eddie had to like being the good guy. Or that he had to answer every one of her phone calls.

Kneeling in front of the cabinet, Eddie inserted shims under the bottom to make the base level. As he worked, though, he felt James's gaze on him, like an unreachable itch between his shoulder blades. Nagging. Irritating as hell.

"Everything okay with you?" James asked.

"Yep."

But James remained rooted to his spot. "Let's go to O'Riley's. Grab a beer." From the tapping going on behind him, James had his phone out again. "But it's your turn to buy."

"I'm working."

"Fine. I'll buy."

Eddie tossed the shims aside. "I don't want a beer."

Actually, a beer didn't sound half bad. If a quick drink had been all James was after, he might have gone along with it. But James was too perceptive to buy Eddie's evasions about Lena. Too damned nosy to let it go. And spending any amount of time deflecting what was sure to be an interrogation sounded like pure hell.

"I'll text Leo," James said. "Have him meet us."

Both brothers yakking at him, questioning him, wanting to know his every goddamn thought? More like pure hell with the flames set to High.

Eddie stood. "Don't you have somewhere else to be?"

Between putting in twelve-hour days for Montesano Construction, family obligations and his new live-in relationship with Sadie Nixon—his best friend since childhood—James always had somewhere to be. Something to do.

"Not for an hour." He didn't even look up from whatever he was typing. "Sadie and I are going to her parents' house for Will's birthday dinner."

"You want to waste an hour while Leo hits on every pretty woman at O'Riley's, that's your choice. Me? I'm going to finish this, pick up my kid and go home."

"You sure?" James asked quietly, but Eddie knew what his brother really wanted to know.

Are you really all right? Do you want to talk about it? What can I do to help?

He was grateful for the concern. He didn't want it, didn't need it, but he could appreciate it just the same. "I'm sure."

Nodding, James stepped forward and slapped Eddie's shoulder. Gave it an affectionate—if heavy-handed—squeeze. "I'll see you tomorrow then."

He walked out, his phone once again buzzing for his attention. Eddie turned to his work. He appreciated his brother's concern. Knew James and the rest of their family were there for him and Max if they needed them. Whenever. Wherever.

It meant a lot.

But there were some things a man had to do on his own.

"I'M TELLING YOU, that woman hates me," Sadie Nixon said with such heartfelt drama, Harper glanced around to make sure they hadn't been magically transported to a Broadway stage. Harper's cousin always had had somewhat of a theatrical streak.

But, nope, they were still in Irene Ellison's gourmet kitchen. The scent of roasting beef filled the air, mixed with the yeasty smell of the rolls in the second oven while potatoes bubbled on the back corner of the six-burner range. Speckled black granite counters topped white cabinets, and green-and-black accents kept the room from being too modern or austere.

"I'm sure that's not true," Aunt Irene told her daughter as she spread whipped white frosting on a triple-layer coconut cake. "Rose is a lovely woman."

"She's a fabulous woman," Sadie agreed, crossing her arms as she leaned back against the counter. "Wonderful, really. Kind. Caring. Considerate. And she hates my guts."

Aunt Irene shook her head. "Now, Sadie—"

"It's true. I've tried so hard to get her to like me. I bake her cookies. Pick up little gifts I think she'll enjoy. Help with the dishes when we eat dinner there. I invite her out for coffee or shopping, just the two of us." Sadie, in bright orange jeans that threatened to cause permanent eye damage, and a silky white top that fell from her shoulder, pouted prettily. Then again, everything Sadie did she did prettily. Hard not to when you looked like a blonde, blue-eyed fairy come to life. "She's always busy."

"Well, I imagine she is very busy, what with going back to school," Aunt Irene said.

Lifting the lid from the potatoes, Harper frowned as steam heated her cheeks, probably curling her hair. "Mrs. Montesano is going to college?"

"She's taking courses at Seton Hill." Sadie swiped her finger through the frosting bowl when her mom's back was turned. "She wants to be a social worker."

Good to know at least one Montesano considered education important. Rose's middle son could learn a lesson from his mother.

Harper gripped the fork like Norman Bates in *Psycho* and stabbed the potatoes with more force than necessary. Not that she was letting grumpy, stubborn Eddie affect the rest of her evening or anything. She'd let all that go. Her frustration with him. Her curiosity as to how someone who seemed so quiet and stoic could also be so blatantly antagonistic.

Her shock over the sense that he just hadn't seemed to like her all that much.

She peeled her fingers from the utensil and laid it on the counter, replaced the lid on the not-quite-done vegetable. How could he not like her? They didn't even know each other, for God's sake. Yes, she'd tutored him, but it wasn't as if they'd had many—or any—deep, meaningful conversations. There was no basis, none at all, for him to form what had seemed to be a distinct aversion to her.

Which was crazy. She happened to be extremely likable. Some would even say to know her was to love her.

Okay, so only her parents had ever said that but that didn't make it any less true.

"Just be yourself," Irene advised Sadie as she moved the remaining frosting out of her daughter's reach. "I'm sure whatever problem Rose has with you will solve itself in good time."

"Please. I broke her son's heart. She refuses to forgive me."

"And he broke yours. But you found your way back to each other and mended those breaks. Forgave each other. It's the way of love."

"It's not that way for everyone." Harper couldn't help but point this out. "Beau and I never fought." And her husband certainly would never have done anything to break her heart.

Sadie raised her eyebrows. "Never?"

"We argued once in a while but nothing major."

Everything between her and Beau had been so easy. So right. They'd fallen hard for each other at first sight, were engaged within a year of that initial meeting and married six months later. They'd rented an apartment, scrimped and saved for two years until they'd had enough for the down payment on their house. Harper had gotten pregnant a few months after moving in and, after eight and a half months, gave birth to a perfect daughter in under nine hours.

They'd done everything right. Everything.

And still he'd been taken away from her.

"No fights means no makeup sex," Sadie said. "Or in-the-heat-of-a-fight sex, which is even better."

Harper sent her a smug grin. "We didn't need to fight to make sex exciting."

Sadie snorted out a laugh.

Irene retrieved a huge glass bowl of salad from the stainless steel fridge. "Before we delve any further into the sex lives of my daughter and my favorite niece—"

"Your only niece," Harper and Sadie said at the same time.

"I'd like to get back to what I was saying, which is that you needn't worry about Rose staying angry with you. She'll eventually forgive you for hurting her child."

"I don't see you holding a grudge against James," Sadie muttered.

"That's because I was on James's side the whole time."

And with that piece of insight, Aunt Irene swept out of the kitchen and into the dining room where Harper's mother, Mary Ann, was in charge of setting the table. Her Uncle Will and dad, Kurt, were entertaining Cassidy in the family room.

"Now that's just mean," Sadie called after her mother.

Harper rubbed her cousin's arm. "Don't worry. Aunt Irene's right. Mrs. Montesano will get over whatever's bothering her. No one can stay mad at you for long."

"She's giving it her best effort." Sadie slid Harper an unreadable look. "Though I'm very glad to hear you say that."

"I don't like the sound of that. What did you do now?"

"Why does everyone insist on asking me that?"

"Because we know you?"

Harper loved her cousin like crazy but that didn't mean she was immune to Sadie's flaws. She tended to leap into situations feetfirst without looking left or right, laugh off the consequences of her actions and follow every whim that floated through her head.

"You know I only ever have the best of intentions," Sadie said, laying her hand on her heart.

Her earnest expression sent a chill of trepidation up Harper's spine. "Uh-huh. Why do I get the feeling those best intentions—" she used air quotes to mark the words "—somehow involve me this time?"

"Because you're incredibly bright and intuitive."

"You're making me nervous, so why don't you tell me what it is you have up your sleeve so we can both move on with our lives."

"Actually, that's what this is all about." Sadie inhaled deeply and when she spoke, her voice was quiet, compassionate. "You moving on. And I know just the man to help you."

Harper's scalp tingled even as a laugh of disbelief escaped her throat. "No. No, no, no. And if that doesn't cover it, let me add a no way, no how, not going to happen."

"But Charlie is a great guy. He's handsome," Sadie said, ticking good ol' Charlie's traits off on her fingers, "charming, successful, funny—"

"Wow. Hard to believe such a man exists in this day and age. Or that he's still single."

"It is a shock," Sadie said as if Harper had been serious. "Because he's so sweet and really smart and—"

"Loves puppies? Takes his mother and grandmother to church every Sunday? Trained to be an Olympic gymnast but gave it up to become a neurosurgeon? Single-handedly stopped a busload of orphans from driving off a bridge and into a river?"

"He's not a superhero, Harper." Shaking her long, puffy hair back from her face, Sadie raised her chin and sniffed. "It wouldn't hurt you to give Charlie a chance. I told him all about you—"

"Oh, Sadie, you didn't."

"And he was intrigued. Extremely intrigued. He's interested in meeting you. It doesn't have to be a blind date or even anything major. We could go out—you and Charlie, me and James—have a nice, casual dinner. If you and Charlie hit it off, wonderful. If not, no harm done."

Irritation burrowed under Harper's skin, rooted itself at the base of her spine. She did her best to ignore it, to keep her expression relaxed. To remind herself that Sadie meant well and was only trying to help Harper, to do what she thought was best for her.

But if she didn't knock it off, Harper might very well smash the cake into Sadie's pretty, interfering face. Except that would be a waste of a really delicious-looking cake.

"Look, I'm sure Charlie is as fabulous as you say." Though Sadie's track record with men before she and James became involved disputed that. "But I'm not in the market for any man. Besides, it would be greedy of me to snag Charlie after I already had the perfect guy. Let's let some other woman have a turn."

"I know it's not easy, believe me, I know better than most how hard it is to get past losing someone you love. But if there's one thing I've finally learned, it's how important it is for those of us left behind to continue living. To move forward with our lives."

Harper softened a bit—but only because Sadie had faced her own terrible loss. Her father died in a car accident when she was nine years old. She'd only recently been able to fully heal from it. "I am living my life."

She didn't have a choice.

"Yes, but are you happy?" Sadie asked gently.

Happy? The question, the word alone, gave Harper pause enough to make her realize she didn't want to answer it. Not if it meant facing the truth.

"I'm not unhappy," she hedged, sounding way too defensive and unsure for her own peace of mind. "I'm content enough."

Yes, that was it. She may not have chosen her current situation, but she'd adjusted to it quite nicely. And even though she may not be ecstatically, blissfully happy all the time, there were still periods of joy in her life—hearing her daughter's laugh, teaching the kids in her class, being around her family. Moments she treasured all the more now that she had firsthand experience of how precious they truly were.

Of how easily they could be taken away.

"I'm sorry," Sadie said. "Maybe I shouldn't have said anything—"

"Hey, at least you got something right today."

"And I hate that you're mad at me—"

"I'm not mad," Harper said, praying that one little fib wouldn't mess up all the excellent karma she'd worked so hard for all these years.

Sadie clasped Harper's hands. "You've been incredibly strong but I'm worried about you. I don't want you to be alone."

Harper's fingers twitched and she tugged free of Sadie's grasp.

And to think, she'd been so excited when Sadie had returned to town two months ago, thrilled when her cousin had moved in with James, settling down right here in Shady Grove after spending so many years flitting from place to place.

Maybe Sadie would get bored soon and go on another of her "life adventures."

One could only dream.

"I'm not ready to date again." Harper held up her hand when Sadie opened her mouth. "I promise when I am, I'll let you know. I'll even give you dibs on being the first person to fix me up. Until that day comes, I'd prefer if you didn't bring this up again."

She turned on her heel and walked out the door, stepping onto the small porch at the front of the house. Hugging her arms against the slight chill in the air, she sat on the top step and rested her head against the post.

Her chest was tight. Her throat scratchy and sore. She sniffed. She was fine. She was 100 percent, absolutely fine.

I don't want you to be alone.

As if that would ever happen. Between her daughter, her family and work, she rarely had a moment by herself. Even as a kid she'd always been surrounded by people—her parents, her friends, teachers and classmates. She didn't know what it was like to be alone.

But in the past year, she'd learned exactly what it was like to be lonely.

"How's that homework coming?" Eddie asked Max, glancing at where his son sat hunched over his books at their kitchen table.

Max—for some reason standing to walk around and around the table—shrugged, a gesture Eddie recognized as one of his own. His brothers were right. It was annoying as hell, especially when he needed to get an answer and none was forthcoming.

Eddie popped a slice of carrot into his mouth then wiped his hands on the towel hanging from his belt. Checked the microwave clock. Almost eight. It would be another twenty minutes before they ate. And, if history proved correct, a good hour until Max was done with his math, reading and spelling.

He'd picked up Max from practice only to be three blocks from home before realizing he had nothing to make for dinner. They'd turned around and hit the grocery store—an errand that should have taken only a few minutes but had somehow dragged into half an hour thanks to Max racing all over the store.

Where the kid got his energy after skating around hell-bent for leather for two hours was beyond Eddie. That last time, when Max had taken off in the frozen food aisle, Eddie thought for sure he'd have to call the cops to hunt him down only to corral him— and the box of cupcakes in his hands—by the deli.

Max had been working on his math since they'd walked in the door twenty-five minutes ago. Eddie would like to blame the long time frame on the amount of work needed to be done but Harper only gave the kids a few addition problems to solve, told them to copy their spelling words and read from their assigned books.

He could blame her for other things, though. Such as him having to stand over his kid to make sure Max not only did his homework but also did it correctly. For Eddie worrying about what would happen if he let either of those things slip.

"Here," Max said, shoving his math paper at Eddie when he reached his side.

Eddie picked it up, his chest tightening at the sight of the messy answers. "Double-check these," he said, pointing to three problems that were incorrect. Three out of the five. Damn.

Sitting on the edge of the chair, his tongue caught between his teeth, Max erased the number he'd written in for the first problem. Frowning, he mumbled to himself. "Twenty-three?" he asked, looking so hopeful Eddie wished he could manipulate the formula for math just to make his kid right.

"Try again. What's six plus six?"

Max swung his foot, his heel hitting the chair leg. *Thump. Thump. Thump.*

Should Eddie be worried it took Max so long to figure it out, that he didn't know it automatically and had to count on his fingers?

Another reason to damn Harper. For making him doubt everything his kid did.

"Twelve."

"Right. So when you take the six of sixteen and add six, the answer is twenty…" When Max remained silent—other than all that thumping—Eddie held up all the fingers on his left hand, the pointer finger on his right. "Sixteen…seventeen," he said, folding his pointer finger down. "Eighteen." The thumb on his left hand. "Nineteen." Left pointer finger.

"Twenty." Max folded Eddie's middle finger down. "Twenty-one." Ring finger, then pinky. "Twenty-two!"

"Good job. Now rework the other ones."

While Max figured out the remaining problems, Eddie put their burgers on the grill, tossed frozen French fries into the oven and threw together a salad.

"Done," Max said, digging into his backpack.

"This one is still wrong," Eddie told him, tapping the incorrect answer.

With a weary sigh—as if Eddie was the one making this process last so damn long—Max slumped into his seat clutching his handheld video game. "I don't know it."

"You didn't even look at which problem it is."

He scanned the paper then shrugged.

"Nineteen plus eight is twenty-seven," Eddie said, erasing the wrong answer. He held out the pencil but Max had his head bent over his game, his hair in his eyes.

Eddie wrote in the correct sum, doing his best to imitate his son's handwriting.

And he could only imagine what kind of fresh hell he'd catch if Harper found out about it. Too bad. She didn't get what it was like, being a single parent, trying to do it all on her own. Besides, he'd make up for it by going over Max's addition flash cards with him this weekend. Twice.

"Put the game away and get your reading book

out," he told Max. "You can read to me while I get dinner on the table."

Eddie grabbed plates, silverware and napkins. When he returned to the table, Max was still hunched over his game, his fingers flying across the buttons.

"I said, put the game away." Max didn't so much as blink. Eddie set the plates on the table with a sharp crack. "Max. Maximilian."

Nothing.

He plucked the video game from his son's hands.

"Hey," Max said, jumping up and reaching for it.

Eddie easily held it out of reach. "You can play later. After you've done your reading and we've had dinner."

In a full pout, Max flopped onto the chair, crossed his arms. "I don't want to read it. Mrs. Kavanagh gave me a baby book."

"She wants you to read a book about babies?"

Max rolled his eyes. "It's a book that babies read."

"Must be gifted babies. Reading before they can even talk."

Another eye roll, this one worthy of a kid twice his age. "It's a kindergarten book."

"If it's the book Mrs. Kavanagh assigned you to read, that's what you'll do."

"I want to read Heroes of Olympus."

They'd just discovered the series over the summer and were on the third book. But there was no way Max could read a book at that level.

Impatience and sympathy battled inside of Eddie

with irritation giving them both a run for their money. Big-time. He dug deep so that patience won in the end. He was tired. They both were. Add in hungry, and the fact that one of them was a kid, and you had the potential for a major breakdown. One Eddie didn't have the time for.

"If we get everything done by nine," he said, "everything being dinner, your homework and your bath, I'll read you two chapters of *The Mark of Athena* before we go to bed. Deal?"

Chewing on his thumbnail, Max nodded. Slid his book—*Pie Rats Ahoy!*—out of his backpack and opened it. "B…b…"

Eddie covered the second half of the word with his thumb. "Sound it out."

"B…beh…"

"Be," Eddie corrected, switching to cover the first two letters. "Now this part."

"Wuh…" Max shook his head. "Ruh…"

"Ware. Now put them together." He covered the second half again. "Be."

"Be."

Covered the first part. "Ware."

"Ware."

"Be," Eddie said, drawing the word out as he slid his finger under the letters. "Ware. Beware."

"Beware. Tuh…huh…"

Eddie curled his fingers into his palms, his nails digging into his skin, but he kept his voice mild as he read over Max's shoulder. "Remember when *t* and *h* are together like that, they make a *th* sound."

Max nodded. "The…there…"

"Good."

"There wa…war…"

"Were. There were…"

Fifteen minutes later, their fries were rapidly cooling on the counter and their burgers overdone. And Max was only halfway through a learn-to-read book about a bunch of pie-stealing rats.

"Let's eat," Eddie said, taking the book from Max and setting it aside. It took every ounce of self-control he possessed not to rip the damn thing into confetti. "We'll finish this after your bath."

"You said we could read *The Mark of Athena*."

"I said if we got done by nine." Not likely now, not with half a book to go plus Max's spelling homework.

Max's eyes welled with tears and Eddie's heart broke. Not because his kid was disappointed—disappointments were a fact of life, one you couldn't hide from or protect your children from. But because Eddie knew exactly how Max felt.

Damn it, he hated that his son had to struggle. Knew all too well what Max was going through. The frustration. The self-doubt. But worse was the wanting—wanting to do better. Wanting to be smarter.

Unable to do either.

"We'll read one chapter before you go to bed," Eddie promised. "No matter how late it is."

"Okay." Grinning, Max lunged at Eddie, wrapped his arms around Eddie's neck. "Thanks, Dad."

Eddie held on tight. He didn't want to let go. He wanted to keep his kid in his arms where nothing bad could happen to him. He wanted to promise him it would all be okay, that *he'd* be okay.

His cell phone buzzed.

"Put your stuff away and wash your hands," he told Max then picked up his phone. "Hello?"

"Eddie," a familiar female voice said. "Hi. How are you?"

He bit back a vicious curse. And wished like hell he'd never turned his cell phone on.

CHAPTER FOUR

"HEY," EDDIE SAID, lowering his voice. Luckily, Max was busy washing his hands and had no interest in his dad's phone call.

"I hope I didn't catch you at a bad time."

Tucking the phone between his shoulder and ear, he dished fries onto Max's plate then his own. "We were just sitting down to eat."

"At eight-thirty? Isn't that a little late?"

He pressed his lips together, squeezed the spatula handle so hard, he was surprised it didn't snap in two. Who the hell was she to question how he did things?

"We had a busy day," he managed to say in a reasonable tone.

"Of course," she said quickly as if trying to appease him. "Did you get my messages?"

Messages? There had been more than the one she left with James?

He grunted in affirmation as he motioned for Max to sit and start eating. "What did you need?"

He could picture her on the other end of the line. Even though it was late, she was probably still at her fancy office, her hair pulled back. When they'd been married, she'd often worked twelve-, fourteen-hour days, put in time on weekends and holidays. She'd had no time and little energy for anything or anyone but work.

Not even her own son.

"Actually," she said, "I'd like to talk to Max."

Eddie turned his back to Max, who now watched him with a frown. Must have picked up on Eddie's tension. "Like I said, we're just getting ready to—"

"I'll only take a moment of his time. I promise."

Your promises don't mean much.

He kept that thought to himself.

"Your mom wants to talk to you," he told Max, holding out the phone.

Max took it. Eddie couldn't tell if the flush staining his son's cheeks was from pleasure or nerves.

"Hello?" Max said.

Eddie plated up his dinner, tried not to listen in on the conversation. Not that there was much said on Max's part other than a few yeses, noes, okays and uh-huhs.

After a few minutes, Max said goodbye and passed the phone to Eddie. "She wants to talk to you again."

Eddie set down his burger. "Yeah?"

"I'd like to visit Max," Lena said without preamble, obviously taking the hint that Eddie had no desire for pleasantries or to drag this conversation out longer than necessary.

His stomach churning, he stood, covered the

mouthpiece with his hand. "Finish eating," he whispered to Max before walking into the living room. "Is that what you talked with him about?"

"No. I wanted to run it by you first."

Thank God for small favors. She had no business saying anything to Max about visiting before she had Eddie's permission.

"Is next weekend a good time for you?" she asked.

There was no good time. After Lena's visits, Max always acted out. Fighting at school. Being disrespectful and angry at home.

How could it be anything other than a disruption? Lena had taken off when their son was two, claiming she couldn't handle the responsibility of having a child, wanting to climb the career ladder more than to be a mother. She'd moved to Chicago and had been on the fast track with her job ever since. Until she got sick.

And now she wanted to see Max next week.

What choice did he have? She was his mother. She had a right to see him. Max had a right to have his mother in his life, even if it was on a temporary basis.

"Yeah, that works for me."

"Great," she said, sounding so relieved, guilt pricked him. He pushed it aside. "Maybe one night," she continued, "he could stay with me at the hotel."

He didn't want to fight her but he had to protect his son. "I don't think that's a good idea."

"It's only one night, Eddie," she said, sounding

small. "I really want to spend time with him. He's my son, too."

"He is your son," he agreed, though it killed him to do so, "but you haven't seen him in months. It's confusing for him to have you pop in and out of his life."

"Now that I'm better, I can see him more often. Can't we work something out?"

She sounded sincere. But actions spoke louder than words and he needed to make sure this wasn't some whim brought on by her illness. "If your visit with him goes well, the next time you come to town Max can spend one night with you."

"I know I haven't been a big part of Max's life up until now," she said softly. "But I want to change that. Are you going to let me? Or fight me?"

Her words, the subtle threat of them, blew through him. Chilled him to the bone. "Goodbye, Lena."

He clicked the phone off, imagined how satisfying it would be to wing it across the room. Instead, he set it carefully on the coffee table and headed to the kitchen. To his son.

Are you going to let me? Or fight me?

He was going to let her. Was going to let her see Max, be a bigger part of his life. Partly because it was the right thing to do. Because he felt sorry for what she'd gone through with her cancer diagnosis. Because he truly was glad she was going to be okay.

But mostly because if he fought her, he was terrified he'd lose.

Two HUNDRED AND ninety-five days.

She hated mornings the most.

Actually, Joan thought, keeping her eyes shut as she lay under the heavy comforter on her bed, she hated every single waking moment of each day. But mornings were, by far, the worst. Because each day there was a moment, just as she awoke, when everything was fine. When she forgot, for the briefest of seconds, that her life had been changed forever.

Each day there were a precious few seconds when she was happy.

And then it all came rushing over her. The pain. The crushing grief. The sense of hopelessness. Of despair.

Her son was gone.

She didn't know what to do. Wasn't sure she could go on. She didn't want to die.

She just…didn't want to live.

Everything inside of her stilled and she held her breath as if she'd uttered her guiltiest secret aloud. Waited for the repercussions, the anger and denial, but none were forthcoming. Not from her husband, who slept next to her. Not from the universe or the God she used to believe in.

Not from herself.

How could she deny what was in her heart? The truth she faced each day. That she kept hidden from everyone. She wasn't okay.

Wasn't sure she'd ever be okay again.

But she'd keep pretending she was.

Everyone told her to take as much time as she needed, but even if she lived forever she'd never get over losing Beau. Her only child.

She was supposed to learn how to live without him. How? He'd been her shining light, her main focus and the best thing that had ever happened to her for so long... How could she possibly go on when he'd been so senselessly taken from this world?

It wasn't right. It wasn't fair. It was the injustice of having him ripped from this world that kept her going. The sense that if she gave up, she'd somehow be letting the monster who'd taken Beau's life win. She had to at least pretend she was getting better. That she was handling her loss with grace and dignity.

When all she really wanted was to curl up into a ball in some dark corner and never come out.

She didn't have that luxury. She had to be there for Harper and Cassidy. Had to be a pillar of strength for those around her. She would not be pitied, would not be looked down upon or thought of as weak.

She'd keep right on pretending she was strong.

Steve shifted, rolled over so that his body pressed against her back, his morning erection solid and warm against the cleft of her rear. A year ago she would have snuggled closer to him, would have lifted his arm and wound it around her waist, led his hand to cup her breast. They would have made love slowly. Sweetly. Or they would have come together wildly. Passion driving them both higher and higher.

Six months ago she would have kept her breathing even and pretended to be sound asleep. Or she would have stiffened and edged away, hoping against hope that he wouldn't touch her.

This morning she remained still. Kept her body relaxed as he rubbed against her, his hand gripping her hip, his breathing growing ragged. He rolled her gently onto her back—he was nothing but gentle, her husband, the man she'd fallen in love with years after thinking she'd never find love again.

They'd gotten married the summer Beau turned thirteen, had said their vows in a small, private ceremony in Steve's backyard with Beau giving Joan away. Steve's son and daughter—sixteen and eighteen respectively—had stood up for him.

It had been such a beautiful beginning. Such a lovely promise to what could have been a long and joyful life together.

But now that life was empty. She was empty. And so alone.

All she could do was hold on to the shell of their marriage. Of herself.

Steve shucked his boxers, slid her underwear down, then lifted the hem of her nightgown. There were no tender words between them. No smiles or laughter like there used to be. He didn't kiss her, had stopped trying to get her to respond—to his kisses, his touch—months ago.

But she wouldn't deny him. Not when she knew sex was a basic human function. Not when he'd been so good to her, helping her keep up her facade in front of everyone else.

She could pretend with everyone else but not with Steve. It shamed her. Humiliated her. But he was the only one who knew the truth. She was broken. Forever shattered.

He slid inside of her and she bit her lower lip, grimaced. She wasn't prepared for him but after a few strokes, her body responded the way nature intended. He grabbed her hips, pressed his face into the side of her neck and pumped into her. His body was warm, his scent familiar.

She could hold on to his strong shoulders. Smooth her hands down his sides, over the soft skin of his lower back. She could lift her hips, meet him thrust for thrust, give a small piece of herself to him, take some comfort for herself.

She kept her hands at her sides, palms up, fingers splayed. Her hips still. Turning her head away from him, she stared blindly into the darkness of their room. The bed squeaked. Her body moved with each of his firm thrusts, rubbed against the softness of the sheet. The numbers on the digital clock changed. Changed again. And again. Until Steve's fingers tightened, his body growing rigid.

He emptied himself into her with a low groan, his breath hot on her neck, his skin damp with sweat. And almost immediately, he rolled off of her and padded into the adjoining bathroom.

Leaving Joan to stare, dry-eyed, at yet another sunrise her son would never see.

EDDIE MONTESANO WAS back at Shady Grove Elementary, back in Harper's classroom.

Max, too, she noted, spying the little boy's head behind his father's legs. Eddie, in faded jeans, a snug T-shirt and a worn Pittsburgh Pirates ball cap, stood in the doorway, almost in the same spot he'd been yesterday when he'd told her he didn't need her help. And he was watching her, his focus so complete, so intense, it was all she could do to take a full breath.

Harper forced her attention to the sleeping newborn in her arms. But even as she smiled at the precious baby, she felt Eddie glowering at her from across the room.

God, talk about unnerving. She was about ready to jump out of her skin. Or hold tiny Dawn Rupert up as some kind of shield against his death glare.

What on earth was he doing here?

"She's beautiful," Harper told Dawn's mother, Lydia. Harper lifted the warm weight of the baby higher and inhaled that sweet, newborn scent. Seriously, they should market this stuff. "And you look great."

Lydia's light brown hair was shiny and in soft waves around her pretty face, no dark circles or breakouts in sight on her clear complexion. Her green top hugged her post-baby boobs, her dark skinny jeans daring anyone to guess she'd given birth just seven days ago.

Good thing she was super sweet and funny, or else Harper would have to hate her on principle alone.

"Thanks," Lydia said with the dismissive wave of a woman well used to not having to try hard to look good. "Honestly, she's been such an easy baby so far, I'm afraid I'm getting spoiled. Not like that one." Smiling, she nodded toward her older daughter, Shana, who skipped happily around her mother while singing the latest Beyoncé song under her breath.

Beyoncé. At seven. Whatever happened to "Mary Had a Little Lamb"?

"If Dawn keeps sleeping so much during the night," Lydia continued, taking the baby from Harper, "I might be able to come back in a few weeks."

Lydia was the classroom mother and a really good one, too. Then again, the woman probably made cleaning toilets look fun and effortless.

"Take all the time you need," Harper said, unable to stop herself from shooting a glance in Eddie's direction, only to discover he was no longer at the door. He and his son were now in the middle of the room. And slowly, steadily getting closer.

"I hate leaving you in a lurch like this but I'll be back before Halloween. If you need someone before then, let me know. I'm sure I can find a sitter."

Harper laughed. "We'll be fine. Don't worry about coming back before you're ready."

"Come on, Shana," Lydia called as she headed toward the door. "Let's get your baby sister home."

"I get to help change her," Shana told Harper proudly. A miniature of her mother, she had long, dark hair pulled back in a ponytail and a penchant for T-shirts featuring Hello Kitty. "But I can't feed her 'cause I don't have boobs yet."

By the door, Lydia groaned and sent a furtive glance in Eddie's direction. "Shana Marie!"

Shana's eyes widened. "What? That's what Daddy told me."

Harper bit her lip to stop from smiling. "I'm sure you're a big help to your mom and dad."

The little girl twirled so that her skirt floated out. "I am."

"Less spinning," Lydia said, "more walking, please."

Harper laid her hand on Shana's shoulder and guided her to her mother. "See you tomorrow."

She waited until the Ruperts were well down the hall before facing her unexpected guests. Making her way slowly to her desk, she sent Max a comforting smile.

He ducked his head and slid farther behind his father. Were those tear marks on his face?

"We need to talk," Eddie said flatly.

She sat behind her desk and linked her hands together in her lap. "Yes, I guessed that was your reason for being here. What can I do for you? From your expression, I take it this isn't a social call."

Or going to be a pleasant visit.

Then again, maybe he just wasn't a pleasant sort of person. His brother James was. He was a complete sweetheart. Friendly. Kind. The type of man a girl could reason with, have a polite conversation with. A truly nice man.

This one storming toward her, his son in his wake? Not so nice or friendly. Which was a pity. She bet he'd be a real heartbreaker if he'd only smile once in a while. Luckily, she wasn't interested in having her heart broken.

"If you have a problem with me," he said, laying his hands on her desk and leaning forward, "you tell me. You don't take it out on my kid."

Eyes narrowing, Harper slid her gaze from Eddie's furious expression to Max's face. Yes, the boy had definitely been crying and she could easily guess why. But she wasn't saying anything until Eddie explained that remark.

Standing, she mimicked Eddie's stance so that they were nose to nose, though she doubted she looked quite as menacing as he did. "Excuse me?"

"Dad," Max whispered, tugging on Eddie's shirt.

Eddie laid his hand on his son's head but didn't turn his way. "Max told me you made him miss recess."

She sent Max a pointed look. The boy stopped

tugging, his face turning beet-red as he stared at the floor.

Oh, Max.

She could, and did, forgive the boy for his part in this little drama. But Eddie? He wasn't getting off so easily.

"I see," she said, tapping her mouth with her finger. "So, to your way of thinking, since you didn't… what? Agree with me? Do as I wanted? I—in a devious and clever act of vengeance—made your son sit on the bench with me while his friends ran around the playground. Wow. I'm really quite the monster. And obviously I don't have enough to do as all that was on my mind from the time you left this classroom yesterday was how I could get my revenge. Want to hear my evil laugh? It's the one I use whenever one of my nefarious plans comes together."

Eddie's frown deepened, turned to confusion. "This isn't funny."

"It's a little funny. Especially from this side of things. Max," she said, "did you tell your father why you had to sit out during recess?"

He lifted a shoulder.

She walked out from behind the desk and crouched so she and Max were eye level. "Do you want to tell him?"

He shook his head so hard, she felt a breeze from the swinging of his floppy hair.

"Tell me what?" Eddie asked.

The little boy wasn't going to budge. Easy enough to tell where he inherited that stubborn streak.

She straightened. "Max had his recess privileges taken away because he misbehaved in class today and at lunch. He disrupted the class several times this morning by walking around during lessons and tapping the other children's desks. And the report I received from the cafeteria monitor stated that Max deliberately poured milk onto Elliott's sandwich because Elliott wouldn't share his cookies. Max and I had a discussion about his behavior and I believe he understands what he did wrong, but since recess is a privilege and not some God-given right, he lost that privilege for today and the rest of the week."

Eddie slid his hand under the bill of his cap and scratched his head. Tugging it down again, he set his free hand on his son's shoulder. "Wait for me out in the hall while I talk with Mrs. Kavanagh, okay, buddy?"

His eyes glistening with tears, his lower lip quivering, Max slunk off.

"Is this the part where you strangle me and toss my lifeless body from the window?" Harper asked, seeing as how Eddie still looked capable of murder. "Because if so, I should warn you that I'm heavier than I look, so tossing might take some real effort."

He flicked his hooded gaze down her body, then jerked his head up. Must not have liked what he saw. And why that bugged her, she had no idea.

He cleared his throat. "I'm sorry."

She wasn't sure which shocked her more—that he'd actually apologized, or that he was blushing.

It should have made him look ridiculous, the color washing up his neck and cheeks. It didn't. He looked approachable and real and not quite as gloomy. And behind his embarrassment, she saw the shyness that'd been a part of him even when they'd been kids.

"You're sorry I'm heavier than I look? Or that you're not strong enough for that tossing?"

"I'm sorry I jumped to conclusions," he said, with no hint of defensiveness or evasion. "And that I jumped down your throat."

His sincerity took her aback, but it was her own sudden softening toward him that caused a weird sense of unease to slide along her skin. As if she were standing on a ledge and needed to be extra careful of each step she took, each move she made.

She should let him squirm. Should, at the very least, let him sweat it out, see how far he'd go to gain her forgiveness, her understanding.

But she'd never been much into making anyone beg. Even when such a prime opportunity stared her in the face.

"It's okay," she said. "We all make mistakes."

"Okay?" he repeated as if trying to decipher her true motives. "That's it?"

"I was going to make you write, *I will not jump to conclusions* on the board one hundred times but I only have so much chalk, and once it's gone I pick up the tab for more, so why don't we skip it?"

He shoved his hands into his pockets. Took them out again, his gaze steady on hers. It set her on edge, the way he looked at her. Which was crazy. She was a grown woman. Had been married, had a daughter. She didn't get all jittery because a good-looking guy stared at her.

God, maybe Sadie was right. Maybe she really did need to get out more.

She picked up a pencil from her desk to have something to do with her hands. "Was there anything else you wished to discuss?"

"I'll talk to Max about his behavior today. He'll have a punishment at home, too."

Some parents went ballistic when their little darlings got punished in school. They took their children's side, blamed the teacher and generally acted worse than whatever their kid had done. Eddie obviously wasn't one of those. She respected that.

"That's up to you, of course." She debated whether to say more but really, when had she ever kept her opinion to herself? "Though—while I'm not condoning his actions in the least—I do think he regrets what he did. He's a good boy. But I can't let bad behavior go, even if that behavior is unusual."

"That makes sense."

"I'm so glad you think so."

He nodded as if she actually needed his permission or his agreement as to how to run her classroom. "You need someone to come in?"

"I hate to repeat myself but... Excuse me?"

"That woman with the baby said she can't help out for a few weeks."

"That's right. She's the room mother."

"Which means…?"

"It means many things."

"Why don't you give me the basics?"

"She posts events and information to the classroom's website, attends all the PTO meetings, organizes class parties and enrichment activities, collects donations from parents for supplies such as tissues, stickers—"

"And she comes in the room? Helps out here?"

"A few times a week, usually on Mondays and Fridays."

He shifted, tapped his fingers on her desk absently, reminding her of his son. "What does she do?"

"Reads to the kids while I grade papers. Helps get snacks. Supervises when they go to the library—"

"I'll do it."

Harper blinked. "You'll do what?"

"I'll come in two afternoons a week," he said, all scowly and defensive, as if she was the one who wasn't making any sense. "Help out with the kids."

"I'm sorry. Shock short-circuited my brain and I must have slipped into a coma for a few moments. I could've sworn you offered to volunteer in the classroom."

His mouth thinned. "I did."

"Why? I mean, you're not exactly what I'd call

sociable.... No offense," she added halfheartedly. Hey, if he took offense it was no skin off her nose. "If you want to observe my teaching methods, all you have to do is ask. You're welcome to sit in on my class anytime you'd like."

"I'm not trying to spy on you. I just thought you could use some help."

"Oh, well...okay then," she said slowly. "That'd be..." Weird. Possibly super uncomfortable. Not to mention having him in her room promised to be nothing but a huge distraction—to her class and her. Too bad she couldn't think of any reasonable excuse to turn him down. "That'd be great. And you'd only have to come in for a few weeks." An assurance for herself as well as him. "I'll...uh...send the paperwork home with Max."

"Paperwork?"

"Forms and regulations. There'll be a background check, too. Have you volunteered at the school before?"

"I chaperoned a couple of field trips last year."

"That'll make the process easier. The checks should still be in place. If they are, you can start whenever you want."

"I'll be here Friday."

"I can hardly wait," she said, trying to sound as if she meant it. Hard to be enthusiastic and encouraging when all she could think was, what had she gotten herself into?

CHAPTER FIVE

WHAT THE HELL was he doing here?

Tugging the brim of his baseball cap down, Eddie slouched against the windowsill. As soon as he stepped into Max's classroom ten minutes ago, he'd known volunteering to be the room dad…parent…whatever…was a mistake. He should have told Harper he'd changed his mind when she'd called him last night and told him his background checks were still good and he could come in today at two-thirty.

Yeah, he'd chaperoned field trips before, but this was different than walking with a small group of kids, getting them from point A of the zoo to point B, or doing a head count on that visit to the dairy farm to make sure no one had been left in the barn.

He didn't know anything about being a teacher's assistant. Had a hard enough time helping Max with his homework. What good would he be to these kids?

But he couldn't back out now. Not when he was already here. Not when Max had been so excited that Eddie was going to help out in his class.

Not after telling Harper he'd do it.

He'd already made an ass of himself in front of her. No sense making a habit of it.

He crossed his arms. Uncrossed them. At the front of the room, Harper wrote a sentence on the board as part of a grammar lesson. Must be casual Friday at the school because she had on a loose white Shady Grove Elementary polo shirt, a pair of shapeless khaki pants and sneakers.

He wished she had on that sweater from the other day instead.

But he liked her hair, how the sides were held away from her face by a clip at the back of her head, the soft sweep of her bangs. The ends grazed her shoulders, curling up slightly as if beckoning him to touch the strands.

His fingers twitched and he deliberately looked away. Kept his gaze somewhere over her shoulder as he tried to pay attention to what she said, in case she expected him to help the kids with their worksheets—dear Christ, he hoped she didn't expect him to help the kids with their worksheets. The differences between a sentence's subject and predicate held little interest.

To Max either. While the other kids kept their eyes on Harper and the examples she wrote on the chalkboard, raised their hands to answer questions and sat still, Max waved his pencil as if fighting off a horde of Stormtroopers.

Eddie gripped the edge of the windowsill, ground his back teeth together so he wouldn't tell his kid to stop playing *Star Wars* and pay attention.

"Max," Harper called as she wrote another sentence on the board.

Teachers, like mothers, had eyes in the back of their heads. Not that Max seemed concerned. He kept waving his pencil around, jabbing it into the air—or the stomach of an imaginary foe.

Eddie straightened, tension tightening his shoulders, the back of his neck. He remembered all too well the humiliation of being called out for his behavior in front of his classmates. He never wanted Max to feel that way.

"Max," Harper repeated in the same mild tone and Max jerked guiltily.

"Listening," he said, turning the pencil to hold it the correct way.

She smiled at him. "Excellent. I'm going to call on you to answer a question after this example."

Max nodded and sat on the edge of his seat, eyes forward, his heels tap, tap, tapping the floor.

Eddie peeled his fingers open. That was it? Harper wasn't going to sarcastically tell Max to get his head out of the clouds? Wasn't going to give him a harsh reprimand or send him out of the room?

Like Eddie's fourth grade teacher had done to him.

"Now, Max, let's try with this sentence. 'The man,'" Harper read, pointing at each word she'd written, "'ate lunch.' As we now know, every sentence has a subject, which is…?" She gestured to everyone.

"Who or what," the majority of the kids responded.

"Exactly. And a predicate…"

A fewer number of kids replied this time. "What the subject does."

"Right." Harper set her chalk on the board ledge. "Okay, Max, what is the subject of the sentence 'The man ate lunch'?" Max hesitated but Harper just re-read the sentence and said, "Remember, subjects are who or what the sentence is about. Could be the house or the car or the awesome teacher…"

Max perked up. "The man?"

"Correct. And the predicate? Or what the subject, in this case *the man,* does? It could be *plays ball* or *ran away*…."

Silence. Eddie squirmed, wanted to blurt out the answer himself, but Harper waited. And waited.

"Ate lunch," Max finally said, leaping to his feet.

"Ding, ding." Harper rang an imaginary bell. "Winner, winner…"

"Chicken dinner," the class shouted.

She walked to a large dry-erase board and crossed Reading Lesson off the day's schedule. "Good job, you guys. Let's take a five-minute break to get your desks cleaned off then we'll take our spelling test. That's five minutes to put your workbooks away and get out a fresh sheet of paper. You may talk quietly amongst yourselves during that time."

Harper erased the board and the noise in the room gradually grew as the students yakked to each other, a few—like Max—getting out of their seats to bounce around the room. And all of them, whether they were talking, sitting or standing, stared at Eddie as if he had two heads and was wearing women's clothes.

He shifted his weight from his right foot to his left. Shit. They probably thought he was nervous. He had to be careful. He couldn't show any weakness. They somehow sensed a man's fear. If they knew he was wondering what he was doing there, what the hell he'd gotten himself into, they'd move in for the kill.

"You okay?" Harper asked as she joined him. At his terse nod, she raised her eyebrows. "You sure? Because you look really freaked out."

He frowned at her but the concern in her eyes remained.

"It's okay," she said in the same tone most people used to soothe a frightened puppy. "Some people aren't comfortable around a lot of kids. Though, those people don't usually volunteer to help in the classroom."

He'd volunteered so he could see firsthand how Max acted in school and be able to nip any more bad behavior in the bud.

And, yeah, because he'd felt like an idiot laying into Harper for taking away Max's recess.

"I'm not uncomfortable around kids," he told her.

He'd just never liked being the center of attention. Some things a man didn't outgrow no matter how much he wanted to.

Harper must have thought he had some deep-seated fear about being surrounded by anyone under four feet tall because she leaned close to him. "You'll do fine," she whispered.

He froze, kept his gaze straight ahead. Max was right. She smelled good. Damn good. Not flowery exactly, but light and fresh.

It took all he had not to turn and simply breathe her in, inhale that sweetness until it filled his lungs to bursting.

"They're mostly harmless," she continued, her tone teasing. He wanted to share in her humor but he couldn't. She stood too close to him, so close her hip brushed his outer thigh. "I promise."

As if to seal that vow, she touched him, the barest brush of her fingers against his forearm. The contact was slight, friendly. But it jolted through him like a shock wave only to settle, warm and humming, in his veins.

Leaving him confused and restless.

While she smiled at her class as if nothing had happened.

She clapped twice. "Hocus pocus."

"Everybody focus," the kids said in unison.

"Thank you," Harper said. "Now, since Mrs. Rupert had her baby—"

"She had my sister," a little girl with a cartoon cat on her shirt said as she danced around her chair. "Her name is Dawn and her poop is *green*."

There was a chorus of *gross* and *ews* and the talking started up again, this time louder and wilder than before.

"Okay, that's enough," Harper said, not raising her voice in the slightest. "Settle down."

The din climbed a few decibels.

Hard to compete with green poop.

Harper held her hand in the air, all five fingers splayed. The movement accentuated the fullness of her breasts, pulled her shirt up, the hem rising a few inches. She folded her thumb in, then each finger one by one. By the time she made a full fist, the kids were all in their seats, their mouths shut.

"Hands free," Harper said, holding both hands in the air and wiggling her fingers. "Eyes on me."

The kids repeated the action.

"As I was saying, Mrs. Rupert won't be able to come in for a few weeks. Luckily, Max's father has agreed to help us out until she returns. Everyone, say hello to Mr. Montesano."

The kids did so in varying degrees of pitch, tone and volume. He inclined his head, coughed softly to clear the tickle from his throat. "Hey."

"How about you read to the kids after they've finished their spelling?" she asked him. "That'll give me time to correct their tests."

Read to a bunch of kids he didn't know? With Harper in the room listening?

Yeah, he read to Max every night—like all the parenting and educational experts said you should—but he'd never be what anyone would consider a fluid reader. Or a fast one.

"Sure," he said with as little enthusiasm as you could use and still be a living, breathing human.

"I got some new books at the library. You can choose a couple of them."

He followed her to her desk, saw the stack of books. Picture books.

Thank you, Jesus.

Eddie leaned against the corner of the desk while Harper picked up the list of spelling words. She recited them clearly and slowly as she walked around the room, used them in a sentence and then repeated the word. The kids were bent over their work, their pencils scratching.

"Please double-check to make sure your names are at the top of your papers," Harper said after she'd read the last word. "Mr. Montesano is going to read to you during circle time."

Harper began collecting tests while the kids gathered in the corner by the rocking chair. Max came up to Eddie. "Can I sit with you when you read?"

"Sure, bud. Why don't you pick out which stories you think your friends would like to hear?"

Max searched through the stack of books. Eddie straightened and, as casually as possible, stepped toward Max's desk. Glanced down at the tests on the three desks surrounding Max's. Names printed on top, lines numbered, each word written neatly and, for the most part, correctly. He glanced back, saw Max was still sorting through the books. Turning to block his son's view, he used a finger to slide

Max's test toward him. Eddie reared back as if the paper had bit him.

Max got two words right. Two out of the ten.

What happened? They'd gone over the words twice each night this week. He'd had Max write them down instead of spelling them aloud. They'd practiced and practiced and practiced some more.

It hadn't done any good. Eddie wanted to crumple the test, toss it into the garbage. He wanted to erase every line and put in the right answers.

He wanted to save Max from going through what he'd gone through. The worries. The doubts. The feeling of failure and not being good enough.

Never being good enough.

Nausea rose in Eddie's throat. It was his fault. He had to fix it. But he couldn't do it on his own.

He had to ask for help.

"WHO COULD THAT BE?" Harper asked Cassidy when someone knocked on their door Friday night.

Sitting on the other side of the table, Cassidy, her blue eyes wide, her mouth smeared with pizza sauce, grinned. "Papa?" she asked excitedly, squirming in her booster seat.

"I don't think so."

"Papa!" Cassidy called. "Papapapapapa!"

Harper winced. Her baby had a set of lungs, God bless her.

"Okay, okay." Harper stood and unstrapped Cass, setting her on the floor. "Let's go see who it is before you have the neighbors calling the police to see if there's a hostage situation over here."

Cassidy raced toward the living room. By the time Harper caught up to her, she was pounding on the inside of the front door. "Papa? Papa, you there? Open up."

"We need to do the opening, kiddo," Harper said, undoing the dead bolt. If she didn't keep it—and the back door—locked, Cass would not only answer the door but also, more than likely, walk out and try to drive the car somewhere.

Her kid had no fear. That was okay. Harper had enough for both of them.

She peeked out the side window only to leap back and plaster herself against the door, arms splayed. For the love of all that was sweet and good in the world, what was Eddie Montesano doing on her porch?

Reaching under Harper's arm, Cass tugged on the knob. Grunted and frowned at her mother. "Stuck."

The door always stuck. Not that Harper blocking it helped matters. "I know. Step back and Mommy will open it." She could do this. She'd just open the door, see what Eddie wanted and then send him on his way.

No problem.

Except, when she pulled on the handle, the door didn't budge. He knocked again.

"Just a second," she said. "I'm having technical difficulties." Planting her feet, she tried again, yanking hard. The door opened, the momentum taking her back two steps.

Regaining her balance, she looked up to find Eddie staring at her in surprise. No, not her, she realized as Cass pushed past Harper to greet their visitor, but her daughter.

Cass had no problem with finding a handsome man on her doorstep—even if that man wasn't her beloved papa. She blinked at Eddie then smiled hugely. "Hi. Want to play with me?"

"Oh, I really hope she outgrows saying that to men," Harper murmured.

Eddie glanced at her, then crouched so he was on Cass's level. "What's your name?" he asked in what could only be deemed a mellowed version of his usual gruff tone.

"Cassidy. I tree." As if to prove it, she held up three of her pudgy fingers.

"Cass," Harper said, "you're not three. You're two."

"No, I tree."

"You're two."

"Tree."

"Two."

"No," Cass said with a fierce scowl and a tiny foot stomp. "I. Tree."

And she stormed off toward the kitchen.

"If you're looking for your birth certificate to alter the dates," Harper called after her, "I hid it the last time we had this conversation."

Harper turned to Eddie. He'd straightened, and the porch light cast half his face in the shadows. The ends of his hair stuck out from under his hat, ruffled in the breeze. "Is Max in the truck?" she asked, peering toward his vehicle parked in her driveway.

"He's with my parents."

"Oh. Well, is there something—"

"You have a daughter."

"Are you asking me if I have one, or telling me?" She shook her head. "Never mind. Yes, I have a daughter. And if left to her own devices for more than a few minutes, she manages to find trouble."

He looked at her like she'd just blasphemed.

That was the problem. Her baby resembled a cherub with her loose blond curls, big blue eyes and round cheeks.

Harper glanced over her shoulder, strained to hear, but all was quiet on the kitchen front. She wasn't sure whether that was a good thing or not. "I realize it's hard to believe that something so sweet and innocent-looking is possible of wreaking havoc but, believe me, wreak it she does."

"Toddlers get into mischief. It's how they learn and play. Start gaining independence."

"Thank you, Dr. Spock," she said dryly. "But Cass goes above and beyond mischief. Two months ago she snuck a marker into her crib and colored all over the walls—and herself—during nap time. She was blue for days. Oh, and then, a few weeks later, during the time it took me to have a ten-minute phone conversation, she climbed onto the kitchen counter, dumped an entire bag of flour onto the floor, then got down and proceeded to throw eggs into it before, for some reason, rolling around in it."

Remembering how long it'd taken to clean up that mess still gave Harper nightmares.

"Learn from me," she continued. "When you get home from the grocery store, put the food away immediately. Don't be fooled into thinking your groceries are safe just because you put them out of reach before taking a call. Kids have ways of getting what they want. My kid especially, so…"

She raised her eyebrows expectantly.

A flush climbed his cheeks. "You want me to go."

"No, of course not." *I just don't want you to come in.* But she couldn't turn him away, not when he seemed so uncomfortable and embarrassed. She stepped back, motioned him inside, then shut the door. "I really do need to check on her, though. Follow me—we can talk in the kitchen."

She was well aware of him behind her, his gaze on the back of her head. Talk about bringing your work home with you. Usually she had paperwork to do in her free time, tests to be graded or lesson plans that needed completing. She'd never had a student or a student's parent in her house.

Now she knew why. It was weird. Tense. Her home was her sanctuary, where she ceased being Mrs. Kavanagh and could just be Harper. Cassidy's mom. Beau's wife.

Eddie being here was ruining that.

She wondered what he was thinking. Worried about it. She bit her lower lip to keep from apologizing about the toys scattered all over the living room, the inch of dust on top of her TV. She had no one to impress here.

In the kitchen they found Cass at the table, sitting on her knees on Harper's chair happily eating Harper's slice of pizza—despite having her own slice cut into bite-sized pieces.

"Want some pizza?" Cass asked Eddie.

"No thanks. You go on and eat yours, though."

"Can I get you something to drink?" Good manners forced Harper to ask. Then again, she didn't know why she was concerned about manners when he was the one who'd shown up uninvited and interrupted her dinner.

"I'm good."

That was too bad. She could use something to do other than smile patiently at him and wait. And wait. And wait some more. After a few minutes, she gave in to the impatience brought on by a long day, hunger pangs and her desire to spend a quiet, peaceful evening with her baby girl.

"I'm going to finish my dinner," she said, reaching over her daughter to pick out a slice of pizza from the box. "You let me know when you've decided whether or not to share whatever it is you're mulling over."

She bit into her pizza. Rude? Maybe. But she

was growing old here waiting for Eddie to speak his mind.

"I didn't know you had a kid."

Whether he sounded put out because of what she'd said or because she had a child, she wasn't sure.

"And here I thought everyone in Shady Grove knew everything about everyone else."

"Guess not," he mumbled, shoving his hands into his pockets.

"I done," Cass proclaimed as she climbed down. She grabbed Eddie's hand. "You play with me now."

"Mr. Montesano doesn't want to play right now," Harper said, going to wet a clean dishcloth at the sink. "Why don't we wash your face—"

"No," Cass screamed and ran off as if Harper had threatened to scrub her cheeks with sandpaper.

"What do I have to do?" Eddie asked. "To help Max improve his grades, get him to pay attention better in class?"

She squeezed the cloth so hard, water dripped off her wrist. "You came over here, to my home, on a Friday night to discuss your son? How did you even know where I live?"

"Sadie told me."

Her cousin always did have a big mouth.

"Do you have any idea how…unusual…this is?" Unusual. Weird. Inappropriate. Did she mention weird? "Most parents don't simply…show up at their child's teacher's house without warning."

"You're not just Max's teacher."

"I'm not?"

"You and me, we're old friends." His tone was low and somber, his expression just this side of grim. Jeez, he could try and charm her with a grin, or at the very least try not to look so foreboding.

"We're not friends, old or otherwise." And where did he get off, using her words from their meeting the other day against her like this, trying to turn them around on her now? "So far, during the brief time we've been reacquainted, you've informed me—in no uncertain terms—that we are not, and never were, friends. That you don't need my help with Max and don't agree with my assessment of what his needs are."

She wasn't going to include his accusing her of taking away Max's recess since he'd apologized for that. Plus he had showed up today to help in class and had done a good job of it—despite her initial prediction that he'd be a distraction to her being right.

"Now, you're here, interrupting my dinner because you've…what? Changed your mind?"

He grabbed the back of his neck. "I didn't mean to interrupt your evening."

She sighed. A man of few words. She did not get why some women found that attractive. "If you want to meet to talk about Max, we can set something up for Mon—"

"I back," Cass announced happily as she dragged

a stroller behind her, four dolls piled in the seat. In her other arm, she carried a naked Barbie which she shoved at Eddie, who took it without even blinking. "Dress her."

"Cassidy," Harper said sharply, "don't be so bossy. It's not nice to tell people what to do."

"Okay, Mommy." She sidled up to Eddie. "I the boss," she whispered. "Dress her."

Eddie's lips twitched and Harper realized she'd never seen him smile, wondered, briefly, inappropriately, what it would be like if he did.

Probably swoon-worthy, if she had to hazard a guess.

"What do you say when you want something?" Eddie asked so kindly, Harper had her mouth open to answer him before realizing he didn't mean her wanting to see him smile. He was talking to Cass.

"I say please," Cass told him, holding out a tiny bright blue dress.

He took the clothes. "That's a good girl."

"I Mommy's best girl. I your best girl, too."

Well, it was easy to see that her daughter had become quickly infatuated with Eddie. And that wouldn't do. Harper stepped forward, ready to shove Eddie out the door if necessary. Then possibly move to some secret location so secluded her cousin wouldn't be able to find her and spill her whereabouts to any of her students' parents.

But Eddie looked at the doll in one hand, the dress in the other and did something so unexpected, so damned shocking, all Harper could do was stare in surprise, horror and, yes, maybe a little bit of appreciation.

He sat cross-legged on her kitchen floor, held out his arms and settled her daughter onto his lap.

Talk about swoon-worthy.

"What's your doll's name?" he asked Cass as he lifted his cap, turned it around and settled it on his head.

"Katrina." Cass named pretty much every Barbie, doll and stuffed animal after her favorite teacher at day care.

"Pretty," Eddie said, earning him an adoring grin. After dressing Barbie, he fluffed the doll's hair and handed her to Cass. "But not as pretty as you."

Cass nodded solemnly. "I know."

Harper covered her eyes with her hand. At least her child didn't have any problems with self-esteem.

"You'd be even prettier if you let your mommy wash some of that sauce off your face," Eddie said, tapping Cass's red cheek.

"You do it." Then Cass stuck her head forward like a turtle, her chin lifted.

"That's okay, Cass," Harper said. "I can do it."

"No!" Cassidy threw her arms around Eddie's neck. "You!"

Patting her baby girl's back with one hand, Eddie reached out the other. What choice did Harper have but to give him the cloth?

He took it, gently disentangled himself from Cass's arms, then washed her face.

It was so sweet, so unexpected, that Harper couldn't take her eyes off of him. His brow knit in a subtle, contemplative frown, his eyes a warm caramel color. Stubble covered his cheeks and jaw, making the angles of his face seem sharper, more pronounced.

She slid her gaze to his scuffed work boots, over his faded jeans. The sweatshirt he wore—the same one he'd had on when they'd met in her class Tuesday—hugged his shoulders, the pushed-up sleeves revealing his muscular forearms.

His hands, oh, his hands, were large and tan, his touch sure and tender as he wiped Cass's face. Harper imagined what it would feel like to have those hands on her, to feel the rough pad of his thumb rubbing against the sensitive skin under her ear, his fingers splayed against the nape of her neck as he held her motionless for his kiss.

The tips of her fingers tingled, her mouth went dry.

Reality crashed in, brought with it shame. And guilt. Shaken by her thoughts, by the flush suffusing her body, the heat skimming along her skin, she averted her gaze. Tried to catch her breath. It was just hormones. Nothing more. She was a woman, made of flesh and blood and flaws. She'd had a healthy, normal sexual appetite with Beau, had enjoyed kissing, touching and being intimate with her husband.

This was nature's way of telling her she was healing. That she could, someday, enjoy those things again. Want them again. But the thought of wanting them with another man had always left her cold.

Until now.

But it was fine. Understandable, even. She was experiencing a physical reaction to a good-looking man, one being nice to her daughter. A reaction to almost a year's worth of lonely nights. Of sleeping alone, waking alone. Of having no one to hold her.

Eddie set the cloth on the table. "All done."

"I prettier now?" Cass asked, staring at him with the complete confidence that he'd say yes.

He smiled, a sweet, shy and totally sexy grin that had Harper's pulse pounding.

Crap. It was even better than she'd imagined.

"You're beautiful," he assured Cass in his solemn way. "Like a princess."

Princess.

Harper's head spun and she grabbed the counter for balance. To ground herself and her thoughts. That was what Beau had called Cassidy. Daddy's little princess.

Now, Cass was in another man's arms, gazing at him with a reverence and trust that should have been reserved for Beau.

It broke Harper's heart, the realization that Cassidy would never know her father, would never remember how much he'd loved her. But Harper remembered. Her memories of him, of how he'd looked at Cass with utter devotion, an all-consuming love, of what it had been like to be his wife, to be loved by him, were crystal clear.

She'd keep them that way, hold them close when the loneliness struck. When she felt weak or needy, as if she couldn't go on by herself. As if she needed another man to take his place.

Looking at Eddie and Cass, she made a promise to herself, and to Beau.

She'd never forget him, what they shared. Never.

CHAPTER SIX

STILL UNSETTLED, HARPER cleared her throat, couldn't do much about how thin her voice sounded when she spoke. "Cassidy, what do you say to Mr. Montesano for dressing your doll and washing your face?"

Hugging the doll to her chest, Cass stood. "Thank you, Mr. Ontsabdo."

"Good first effort," he told her. "But, if it's all right with your mom, you can call me Eddie."

"It's all right, Deddie," Cass assured him breezily.

Yes, it was just fine. Be on a first-name basis with him. What could possibly be wrong with that?

"Why don't you take your dolls into the living room?" Harper asked her. "It's almost bath time."

"Katrina wants to take a bath, too."

Water and shampoo weren't all that good for Barbie's hair but unmanageable tresses were a small price to pay for a stress-free bath time.

"The more the merrier, I always say. Bring her along."

Looked like Katrina wasn't staying in that dress long. Some days Harper felt like she lived in the midst of a Barbie nudist colony.

Cass tucked the doll under her arm then pushed

the stroller into the doorjamb—twice—before clearing it and making her merry way into the living room.

Eddie got to his feet, his movements surprisingly graceful for a man she'd seen get stuck in one school desk and bump into another. "I should go. Sorry I interrupted your evening."

Darn right he should go. She wanted him gone, out of her home, leaving her in peace.

Watching his broad back as he walked out of the room, she tried not to feel bad. But he had come all the way across town to speak to her about Max. Okay, so *all the way across town* didn't exactly mean he'd traveled a hundred miles across frozen tundra—or any tundra, really—but still…

He needed her.

"I'm not sure what you're looking for here," she admitted when she found him wrenching open the front door. "I want to help Max, of course, but I've already explained to you what I feel the best course of action is to take. Have you changed your mind?"

He shut the door. Opened it again. Shut it again then turned to her. "No."

She hadn't thought so. He'd asked what he could do to help his son, hadn't given any indication he'd realized Harper's assessment was correct. "Then I don't know what else I can do."

"Today in class, when you were teaching that sentence stuff, why did you tell Max you were going to be calling on him next?"

Of all the things she'd thought he would say, that one hadn't made the top twenty. "I wanted him aware of what was going to happen and that I expected him to pay attention."

"You didn't do that for the other kids."

"Actually, I did the exact same thing for Rory Chapman not two minutes before you arrived."

"She have problems focusing, too?"

"He. And yes, he does." Rory had been diagnosed with ADHD last year.

"When you asked Max the question about subject and predicate, you practically spelled it out so he'd get it right."

"Not quite. More like I…led him in the right direction."

"You gave him special treatment."

She couldn't tell if that upset him or not. "No, what I did was use different teaching techniques. Kids with ADHD sometimes do better if they can prepare in advance for when they'll be called on, are given probing questions and plenty of time to think through their answers."

While she couldn't individualize every lesson plan, assignment or test, she could and did tweak how she taught to help each and every one of her students achieve their highest potential.

"Can you do that even if Max isn't diagnosed as ADHD?" Eddie asked.

Slippery ground here. "Since I already have, you

know the answer to that. But I still think it's in Max's best interest to have a proper diagnosis."

Eddie's jaw was tight, his shoulders rigid. "Maybe we could try this first. You using some of those different techniques in class and me working with Max at home."

She tossed her hands into the air, barely missing clipping him on the chin. Honestly, it was as if every word she said bounced right off his stubborn head. "I don't get it. You obviously love your son and want what's best for him. So why on earth are you so against him getting the help he needs?"

He stared at a spot above her head, stayed so still, she didn't think he'd ever breathe again, let alone answer. But then he exhaled heavily and met her eyes. "Because of my learning…problems, I was sent to special classes, kept separate from most of my peers. I always felt…different," he said slowly, as if he'd never spoken these words before and was figuring out how best to get them out of his head. "Like there was something wrong with me."

"There was nothing wrong with you," she said, her soft tone no less adamant, her heart aching for the boy he'd been. "And there's nothing wrong with Max."

"I still felt like I was never good enough. Smart enough. Like I was lacking in some fundamental way. And I need to do everything I can to protect Max from ever feeling that way."

He was trying to save his son from what he'd gone

through. She understood that, sympathized with it, but this wasn't some TV cop show where the main characters could go rogue and be rewarded as heroes for it. This was real life. And her very real career and professional reputation could be on the line if she stepped too far out of bounds.

What he was asking went against the school district's guidelines for helping students who were struggling. There were rules to follow, put in place to protect both the children and the teachers. It also went against her own instincts. Max needed to go through the steps outlined by the district—she'd already taken the first one by meeting with Eddie and discussing her concerns. The second one was to have Max diagnosed by one of the district's psychologists and, ideally, his pediatrician. Then they could develop the best strategy to help him succeed.

So why hadn't she told Eddie no already?

"What if you do everything you can and Max is still struggling?" she asked. "At what point do you admit there might be a bigger problem, one that you or I aren't able to solve on our own? Or even with our collective powers?"

"You mean because kids with ADHD have trouble learning?"

"There's a chance that children diagnosed with ADHD have a learning disability, but it's relatively small. A quart—"

"A quarter to a third."

"Someone's been doing internet research." Maybe he'd listened to her after all.

"I stumbled on a few sites about it." He sounded guilty, as if he'd admitted to downloading porn.

Cass shrieked in pure joy—never a good sign—and Harper peeked around the corner into the living room and found her using the sofa as a trampoline. "No jumping on the couch, Cassidy."

"Okay, Mommy!" Another shriek and the unmistakable sound of the couch springs groaning.

Harper sighed. "I appreciate what you're doing," she told Eddie, "and I get your reasons behind it. I do. But I still feel the best thing for Max is to go through the steps already in place, to utilize the school district's programs and support network."

"We could try it…you working with him…for a few months. If there's no improvement, I'll—" He pressed his lips together. Swallowed. "I'll agree to go through with the district plan."

When she hesitated, he stepped toward her, leaving a few feet between them, but he was close enough she smelled the spicy scent of his soap, could see the faint lines fanning his eyes.

"Please," he said, his rough voice seeming to rub against her skin.

God, who knew one word could be so…potent? So hard to refuse?

"I'll tutor Max," she grumbled, not bothering to hide her reluctance. "For one hour a day, Monday through Thursday right after school. Friday you and

I can meet to go over his progress and I'll give you some tips about helping him at home."

"I appreciate it."

He should. Talk about going above and beyond the call of duty. But she'd do it for Max.

"I'll tutor him," she repeated, "but if he shows little or no improvement by the end of the second marking period, you agree to try things my way."

She could see his mind working, could imagine the inner debate he was having with himself. Hadn't she had one of her own not two minutes ago? But this might be a good thing, this unexpected compromise they'd reached. She'd have a chance to work one-on-one with Max, giving her an opportunity to better assess his needs as well as his strengths and weaknesses. And if in the end she was able to help Max and know that she'd given Eddie peace of mind? Then it would be worth it.

"Agreed," he said and finally, thankfully, walked out her door.

Leaving his scent and the image of him holding her daughter etched in Harper's mind.

PASTOR ARROWSMITH WOULDN'T let go of her hands.

Keeping her expression clear, her fingers relaxed, Joan smiled at the older gentleman. "Lovely sermon this morning, Pastor."

She had no idea if it'd been lovely. For all she knew he'd gone on a rampage about fire and brimstone and the evils of sin leading straight to hell. She didn't listen to him anymore. Couldn't believe in forgiveness and eternal salvation, had no desire to trust in a God who'd let her son be taken away from her.

"Ah, thank you, Joan. Thank you." The pastor, a rather rotund man in his early seventies with silver hair and a chin beard that made him look like a leprechaun, squeezed her hands. Held on tight as he leaned forward and lowered his voice. "Mitzi and I have been thinking about you, what with the one-year anniversary approaching. And, of course, we keep you and your family in our prayers. How is everyone holding up?"

Joan's fingers went numb. Her heart raced, her stomach churned with a toxic combination of pain and anger. How dare he bring it up? She didn't need reminding of how long it'd been since Beau had died.

Two hundred and ninety-three days.

And she certainly didn't need his concern or the sympathy softening his expression. Did he really think she'd tell him her innermost thoughts and feelings? That she couldn't hold up under the stress and strain?

She didn't need a shoulder to cry on or a sympathetic ear. Didn't need to lean on anyone. She'd withstand her loss on her own two feet.

"How is Mitzi?" Joan asked smoothly, the only telltale sign of her distress being the slight rasp of her usually clear voice. "I didn't see her in church."

He hesitated, as if unsure about whether he should push. Joan met his gaze equably. No one watching would ever guess she was anything other than completely calm and in control.

"Unfortunately, my better half is a bit under the weather. She'll be sorry she missed you."

No longer caring how it looked, what he would think, she yanked her hands free, tucked them behind her back so he couldn't reach for them again. He was just being kind, letting her change the subject. Trying to help her by being placating and sensitive to her feelings. She should be grateful.

Instead, she hated him for it.

"I was hoping to discuss setting up a meeting of the Women's Club but I'll catch up with her next week. Oh," Joan continued, spying Steve near the corner, "there's my husband. I'd better join him before he goes home without me. Please tell Mitzi I hope she feels better soon."

Without waiting for his reply, she walked off, the heels of her pumps sinking into the grass as she crossed the neatly trimmed yard in front of the church. Her fellow parishioners greeted her with a friendly word or wave. She responded to each and every one, stopping to chat for a moment, laughing at each inane comment about what a nice day it was, answering questions about Cassidy, pretending she cared about what was being said.

She wanted to go home. To sit in her bedroom, nurse her throbbing headache with some tea and the dark. The quiet. But Steve was engrossed in conversation with a dark-haired, curvaceous woman a few years younger than them, one Joan recognized as a new member of the congregation but couldn't name. They obviously knew each other, though. If their body language was anything to go by, they were comfortable around each other.

Very comfortable.

Joan couldn't make herself care. Couldn't work up even the tiniest twinge of jealousy, of doubt or worry. The other woman stood close to Steve, her body leaning ever so slightly toward him. As Joan watched, the woman threw her head back and laughed at something he said then playfully patted his arm.

Typical signs of interest. Attraction. She was flirting with him, from the way she kept touching her glossy black hair to the way she made eye contact then looked away. Not that Joan blamed her. Steve was a handsome man, his brown hair only beginning to show signs of gray, his body toned and slim from his daily swim and workout at the gym. A handsome man with a quick, sharp sense of humor and a deep devotion to his family.

He was a good man. Her husband. And she could no longer stand him touching her, had no desire to be intimate with him—physically or emotionally. Wished on most days that he'd leave her alone. All alone.

He didn't deserve to be treated that way. Didn't deserve her turning him away time and time again. But she couldn't stop herself.

Since he had yet to notice her, she worked to keep her expression pleasant and joined him. "Sorry, sorry," she said to Steve with a breathless laugh as she reached him and the other woman. "I was chatting with Pastor Arrowsmith. Poor Mitzi's under the weather." With a smile, she turned to the woman. "Hello."

"Dr. Crosby, it's so nice to see you again. You might not remember but we met shortly after my kids and I moved here." She offered her hand. "I'm Carrie English."

Yes, now Joan remembered. Carrie English, moved to Shady Grove after her divorce, worked as a paralegal or some such thing. "Of course. It's so nice to see you again."

"Oh, you, too," Carrie said. "I'm afraid I've been monopolizing your husband's time. My oldest just got his driver's permit and I've been drilling Steve about insurance rates."

"That's such a wonderful milestone." Beau had been so excited about learning how to drive, thrilled with the prospect of freedom, then so nervous when he'd first gotten behind the wheel. "How are your children?"

She gave a rueful shrug. "They're teenagers. What else can I say? Every word I utter is wrong and starts an argument. They eat me out of house and home, and are either texting on their phones or fighting with each other. I love them, don't get me wrong, but there are times I want them to hurry and grow up already."

And she laughed.

Anger flowed through Joan, left her trembling with the effort to hold it inside. A scream burned in her throat.

Shut up! Shut up, you stupid cow! You don't know how lucky you are to be able to see your children every day, to hear their voices, to hold them close.

"The teenage years can be trying," Steve said. "Our kids gave us a run for our money a few times, that's for sure." He looked at Joan expectantly as if waiting for her to agree.

Steve's children, Michael and Miranda, *had* been difficult teenagers. Rebellious. Defiant. But Beau had never given them any trouble. He'd been such an easy child, his middle and high school years had been uncomplicated and enjoyable.

When she kept silent, hurt crossed Steve's face but he masked it with a grin and turned to Carrie. "But to be honest, I wouldn't trade those years for anything."

"I'll keep that in mind," Carrie said. "As long as you promise things really do get better and they start acting like humans again."

"We should get going," Joan blurted, unable to hear another word from this woman, this woman who had what Joan didn't—her children healthy and whole and alive. She linked her arm through Steve's, ignored how he stiffened. "I know how you hate to miss opening kickoff."

He nodded curtly then smiled at Carrie and offered her his card. "If you want us to take a look at your policy, give you a quote on what our rates would be, just give me a call at the office."

"Oh, you'll be hearing from me," she said, her voice turning husky.

Joan kept pressed against Steve's side as they crossed to the parking lot, only pulling away when they reached their car and he opened her door for her. She slid into the passenger seat, stared straight ahead while he got in and turned on the car.

He looked at her, the engine idling. "Are you okay?"

She yanked the seat belt across her chest, clicked it into place with a hard shove. "Why does everyone insist on asking me that?" Was she okay? Was she all right? How was she coping?

It was none of their damn business.

"They ask," he said, "because they care about you."

She didn't want them to and she didn't wish to discuss this any further. "The next time you flirt with another woman, please try and be more discreet."

"Is that what this is about?" he asked. "You're jealous?"

He sounded hopeful but she refused to lie to him. He was the only person she wouldn't lie to. "Not at all. But I have a reputation in the community, one I don't want tarnished."

"I don't see how you could be held accountable for my behavior."

She gaped at him. "Of course I can. Your behavior reflects on me and vice versa. We are a couple, both successful and are thought of in a certain way." Steve owned a thriving insurance business. "People have expectations of how we should act, how we live our lives. One mistake, one moment of weakness could set tongues wagging." And everyone would know she was broken.

He jerked the car into gear, slowly pulled out of the lot. "I don't give a damn about gossips."

"Maybe not," she said, her lips barely moving, "but I do. All I'm asking is that if you do find yourself in a…compromising position…you make sure no one discovers it."

He slid a glance at her, his expression unreadable. "I'm not Bruce, Joan."

No, he wasn't her first husband, was nothing like the philandering playboy she'd made the mistake of marrying right out of college. But he was a man.

And she was no longer the woman he'd married, the wife he'd shared his life with all these years. She'd changed, and she wasn't sure she would ever change back.

They drove in silence the remaining mile home. Turning into their driveway, he pressed the garage door opener clipped to the visor.

"You're an attractive man," Joan said as the door slowly rose. "An attractive man in the prime of your life. Our sex life has been far from satisfying for you lately so it's understandable if you find yourself searching for another woman to be intimate with." She met his eyes, kept calm under the heat of his narrowed gaze. "I would understand."

"You'd understand if I took a lover?" he asked in a quiet, dangerous tone she'd never, not once, heard from him before. He put the car into Park and turned off the engine, his words low, his movements controlled. "My being with another woman wouldn't bother you?"

She thought of him with another woman, a woman like Carrie, imagined him touching her, making love to her the way he used to make love to Joan.

She shut her eyes and scanned her body for a reaction, any sort of twinge of regret or panic, but there was nothing. No pain. No anger. No sadness.

Nothing.

"If you were to seek female companionship outside of our marriage, if you did so in a tasteful manner, a manner in which nobody ever found out about it, I wouldn't hold it against you."

He laughed, a harsh, bitter sound that filled the car, chafed her nerve endings. "That's big of you. And now, because you are such an enlightened woman, so magnanimous, you're giving me your what? Blessing to have an affair?"

She shifted, tugged at the seat belt which seemed

to be strangling her. She unhooked it, let it snap back. Why couldn't he see this was the perfect solution? He deserved more than she could give him right now, maybe more than she could ever give him again.

"Not my blessing. My understanding. And," she said, rubbing her palms along the legs of her dress pants, wrinkling the silky material, "if it suits you, my permission."

"If it suits me? What the hell is wrong with you? If you think I want your permission, if you think I'm the type of man who'd cheat on you, treat you like your bastard of a first husband, then you don't know me at all." He opened the door, his chest rising and falling rapidly with his quick breaths, but when he spoke, his voice was low, the words barely a whisper. "And I sure as hell don't know you."

"PUT THE GAME down," Eddie told Max for the third time, "and get out of the truck already."

Standing in Harper's driveway, he held the driver's side door open while his kid's fingers pressed button after button on his video game. Some days he wished he could toss the damn thing out the window.

"Max. Now."

Still playing, despite Eddie's enough-of-this-bullshit tone, Max slid along the seat, finally looking up when he sat behind the steering wheel.

"Are you sure Mrs. Kavanagh lives here?" Max asked.

"Positive."

"How do you know?"

Because he'd shown up here, two nights ago, without warning to beg for her help.

It'd been humiliating, having to tell her why he was so worried for Max, spilling a few of his secrets. Luckily, it'd been worth it.

"I just know. Are you coming or not? Because in ten seconds I'm shutting the door—"

Max jumped down, landing with his chin practically touching his bent knees. He popped up like a spring and followed Eddie to the rear of the truck.

"I didn't know she lived in Shady Grove," Max said in a hushed voice.

"Where did you think she lived? The moon? That'd be one long commute."

He rubbed the side of his nose. "I thought her house would look different." He glanced at the green cottage-style house, his shoulders drooping in disappointment. "It's just regular."

Eddie opened the tailgate and slid his toolbox toward him, checked to make sure he had what he needed, then lifted it. "What would you have preferred? An igloo? A thatched hut?"

Max shrugged.

"Teachers are people," Eddie told him as he hoisted his toolbox. "Just like you and me. They live in regular houses, buy groceries, go to the movies, cook dinner, get sick and…"

And Max was playing his game again, his

head bent over it as he softly chanted, "Come on, come *on*..."

Eddie walked to the house. Max would come up for air eventually. He could find Eddie then.

He knocked on the door. A moment later he heard the pounding of little feet running, then the doorknob jiggled. "Hello?" Cassidy called.

For such a little thing, she had a booming voice.

The door opened and Harper blinked at him. Blinked again. "Have I stepped into a time loop? Because I could've sworn we were here just the other day."

He searched for something to say, some funny, witty, smart response. James would smile and laugh, make a joke of his own. Eddie's younger brother, Leo, would go right for the charm that was as much a part of him as breathing, giving her a wink and some slick come-on.

But Eddie's mind was blank. Her fault. Her and that outfit she had on—a snug, black Pittsburgh Steelers T-shirt and dark jeans that molded to her curves. Her hair was pulled into a ponytail, just like the one she used to wear when she'd cheered at the high school football games, and he scanned her figure again, wondered what she'd look like now wearing that little skirt.

Wished he could find out.

"Deddie!" Cass cried, running up to him in a pair of jeans and a tiny Steelers football jersey with the number forty-three on the front. "Hi! Hold me."

She lifted her arms.

Harper's sigh was a work of art, one most parents had heaved at one point or another. "Cassidy, do you have to be so bossy all the time?"

Cass hopped up and down, her arms still up. "Yes."

Christ, but she was about the cutest thing he'd ever seen. He set his toolbox on the porch then picked her up and settled her on his hip. He grinned. "What are these?" he asked, tugging playfully at one of her pigtails. "Handles?"

She slapped both hands on her head, her little fingers getting tangled in the black-and-gold ribbons tied around her hair. "Piggy-tails. 'Cept I not a pig. I a big girl."

"I hate to be the bearer of bad news," Harper told her, "but big girls use the potty."

"No, Mommy," Cass said solemnly. "Big girls wear diapers."

"Then I guess you're all set. Because the way things are going with your potty training, you'll still be in diapers at your high school graduation."

That fact didn't seem to bother Cass one bit.

"Max wasn't fully potty trained until he was almost four," Eddie said, knowing how frustrating it was to be in charge of potty training. To be solely responsible for every aspect of your child's development.

"So you're saying there's still hope?"

"There's always hope. Not sure why it's so hard to

teach them something so basic and simple as using the toilet, though."

She smiled. It lit her face. And took his breath away. "I know. After I told Sadie how Cass wet her pants four times in one day, Sadie started bragging about how she house-trained her puppy in a few weeks. I considered killing her and burying the body but then I figured I might need her to use those dog whispering skills on Cass."

One of the first things James had done when Sadie finally realized they were meant to be together was get her a puppy. At least it wasn't as binding as an engagement ring. Eddie still wasn't sure one of them wouldn't change their minds about the whole *being in love and together forever* thing.

"Cass'll get the hang of it," Eddie promised. "She's a smart girl."

Harper snorted. "I'll say. She's outsmarted me on this so far." She glanced behind Eddie. "Hello, Max."

Eddie turned as Max climbed the steps. "Hi."

"Hi!" Cass wiggled like a fish on a hook and Eddie set her on her feet before she did a nosedive onto the porch. She grinned at Max. "What's you name?"

He sidled next to Eddie. "Max."

"Play with me, Max."

Harper stepped onto the porch. "Max may not want to play, Cass."

"Yes, he does. Come on," she told Max, taking his

hand but unable to move sixty pounds of shy, stubborn boy. "Come." Another tug. "On."

"Enough." Harper's stern tone got through and Cass, with a pout worthy of an Oscar nomination, dropped her chin to her chest and let go of Max's hand. "Let's find out what Max and his father are doing here and then, maybe, if you ask politely— that's ask, not tell—Max will play with you. Okay?"

Cass nodded but didn't look up.

Harper winked at Max. "Now, to what do I owe this unexpected pleasure?"

Don't think Eddie missed the way she emphasized *unexpected*.

"We're gonna fix your door," Max told her.

"Is that right?" Harper raised her eyebrows at Eddie. "And why would you do that?"

Did he really have to answer when it was so obvious? From the way Harper watched him, he guessed he did.

"It sticks," he said.

"Yes. But you don't have to fix it."

"I'm here. My tools are here." He shrugged. Couldn't she just leave it at that?

"Now can Max play with me, Mommy?" Cass asked. "Please?"

"That's up to him. You don't have to if you don't want to," Harper told Max.

He straightened with all the bravery and enthusiasm of someone facing a firing squad. "It's okay." He looked at Cass. "I'll play with you."

"Yay!" Cass grabbed his hand.

"The Montesano charm strikes again," Harper murmured as her daughter dragged Max inside. "But then, it's as I always suspected." She held Eddie's gaze, curved those glossy lips that drove him mad into a playful grin. "It's the quiet ones a girl has to watch out for."

CHAPTER SEVEN

IT'S THE QUIET ones a girl has to watch out for.

She was teasing him, Eddie realized. Making a light, almost flirting comment because she felt it safe to do so. She probably thought because he kept his thoughts to himself, didn't blurt out everything that popped into his head, that he was harmless.

He wanted to prove he wasn't. That she had reason to be wary of him, of his true intentions. He wanted to invade her space, press his nose against the long line of her neck and inhale her scent. Taste her there, where the pulse beat at the base of her throat.

And that would be the end of her helping him and his son.

"I'll need to take the door off its hinges," he told her, "but it should only take a few minutes to plane it."

She laughed as if he'd made some hilarious joke. "You're not fixing my door."

He'd already said he was—or, actually, Max had. But it was the same idea so he didn't bother correcting her.

His mother and sister had taught him exactly how impossible it was to win an argument with a woman.

He knelt at his toolbox. As he retrieved what he needed, Harper called for the kids, asked them if they'd like to play outside. By the time she zipped Cassidy into a pink jacket, gave them a bucket of sidewalk chalk and asked them to draw her pictures on the cement sidewalk, he'd grabbed a chunk of chalk for himself and rubbed it along the latch side of the door and opened and shut it several times.

"Wait, wait, wait," Harper called, hurrying up the porch steps. "We have to discuss this."

"Not everything needs to be talked to death."

During the time they had their little *discussion,* he could be done and on his way back home.

"Be that as it may, you seem to have forgotten one itsy-bitsy—but very important—thing."

Frowning, he glanced into his toolbox. He didn't need much for this job, chalk—which she'd provided—and a hand planer. It wasn't rocket science. It was planing a door so it opened and shut smoothly. "No, I didn't."

"You forgot," she said in a calm, patient tone she probably used when trying to get through to the kids in her class, "that I did not hire you to fix my door."

Was that all? "I'm off the clock. No charge."

But when he knelt to tap the pin free of the bottom hinge, she blocked him. "Eddie, I didn't ask you to fix my door. I didn't hire you to fix my door. I do not want you to fix my door. Clear?"

"Crystal."

She nodded, all self-satisfied as if she'd won some battle.

"You didn't ask me to fix your door," he repeated, straightening. "I'm offering. To…thank you. For helping Max."

"Oh. Oh," she repeated, drawing the word out so that it was three syllables long. No easy trick, that. "What you mean is, you want to fix the door so you won't feel beholden to me."

"I don't usually use words like *beholden,* but yeah. That about sums it up." And he didn't like that she'd read him that correctly. That easily. "But if you don't want it fixed—"

"Far be it from me to stand between a man and his pride," she said, stepping aside and gesturing grandly. "Please. By all means, do what you have to do."

He would. He just hoped like hell she didn't keep staring at him as if trying to bore a hole into his skull so she could read his mind. Women, they all wanted to know every thought a man had, every feeling.

He was entitled to his own thoughts and to the right to keep those thoughts to himself.

Using a hammer and nail set, he tapped the pins free from the hinges. He wiggled the door free only to freeze when she laid her hand on his back. It was only for a second but it was long enough for her warmth to burn through the fabric of his T-shirt, to heat his skin.

He whipped his head around so fast, he was surprised he didn't dislodge a few vertebrae.

She didn't notice. She was too busy peering over his shoulder. "Why don't you unscrew the hinges from the wall?"

"Easier this way."

"Don't you have to measure it?"

He carefully opened the door, pointed to the chalk. "See where it's rubbed off?" She nodded. "That's where it's swollen."

She smiled. "That's really clever."

Yeah, that was him. Clever. He wiggled the door free, let her help him lift it and lay it on its hinge side.

"Want me to hold it?" she asked.

"Why don't you do the planing?"

She laughed, the light sound carrying on the breeze to wrap around him. "I don't think that's a good idea."

"Why not?"

"Because I've never done it before?"

He held out the hand planer. "First time for everything."

She hesitated then accepted the tool. "What do I do?"

"Just run it along the edge," he said, pointing again to where the chalk was gone. "Hold it with both hands, flat against the wood. You don't have to press hard, let the blade do the work and just…" He made a pushing motion, going up at the end as if ascending an incline. "Don't stop dead when you reach the end, sweep it up."

"Sweep it. Okay. Sure."

He kept the door steady while she laid the tool on the wood.

"Sweep it," she repeated in a whisper. She bit her lower lip, frowned in concentration and pushed the planer. "Like that?"

He nodded and couldn't stop from smiling at how serious she was, how intent, as if he was going to grade her. "It probably doesn't need much, maybe two or three more times."

While she went over the door, he glanced at the kids. Max was on his stomach, making what looked to be an apple orchard on the sidewalk. Cass mimicked his pose, from her feet being in the air to her hand holding up her chin. Looked like his kid had his first female admirer.

"Well," Harper said, as several thin sheets of wood curled at her feet. "What do you think?"

"Let's try it out. See how we did." Together, they lifted it upright and set it back into the hinges. "Much better," he said after shutting it and opening it a few times. "Can you hand me those pins?"

She picked them up from where he'd laid them by his toolbox. She was quiet. He didn't like it. Not when he was getting used to hearing her talk.

Her silence made him nervous. Made him think he had to find something to say to fill it.

Shit.

"So…uh…" He tapped the top pin into place, cleared his throat. "You like the Steelers, huh?"

He winced, felt a blush creep up his neck. *Of course she likes the Steelers, you idiot. Look at her clothes.*

"Like is such a weak word to describe what I feel for the boys in gold and black."

She sounded so serious, so devoted to Pittsburgh's professional football team, he glanced over his shoulder. She wasn't kidding.

"I never would've pegged you as a football fan," he said. Weren't women like her, smart, educated women, into finer pursuits? The ballet or opera?

"I get that a lot. When we were first dating, Beau thought I only spent Sundays watching the games because he liked to."

Beau, her dead husband. "He liked the Steelers, too?"

She nodded. "He preferred baseball, though." Glancing around, she leaned in close and lowered her voice. "He was a Yankees fan."

Only a foot separated them, a mere twelve inches between him and those lush curves, that perfect mouth. His brain screamed at him to retreat, his body told him to get closer. He didn't move. Couldn't. "That's a bad thing?"

"Hey, I didn't make the rules. You either love the Yankees or hate them."

He couldn't help it. He grinned. "But you still married a Yankees fan."

She sighed dramatically, but couldn't hide her own smile. "Everyone has their flaws. That was Beau's. Luckily, I'm a very tolerant and forgiving soul."

"He was a lucky man."

Staring at her daughter, she rubbed her thumb over the base of her wedding rings. "I was the lucky one."

He hated the sadness in her eyes, the thickness of her voice as if she was fighting tears. Hated that she'd been so hurt, that she still dealt with that pain. He had no clue what to do, how to act. He felt useless and more tongue-tied than usual, afraid if he opened his mouth, he'd say the wrong thing. Make everything worse.

But she was sad. And that wouldn't do.

"I'm sorry," he said, hoping she understood what he truly meant.

I'm sorry for your loss. So sorry your daughter will never know her father, that you have to live the rest of your life without the man you so obviously loved.

"Thank you. It was hard. Some days it's as hard as the day he was killed. Others..." She shook her head. "Others it's as if he's been gone forever. Almost as if he never was a part of our lives."

"He's still a part of it," Eddie said softly. "He always will be." He nodded toward Cassidy, who was talking a mile a minute to a patient Max.

Harper followed his gaze then looked back at him. "Wow. Who would've guessed behind all that—"

she waved a hand at him vaguely "—stoic silence, were such deep, insightful thoughts?"

She was teasing him again. He could handle good-natured ribbing. He had two brothers who excelled at it, a sister whose tongue was as sharp as a blade.

But he didn't like the idea of Harper thinking he was some dim-witted fool, someone who kept his peace because he didn't know what to say.

Even if there were times that assessment was correct.

He stepped closer to her, noted the small frown that formed between her eyebrows, the way her throat worked as she swallowed. "I don't say every thought that pops into my head," he told her, his words low, his tone mild. "If I did, I would've told you, as soon as you opened the door, how pretty you look today."

She flinched as if he'd slapped her instead of complimented her. "I…you…"

He grinned. He liked that he could make her stutter, could make her speechless. "I would have said," he continued relentlessly, "that I like your hair pulled back because it shows off your neck and reminds me of when you used to cheer at the football and basketball games. It seemed every time I happened to glance your way, you were smiling. Laughing." He dropped his gaze to her lips. "I used to dream about your mouth."

She inhaled sharply, took a quick step back.

Shoving his hands in his pockets where they

couldn't get him into trouble—like his mouth probably had—he met her eyes again. "Those thoughts deep enough for you?"

IT'S THE QUIET ones a girl has to watch out for.

Dear, sweet Lord, but she'd hit the nail smack dab on the head with that one.

Harper's scalp prickled, sweat formed between her breasts as if the air temperature had suddenly shifted a good forty degrees or so. Two minutes ago she'd been perfectly fine, calm and cool. Comfortable and at ease with quiet, shy Eddie Montesano. Teasing him a bit, being her usual oh, so witty self, saying—as he'd put it—every thought that had popped into her head.

She should take a lesson from his book.

Because now she was hot, sweaty and a cluster of nerves. Flustered beyond anything she could recall in recent memory.

Stepping back again, this time trying to make the move as casual as possible, she linked her hands together at her waist. "Uh...yes. Those were...that was..."

Bizarre. Disconcerting. And very, very confusing.

Not that Eddie seemed bothered in the least. Oh, no, he was just fine, thank you very much, watching her in that careful, assessing way of his. As if he hadn't shared words that had the power to turn her safe, settled world upside down.

Well, she wouldn't let them. Wouldn't let Eddie change anything about her, about her life. Including how she dealt with him.

"Kids," she called, sounding desperate to her own ears. Okay, so maybe she would let him change how she dealt with him. A woman had to be smart, had to protect herself, didn't she? And if there was one thing Harper was, it was smart. She forced a smile when Cass and Max looked up. "Why don't you come inside? We'll have milk and cookies."

"Cookies!" Cass cried, doing a decent imitation of *Sesame Street*'s Cookie Monster as she clambered to her feet. She tugged on the slower-moving Max's arm. "Come on, Max! Come on."

"I'll just clean up here," Eddie said.

Was that humor she heard in his voice? Figured, the first time she'd seen him amused it was at her expense.

"Sure. Fine." She put her hands on her hips as Cass and Max raced between them and into the house. Dropped them back to her sides. Felt like wringing her hands but that seemed a bit overly dramatic. "Come on in when you're done. We'll be in the kitchen. And…uh…thanks again. For fixing the door."

No matter what anybody said, Harper did *not* bolt as if her rear was on fire. She walked, rather sedately if you asked her, her head held high, her arms loose and swinging naturally. If she so happened to slam the door shut with more force than necessary, it was only because she wasn't used to it swinging into place so easily.

"Cassidy," Harper said on a groan when she stepped into the kitchen and caught her baby sitting on her knees on the counter. "What have I told you about climbing onto the counter?"

Happy as you please, Cass bit into a chocolate chip cookie, leaving a smear of chocolate on her chin. "I not 'posed to."

"Exactly. You're not supposed to. So why are you?"

Cass widened her big blue eyes and held out a cookie. "Want a cookie, Mommy?"

Harper sent a pleading look to the heavens. Both Cass and Max looked up as well as if to see what the heck she was looking at.

"No, I do not want a cookie. But thank you for asking and trying to distract me from you breaking the rules."

"You welcome."

Some days Harper wondered why she bothered. She set Cass on the floor. "Let's go into the bathroom and wash your hands."

Cass wrapped her arms around Max's waist, squeezed him so hard, Harper was surprised his eyes didn't pop out of his head. "I want Max to wash them."

"Max has to wash his own hands."

"I can help her," he said. "If you want."

"That's very nice of you, Max, but you don't have to."

"It's okay. I want to."

Harper shouldn't let him. God knew Cassidy didn't need to get her way all the time—and she didn't. But Harper wouldn't mind a few minutes alone to gather her thoughts. Get herself back on steady ground.

"That would be great. Thank you. Let me get the water going so it's not too hot for her."

After leaving them in the bathroom, both of them sudsing up their hands, she poured milk into plastic cups, put a lid on Cass's. She plated some chocolate chip cookies and laid them on the table, then took a deep breath. Shut her eyes and cleared her mind. Exhaled. There. Much better.

I used to dream about your mouth.

Her eyes flew open and she glanced around, but Eddie hadn't appeared in the kitchen. His words, that particular statement, however, kept playing over and over in her head.

I used to dream about your mouth.

Oh, jeez. Oh, God. That was…that meant…

Her mouth dried. Her palms grew damp. She lifted the gallon of milk, drank deep straight from the container. She lowered it and wiped the back of her trembling hand over her mouth. No. No. It couldn't mean what she was thinking.

He probably meant it in an innocent way. Kissing or…or…

She rolled her eyes. Or what? He'd been a teenage boy. Who knew what sort of things they thought about, what with their rampant hormones and wet dreams and all.

Had he fantasized about them? Him and…and… her?

She sagged against the table. The mere idea of something so intimate, so raw and basic between them, between her and another man, a man who wasn't her husband, should send her running, screaming in terror. In offense. And mortification.

It did. Of course it did. She was a nice girl and a nice girl did not think about even the possibility of oral sex with the father of one of her students. Not while their children were splashing in the sink in the next room, their giggles high-pitched and infectious.

Unless that nice girl also happened to be a grown woman. A woman who'd been married for years and had a child. A woman who enjoyed sex very much. Very, very much.

A sudden image slammed into her, a familiar fantasy, one she'd had often of Beau, one they'd lived out many times. She, on her knees in front of him, his hands tangled in her loose hair, his head thrown back as she took him into her mouth.

It was so clear, so intense and erotic, she bit her lower lip to stop a whimper. Lust pooled in her stomach, swept through her veins even as tears stung her eyes.

Because this time, it wasn't Beau she was pleasuring.

It was Eddie.

She slid onto a chair, grabbed a cookie and viciously bit into it.

Joan would say she was transferring what she really wanted into a desire for chocolate.

So be it. Chocolate may add a few more pounds to her hips—and was already to be blamed for the extra ten she carried there—but at least she didn't worry about what it would do to her reputation. And having sexy Eddie Montesano at her house, telling her things he had no right telling her was messing with her brain. And her willpower.

It was putting ideas into her head. Enticing, highly-charged, lust-filled thoughts that had no right being there.

Only because she hadn't had sex—real, live sex with a real, live man—in almost a year. Because she was a woman in her prime. Not because she was attracted to Eddie.

She ate another cookie. Yes, he was attractive with that shy grin, his golden eyes. More so than she may have realized until now. Much, much more than she would have liked.

The kids came in, their feet pounding on the wood floor. Thank God. Without a distraction, she didn't trust herself not to create other dangerous, porno-graphic scenarios starring her and Eddie.

"Have a seat," she said, pulling a chair out for Max. "Help yourself."

He sat and Cass immediately shoved a chair next to his and climbed up.

"You my boyfriend," she told him in the same no-nonsense tone most people used when informing someone that the sky was, indeed, blue.

Max, in the act of reaching for a cookie, froze, complete terror crossing his face. His panicked gaze flew to Cass and then to Harper. "Uh…"

"How about if Max is your friend who happens to be a boy?" Harper asked Cass.

Cass frowned, looking so much like her father, Harper's heart broke just a little. "No. He's my boy-friend." She turned to Max, hands on her hips. "You my boyfriend."

"I thought Hunter and Travis at day care were your boyfriends?" Harper said. "And Nate? Nate's the paperboy," she explained to Max.

"They my boyfriends, too."

Harper winked at Max. "She's fickle. Pretty much every boy under the age of twenty is her boyfriend." She added air quotes around the last word.

"Oh. I get it." He sent Harper a small smile at their shared secret. "I'll be your boyfriend," he said to Cass.

She looked at him as if she never doubted he'd

come around. And how she got chocolate on her eyebrow, Harper had no idea.

But at least she'd picked a winner for her latest conquest. Max was such a sweet kid, always the first to offer comfort when one of his classmates got hurt—physically or emotionally. He didn't say much. There were days she didn't think he said anything at all, but he'd sit next to an injured child just to…be there. Though he had his troubles focusing, she'd noticed he was very quick to pick things up, read situations and people clearly.

Like father like son.

"Me and Mommy made cookies," Cass told him. She drank some milk, slammed the cup down like a cowboy at a saloon. "I stirred them. I the best stirrer."

"You are tops when it comes to stirring," Harper said.

Cass climbed down and ran around to the other side of Max's chair. "Let's play. I be the mommy and you the daddy."

Max was only halfway finished with his second cookie. "Why don't you get out some of your puzzles instead?" Harper suggested to Cass. "You and Max can put them together in here on the floor."

"Okay, but I still the mommy."

"More milk?" Harper asked Max after Cass ran out of the room.

He shook his head and she stood to put it in the fridge.

"I make cookies with my nonna." His voice was

soft, as if confessing a crime. "She lets me turn on the mixer. And crack the eggs."

"I bet she loves having you help her." Though Mrs. Montesano must have a few tricks up her sleeve to keep Max engaged in an activity that wasn't computer or video game related. Harper had found he lost focus if she didn't repeat what she wanted him to do calmly and patiently, and checked on him often to make sure he was on task. "What kind of cookies do you make?"

He shrugged. Guessed they were back to his father's way of communicating—shrugs, nods and the occasional grunt. But then he lifted his head and met her eyes. "All kinds. But chocolate chip are my favorite."

"Mine, too." She wished celery sticks were her favorite but you couldn't have everything in life.

He broke a piece of cookie off, mashed it into his paper napkin. "My mom doesn't make cookies."

"No?" she asked, super casually. This was the first time Max had ever mentioned his mother to her. She needed to be careful. "Well, not all moms like to bake cookies. But some dads do."

"My dad never makes cookies. He builds stuff." Max finished his drink then lowered his glass to reveal a thick milk mustache. "My mom's too busy to make them. She works all the time."

She knew from Max's records that his mother lived in Chicago. He obviously didn't have much to do with her. She wasn't even listed as an emergency contact for him. Instead, Eddie had put down his parents and then his sister, Maddie.

Harper retook her seat. "Do you miss her?"

He shrugged. But his expression said he did miss her. Or at least, he missed having a mother in his life. "She called me the other night."

"So you get to talk to her on the phone a lot? What about video chatting? You know, like what we did when Hannah was sick?" Hannah had missed two weeks of school with a severe case of strep throat so her parents and Harper had set up a video chat between her and the class to cheer her up.

"We used to," Max said. "But Mom stopped." He broke his cookie in half. Then in half again. "Dad told me you said I hafta stay after school every day," he blurted.

She heard the front door open followed by Cass's voice, Eddie's low response. "Didn't your dad explain why I want you to stay after?"

He shook his head. "Is it 'cause I was bad the other day? I'll be good. I promise."

Eddie, you numbskull. What did you tell this boy?

"I appreciate your apology but you're not in trouble."

"I'm not?"

"No. The reason I want you to stay after school is so I can give you extra help with your schoolwork."

He swung his leg, his foot brushing against the floor. *Swish...swish...swish...* "Oh."

"It'll be fun," she said.

His look said, *you have got to be kidding.*

She laughed. Reached over and squeezed his forearm. "Really. I promise I'll do my best to make it as painless as possible."

"You ready to go, Max?" Eddie asked from the doorway.

Just having him in the same room after what he'd said, what she'd imagined, was enough to give her heart palpitations. She wanted him gone so she could give her brain a mental scrubbing, rid her thoughts of him.

But he couldn't leave. Not quite yet.

"Max," she said, getting to her feet, "why don't you go in the living room with Cass while I pack up some cookies for you to take home?"

"Okay."

At the same time Eddie spoke. "We don't need any cookies."

"That's crazy," Harper said as Max ran off. "A seven-year-old boy definitely needs cookies. Besides, I was hoping you and I could have a little chat."

He raised his eyebrows until they disappeared under the brim of his ball cap. "Another one?"

Her mouth dried remembering their last talk. Staring at his throat—the only place she seemed capable of looking at without blushing—she nodded. "How about a beer to help you get through it? I won't add it onto the mental list of ways you owe me."

He glanced longingly at the doorway then gave

a resigned sigh. "I'm driving. But I'll take a soda if you have one."

She grabbed a can from the fridge, handed it to him, careful not to let their fingers touch. "Look, I hope you don't think I'm sticking my nose in where it doesn't belong, but does Max get to see his mother often?"

He paused in the act of taking a drink, his body stiff, his shoulders rigid. "No."

"Because," she continued, though she was obviously treading on dangerous ground here, "we were talking about her and—"

"You asked about his mom?" he asked, all flinty-eyed and suspicious.

"That's the thing." She got a plate from the cupboard, began setting cookies on it. "Usually with Max I have to drag the words out of him to make sure his vocal cords are still working, but today he offered the information himself."

"What did he say?"

"He said his mom didn't make cookies. That she was too busy working."

"Lena's a fashion buyer for a major department store in Chicago. She works a lot of overtime and travels often."

"He also said he spoke with her the other day."

"She called." Eddie stared at the soda can, rubbed his thumb up and down the side, wiping off the condensation. "She wants to see him next weekend."

"He didn't mention that."

"He doesn't know."

"How can he not know?"

"I didn't tell him."

She wished she could coldcock him over his stubborn head. "Like you didn't tell him you were the one who asked me to help him with his schoolwork? Or that the reason he needed to stay after school was for tutoring? He thought he was in trouble."

"I never said it was punishment."

"You never say much." She set the plate down with a sharp crack. A cookie slid off. "Have you ever considered that's part of the problem?"

His eyes narrowed. "Lena's been…under the weather. I don't want Max to get his hopes up only to have him disappointed if she has to cancel."

Okay, so maybe he didn't deserve a bump on the head. He was looking out for his son, trying to do what was best. Wasn't that what all good parents did? The best they could?

"What are you going to do if she does show up?"

"I hadn't thought it through that far."

Harper covered the cookies with plastic wrap. "It might not be any of my business, but I think it would do Max a lot of good if you talked to him about his mother."

"You're right." He took a drink. Set the can on the table. "It's none of your business."

"All I'm saying is you might want to have a conversation with your son, a real conversation that includes actual words, about how he feels about his mother. He seemed very…conflicted."

Conflicted. Confused. Hurt. He needed someone to talk to.

To talk to him.

"His mother," Eddie said, still in that low, soft voice, "left him when he was two years old because taking care of him interfered with her career. How do you think he feels?"

Harper's heart ached for Max. And maybe just a little bit for the hard-eyed man in front of her. "I don't know. There's no right or wrong way for him to feel and he needs to know that. And I think it'd do Max some good to express his feelings."

"Max is fine. I'll take care of it."

"That's your answer for everything, isn't it? You'll take care of it. You'll fix it. You don't want any help."

"I don't need any."

"Must be nice. But the rest of us mortals get by with a little help from our friends." She handed him the plate, held on when he reluctantly took it. "Oh, wait. You don't have friends. You're one of those lone wolf types."

For a moment, he looked as if he would argue, but then he tugged on the plate, pulling her a step closer. Her heart picked up speed, her eyes widened. A mix of fear, horror, excitement and, yes, attraction kept her immobile.

With a sharp, and definitely wolflike, grin, Eddie leaned down. And howled.

CHAPTER EIGHT

HARPER STARED AT him for a moment as if he was crazy but then, as Eddie had hoped, she smiled. Kept smiling. Better yet, she hadn't stepped back, not like when they'd been on the porch. She hadn't run away.

Thank God. He'd been afraid he'd made a complete idiot of himself, baying that way. At least he'd done it softly so the kids couldn't hear him.

Still, he couldn't help himself. She thought he was an island among men, a recluse who shunned all human interaction or some such bullshit, when in truth, he relied on others all the time. His family, mostly. He wasn't sure how he would have managed after Lena left without his parents pitching in, his mother watching Max while Eddie worked, his brothers stopping by on the weekends for a beer or to watch a baseball game, Maddie having him over for dinner.

He'd just meant that when it came to the situation between Max and Lena, he had things under control.

Mostly.

"I'm not sure whether to laugh because you're

joking," Harper said, "or cry tears of joy to discover you have a sense of humor."

Wincing, he was the one who stepped back. Was that really how she saw him? What she thought of him?

"Being quiet isn't equal to being a humorless asshole." He hoped.

She went white. "No. I didn't mean it like that."

He turned, ready to get his kid and get the hell out of there but she stopped him with a hand to his arm. "Eddie, I'm sorry. Really sorry. That's the problem with being chatty. When your mouth's open so much of the time, you're bound to put your foot in it more often than not."

She sounded so sincere, so apologetic, he faced her. "Makes sense," he said. And that was a big reason why he preferred keeping his mouth shut.

He'd never acquired the taste for his own feet.

Yet, thanks to his ego, he might have wedged his size tens in there nice and tight earlier. He'd told her exactly what was on his mind, hadn't held back. He hoped that wasn't a mistake.

"You going to hold it against me?" he asked. "What I said on the porch."

She swiped up the kids' cups, carried them to the sink, kept her back to him as she answered. "Of course not. I'm flattered."

She didn't sound flattered. Didn't act it either. She acted freaked out. Panicked. "Flattered?"

Now she faced him, as serene as a nun at mass.

But she linked her hands at her waist, which he'd noticed she did when she was nervous. "That you had a crush on me in high school."

"I didn't have a crush on you."

She dropped her hands. "But you said you watched me at the games, that you used to…that you dreamt…"

"You were a pretty girl in a short skirt, of course I watched you. You and the other cheerleaders. Plus a number of the girls from the softball team." He scratched his chin. "And that chemistry teacher, the brunette with the big—"

"Mrs. Wilton?" she asked, incredulous. "She was married. And at least thirty."

"Ancient."

As if realizing they were both past that age now, Harper snapped to attention, grabbed the dishcloth from the sink and started scrubbing the counter. "Well, I guess that clears that up."

Now she was mad he hadn't been jonesing for her all those years ago? It was like he was walking on a tightrope. One wrong move—or in this case, one wrong word—and he was taking a header onto the concrete.

Story of his life.

What the hell? He'd already come this far today, sharing a few of his innermost thoughts, he might as well go for broke.

"I didn't think of you that way in high school—"

"Yes," she said, her voice tight and, if he wasn't mistaken, offended. "You've made that perfectly clear."

"That may have been a mistake. Thanks for the cookies," he added quickly, walking out before she could respond.

He collected Max, having to sneak him out of the house when Cassidy's back was turned. When they reached the sidewalk, they could still hear her screaming their names as if her little heart was breaking. It took all Eddie could do not to rush inside, see if he could calm her down. But Cass wasn't his responsibility. He had no right thinking she needed comfort from him, not when she had Harper. Not when she wasn't his daughter.

They climbed into the truck and drove off, Max wasting no time before pulling out his video game, losing himself in the electronic world of pissed-off birds and Pokémon. Which suited Eddie fine. Silence was good for the soul. He didn't understand most people's desire to fill it constantly with music or the noise of a television. With endless, pointless conversation.

You never say much. Have you ever considered that's part of the problem?

At the corner stop sign, he hit the brakes too hard and had to fling his arm out to stop Max's forward momentum.

"Sorry," he muttered when his son looked at him questioningly. He drove on. "Squirrel in the road."

Max went back to his game.

Eddie tapped his fingers on the steering wheel. Maybe Harper had been right about Max needing to talk about his mother. But it wasn't easy. Eddie had never been big with words, always felt as if someone was judging them. Finding them, and him, lacking.

But for his son, he'd try.

"Harp...I mean...Mrs. Kavanagh said you told her your mom called the other day." He glanced over but his kid kept right on playing. "Max." They drove another block. "Max."

Finally, his son looked up, frowning with massive impatience as if he'd been interrupted during brain surgery. His own. "Huh?"

"Why'd you tell Mrs. Kavanagh your mom called?"

With a shrug that was more a twitch of his shoulders, Max slid down in the seat until his chin touched his chest.

Shit. That hadn't come out right. "It's okay that you did. Do you...uh...did you have a nice talk with her?"

"With Mrs. Kavanagh?"

"No, with your mom."

Another shrug.

"She's going to be in town next weekend," Eddie said. "She wants to see you."

Max looked at him, his eyes huge. "She does?"

"Yeah." He cleared his throat and hoped like hell

he was doing the right thing. "Do you…do you want to see her?"

Do you think about her? Do you miss her? Do you wish you were with her instead of here with me?

"She didn't come the last time," Max said.

"She was sick," Eddie reminded him. But he hated how disappointed Max had been when Lena had called to say she couldn't make it after all.

Hated himself for being so relieved.

"Maybe she won't come this time either."

Eddie inhaled deeply. "I think she will. She sounded like she really wants to see you."

"She said she misses me," Max whispered. "What will we do if she comes?"

"She'll probably want to take you out to eat, then you could do something fun like go to the movies."

Max rubbed the side of his nose, a sure sign he was doing some deep thinking. "Okay. Dad?"

"Hmm?"

"Can I sit next to you?"

"Sure, bud."

Max undid his seat belt and slid over, buckled up again then snuggled against Eddie's side. Eddie slid his arm around his son's shoulders and held on tight.

Prayed he'd never have to let him go.

THE KNOCK—THREE quick raps—late Friday afternoon, floated through the foyer, echoed in the living room where Eddie folded towels. They filled the air, had Max stopping midtwirl in some faux karate move, stilling his flying fists of fury. They tapped on Eddie's brain like a hammer.

Lena was there.

"She's here," Max said in an awed undertone. He looked at Eddie, his eyes wide, his lips curving in the smile Eddie would never get tired of seeing. "She's here, Dad."

"I hear that."

Max ran down the hall only to whirl around. "I forgot the present!"

Leaving Eddie to open the door.

He set a hand towel in the laundry basket, then made his way as slowly as humanly possible toward his ex-wife. Ever since Eddie had told Max Lena was coming, he'd done his best to bring up the subject, as casually as possible, at least once a day. It hadn't been easy, but Eddie wanted Max to feel comfortable talking about his mom. Wanted his son to know it was perfectly natural for him to be excited about spending time with her. Not that Max acted excited.

Until now.

He'd done a good thing, Eddie assured himself. Was doing the right thing, for both Max and Lena, by telling Max his mom wanted to see him, letting Lena take him out to dinner and a movie. He just wished doing the right thing wasn't so damn hard.

She knocked again.

He reached out but yanked his hand back before touching the knob. Rubbed his fingertips against his palm. Heard Max's clomping footsteps in the kitchen.

He opened the door.

"Hello, Eddie," she said, her voice unsteady, anxiety clear in her brown eyes.

"Lena," he said, stepping aside so she could come in. "Max will be out in a second."

She'd lost weight. She'd always been slim, her legs and arms long, her figure more angles than curves, but now her cheeks were sunken, her collarbones standing out in sharp relief. Her hair, the same oak brown it'd always been, was short as a boy's, the strands barely two inches long.

From the cancer, he realized, his fingers tightening on the door handle. From the disease that could have taken her life and the treatments used to save her.

He shut the door. Cleared his throat. "How are you feeling?" he asked, speaking more gently than he had since their first year of marriage.

She smiled, a quick, unsure quirk of her lips, as if she didn't quite know whether his concern was real. "I'm good. I still tire easily but I'm getting stronger every day."

Nodding, he shoved his hands into his pockets. "I'm glad."

He never wanted her sick or suffering. They'd loved each other once. He may not trust her change of heart concerning Max but he didn't want anything bad to happen to her.

He just didn't want her in his son's life.

Max hurried down the hall. Lena's entire face lit

with joy. Love. "Max. Hi. Oh, my goodness, you've gotten so big."

She dropped to her knees on the tile floor but Max froze. Frowned. "Where's your hair?" he blurted.

Lena touched the side of her head. Cleared her throat. "I got it cut. What do you think?"

Max's horrified gaze flew to Eddie. "It looks pretty," Eddie said. "Right, bud?"

It was never too early to learn how to say what a woman wanted to hear.

Too bad Max didn't seem to agree. "Uh…"

Lena laughed. "Don't worry. It'll grow back."

"Good," Max whispered, stepping close enough for Lena to pull him into her arms.

She gave him a smacking kiss on the cheek. "You must have grown three inches since the last time I saw you!"

After his mother finished squeezing the breath out of him, Max patiently endured her inspection of his person. She ruffled his hair, commented on his new tooth coming in, told him how much she loved his *Star Wars* T-shirt.

"I made you something," Max told her, holding out a messily wrapped gift.

"You did? That is so sweet. Thank you." Lena took the present, leaned back on her heels and opened it. She gasped, covered her mouth with her hand, her fingers unsteady. "Oh. Oh…"

Her eyes welled with tears and Max shot Eddie a panicked look, slid over to press against his side.

"Sometimes women cry when they're happy," Eddie told him, gently squeezing his shoulder.

"Like when Nonna cried on her birthday?"

"Yep." Rose had been touched by the week-long trip to Toronto her kids had all gone in on together, but Eddie suspected a few of his mom's tears were for the fifty-five candles on her cake.

"It's beautiful," Lena said, running her fingers over the glass.

It was. Max and Harper had read some book about a hungry caterpillar this week during their first tutoring session. When Max mentioned how much his mom loved butterflies, Harper had given him time each day to work on a painting for Lena.

The background was a blending of light blue and white, the butterfly a deeper blue. He'd added white swirls of varying widths and lengths to the butterfly's spread wings and outlined the creature in a bright gold.

"Dad helped me make the frame," Max said.

Lena glanced at Eddie, sniffed. "Thank you."

He hadn't done it for her; he'd done it because Max had been so excited to make something for his mom. But now, seeing the very real gratitude on Lena's face, Eddie was glad he'd been a part of it.

But ultimately, it had all been Harper's idea.

"I can't wait to hang it up in my apartment," Lena said as she straightened. She smiled at Max. "Maybe someday you can come to Chicago. See how it looks in the living room."

Max had been to Chicago only once. It'd been six months after their divorce had been finalized, and Lena had flown to Pittsburgh, then taken a three-year-old Max with her. He was supposed to stay two weeks.

She'd brought him back four days later when she'd been asked to fly to New York for a fashion show.

"Well," Lena said. "Shall we go, Max? I'm starving. I thought we'd eat at Panoli's."

Panoli's was Shady Grove's best pizzeria. And Max's favorite place to eat other than his nonna's.

"Can we go to the movies?" he asked her, still leaning against Eddie's side.

"We can do whatever you want to do."

"We checked out the movie listings," Eddie said when Max stayed quiet. "There are two shows he wants to see, one starts at seven, the other at seven-twenty."

She checked the chunky, silver watch on her wrist. "We'd better get going then."

She held out her hand.

Eddie's fingers tightened slightly on Max's shoulder and he quickly relaxed them. Gave his son an encouraging pat. Max hesitated then stepped forward, linking his hand with his mother's.

Forcing Eddie to let him go.

THE MOMENT EDDIE stepped inside Harper's house, it started raining.

With the grim mood he was in, Harper couldn't help but think it wasn't just coincidence.

Now they sat across from each other at her kitchen table, Max's schoolwork from the week in front of them, light static crackling from the baby monitor on the counter. Cass had fallen asleep on the way home from day care, had stayed dead to the world as Harper carried her inside and put her in her crib.

Thank God. If she knew "Deddie" was here, they'd never get anything done.

"As you can see," Harper said to Eddie, "Max did a little better on this week's math quiz."

Eddie studied the quiz as if the answers to world peace were on it. "So the tutoring's helping."

"He did a *little* better." She pointed to the grade in the corner—a D. "But you have to take into consideration that it was a review quiz, which gives me a better sense of where everyone is at before moving on to the next section. And he was able to focus because he took the test while the rest of the kids were at the library."

Because he hadn't finished in the time allotted. When she'd collected the quizzes, she'd noticed he'd completed two of the problems and had sent the rest of the class to the library, keeping Max in the room to get through the quiz in peace.

All of which Eddie knew. He'd been in the class today helping, had taken the kids down the two flights of stairs to the library, stayed with them while the librarian had read them a story and checked out their books.

He'd looked a bit glassy-eyed and pale by the time

he'd ushered them into their classroom, but he'd survived. Of course, he'd been short two girls, but he'd found them playing in the stairwell quickly enough.

"Unfortunately, Max struggled again on his spelling test." Harper handed that paper over along with the progress report she'd written. "I noted what he and I did during each tutoring session, as well as whether the technique we implemented helped."

"He pays attention at home," Eddie murmured. "Once I pry that video game out of his hands, anyway."

"That's not unusual. Most kids with Max's problem—" no sense calling it ADHD before Eddie allowed him to be officially screened for it "—do better without all the distractions that come with being in a class filled with other kids. But if you do find him daydreaming or losing focus, try letting him stand to do his work or he can walk around the house once for each math problem he finishes."

Eddie wrote that down. His head was bent, his dark hair recently trimmed—he and Max had gone to the barber Tuesday night—so that it lay in soft, messy waves. A frown of concentration wrinkled his brow, and his mouth was tense.

She suppressed a smile. He was so cute, so sweet, jotting down notes of ways to help his son.

And believe her, *cute* and *sweet* were not words she ever would have thought she'd use when describing Eddie.

I didn't think of you that way in high school. That may have been a mistake.

She'd had no clue what he'd meant when he'd murmured those words to her. Still didn't. But she'd wondered about it, oh, only a hundred times or so since Sunday. Worse, she'd dreamed of him. Just once, just that Sunday night, but it had been so steamy, so erotic, she'd awaken sweaty and aroused.

And so guilt-ridden she hadn't been able to get back to sleep.

After that, she'd stayed up late each night until she hadn't been able to keep her eyelids open another moment. Only then would she fall into bed and slip into a dreamless sleep.

"Anything else I should try?" he asked.

She pulled out the paper she'd typed up during last night's stay-up-to-the-point-of-exhaustion-so-you-don't-have-the-energy-for-sexy-dreams-about-the-man-across-from-you session. "I thought it'd be better if you incorporate a few techniques a week—one to three. That way Max won't feel overwhelmed with changes, and we can build on each step."

He read the list. Scowled. "I don't see how his having a clean work area is going to help him bring his math grade up."

"Like I said," she told him, striving for patience, "we're building on each step. These are just the beginning." She got up and moved to the seat next to him. "These are all things to help him focus and complete his tasks. Having an uncluttered workspace will give him fewer distractions. Where does he usually do his homework?"

"At the kitchen table. While I'm making dinner."

"Okay. So, the first thing you can do is review the daily homework schedule with Max. I'll write one up and send it home with him when there are assignments due. Have him read it to you, then go over it again together. Next, make sure the table is clear of any clutter, then have him list the items he'll need to do his assignments and have him get them out. Pencil, worksheet, spelling list, et cetera. Just don't let him bring anything to the table that is not necessary to accomplishing his homework. No rubber bands, not an apple left over from lunch, or the baseball card he brought in for show-and-tell.

"And if you could keep track of how well Max does with each assignment—was it difficult for him? Did he get frustrated or angry? How long did it take him to complete the assignment? That'll give me a better idea of what areas we need to tweak. Oh," she added excitedly, "I came across this book online I thought could help." She dug through her papers, found the printout of the website page. "*Using Art to Teach Reading Comprehension Strategies.*"

He didn't even look at the paper. He was too busy staring at her face. "You love it," he murmured.

"I'm not sure. I haven't actually seen it yet, let alone used it."

"Not the book. Teaching."

"Believe me, most teachers love what they do or they wouldn't do it."

"Not even for summers off?"

"It may be why some people choose to go into this profession, but for most of us it's not that. Don't get me wrong, summer vacation is a nice perk, but the way I see it, all those three months do is help counterbalance the other issues teachers have to deal with the remaining nine months."

"What issues?" he asked, sounding sincere. Interested.

"Upper administration and their never-ending political wars. Budget cuts, long days and a salary that's lower than that of other workers with college degrees. We're also on the front lines when it—"

"Now who's been doing internet research?" he asked, his mouth twitching as if he was fighting a grin.

"Just because it's online doesn't mean it's not true. I think. Anyway, we're also on the front lines when it comes to parents. Parents who are uninvolved to the point of neglect, those who are too involved—coming in the room every day, pushing their kids to be number one. Parents who believe their little darlings are perfect and blame their child's bad behavior on everything and everyone but the child."

"Like I did."

"No and yes. When Max misbehaved you didn't go to the principal and tell him I was picking on your kid and demand his recess privileges be restored.

You backed me up and, as an educator, I appreciate that. But, you were also the first one who accused me of not doing enough to help him learn."

"I was wrong."

"I believe I made that clear when it happened."

"I was wrong," he repeated gruffly, leaning across the table to cover her hand with his. She froze, her breath locking in her chest. "I'm sorry."

His hand was warm, the pads of his fingers rough as he brushed them back and forth against her knuckles. She jumped to her feet and gathered her papers. "That…it's okay. Do you have any other questions for me about Max?" she asked, keeping her gaze on the table.

"I think I'm good. I'm just…"

She looked up. "You're just what?"

Eddie drummed his fingers on the table. "I'm worried about making all of these allowances for Max. Giving him extra time to finish his math quiz. Letting him stand while he does his work, going over the directions three times to make sure he gets them.… What if he starts to think that's how it's supposed to be? Him getting special treatment? That's not real life."

"He's seven. He shouldn't have to face real life yet." But she understood his worries. "Think of it this way—kids who are advanced get certain concessions an average student doesn't. They're part of enrichment groups, get to leave class for reading and math, have extra spelling words added to their list.

What we're trying to do with kids at this age is figure out how best they learn so they can use these tips and tricks throughout the remainder of their schooling and their lives."

He blew out a heavy breath. "Yeah. Okay." He stood, picked up his paperwork, flicked the corner of the folder with his thumb. Flick. Flick. Flick. "I appreciate this." He tipped his head toward the table. "You taking the time to meet with me."

"I'm happy to do it. Do you mind meeting here every week? I like to pick Cass up from day care as early as possible on Fridays." With Eddie having to get Max home to wait for his mom, Harper had suggested he come over instead of meeting at the school.

"I could come to the school before four if that helps."

"It's just…easier for me if we do it here."

Though her daughter wasn't the only reason she wanted to continue meeting at her home. She didn't want too many people to know exactly how many *allowances* she was giving Max and, in effect, Eddie.

He shrugged, which she was taking as a yes—mostly because she needed it to be a yes.

"Great. If you have any questions or concerns before next Friday, you can send a note in with Max or call me during school hours—"

"Or I could tell you when I come in."

She shut her eyes briefly. "Right. Of course."

He was the classroom helper for a few more

weeks. Seemed as if just when she finally rid her thoughts of him, he showed up, live and in person, and the torment started all over again.

"I'd better get going," he said. "I'm sure you have plans."

Was he asking if she had plans? And if he was asking and she didn't have plans, did that mean he was going to ask her to make plans with him?

"Actually," she said as they walked through the house, "Sadie invited us over for dinner but I declined. Sometimes it's nice to stay at home. Catch up on a few things."

There. That should make it clear she wasn't some lonely widow, jumping at any chance to leave the house.

Even if the few things she needed to catch up on were laundry, dishes and reruns of *Friends*.

"I'd rather stay home," he said, "but Maddie—my sister—badgered me into going out to eat with her."

Guess he hadn't been fishing about her plans, hadn't been trying to see if he'd have an opening to ask her to spend the evening with him.

If she was disappointed, no one had to know but her.

CHAPTER NINE

FOR THE FIRST time since he could remember, Eddie hoped a woman would keep talking.

He must be losing his freaking mind.

But when Harper stopped chatting with him about Max or her job or asking him once again if he had any other questions, he'd have no reason to stay. When they reached her door—in a matter of mere seconds—he would have to leave.

He didn't want to. He still had half an hour until he needed to be at Maddie's. He could go early or, since Maddie lived across the street from their parents, he could stop there, see how his mom was doing with her college courses, have a beer with his dad.

He had places he could go. People he could see, people he cared about, who he enjoyed being with.

He didn't want to leave.

Not yet. Not when the tension riding his shoulders since Lena knocked on his door was finally fading. His stomach no longer felt twisted and tied in knots, the tightness in his chest had eased.

Part of it, he knew, was relief from hearing Max was doing better. No, a D wasn't anything to cheer about but the tutoring—the individual attention—

was helping. And the tips and techniques Harper had taught Eddie gave him a sense of control. A sense that he could help his son.

The other part was Harper.

He hadn't stopped thinking about her since Sunday. Had wondered if he'd gone too far that day. Or if he hadn't gone far enough.

They turned the corner and her arm brushed his. She moved away. And then, there they were. At the door.

She reached for the handle and sent him a polite version of a don't-let-the-door-hit-you-in-the-ass-on-the-way-out smile. "I'll see you Tuesday then."

Four days until he'd have a reason to be near her. And then, they'd be surrounded by eighteen kids.

There was only one thing to do, one way to delay the inevitable.

"You didn't ask about Max's mom getting him."

"The last time I asked you a personal question regarding your son and your ex-wife, you told me it was none of my business."

"That didn't seem to bother you." It sure as hell hadn't stopped her from giving her opinion.

"I'm changing my ways," she assured him as she opened the door.

For some reason, that annoyed him. He didn't want her to change.

Except maybe out of that Shady Grove Elementary polo, those ugly khakis. He wanted her in those jeans from the other day. Or maybe a dress, one that swirled around her legs, hugged her ample curves.

He wanted her in his bed, under his body. He'd only now realized how much.

He stepped into the doorway then faced her again. Rain hit the roof in a steady beat. A strong breeze blew it across the porch, wetting the back of his jeans. He remained rooted to the spot.

"Lena loved the butterfly Max made," he said, as if daring her not to pick up the conversational gauntlet.

Her grip on the handle loosened. "I'm so glad. He had fun making it and I think he picked up a few vocabulary words, so it was a win-win situation."

Leave it to a teacher to make everything, even an art project, educational.

"Did Max say anything? About seeing Lena?"

"Yes."

He waited. She sent him an innocent look, an expectant one.

"Well?" he asked.

"Well what?"

"What did he say?" Eddie ground the words out from between clenched teeth.

She leaned her head against the door, her hair sliding off her shoulder. "A few things."

He narrowed his eyes. "Care to be more specific?"

"Not really." She straightened. "If you want to know how your son feels about his mother, or anything else for that matter, I suggest you ask him.

That's what I did. It's really not that hard. You just say, 'Hey, Max. Your mom's coming. Are you excited?' The nice part about it is you can use other words for excited—nervous, scared, angry. Your pick."

"I did ask him," he admitted.

"And you can't—" She frowned. "Wait? What? You did?"

"Yeah." He'd wanted to know what his kid was thinking. Feeling. Before, he'd wait, let Max come to him, but with Lena's visit approaching, Eddie had felt as if they were running out of time. "I asked if he was looking forward to seeing her. He shrugged. I told him it was okay if he was nervous or if he wants to come home after dinner and skip the movie. He nodded."

Her lips quirked, elongating that perfect heart-shape. "Wow. That must be so frustrating, talking to someone who doesn't talk back. If you get stuck on deciphering all those shrugs and nods and head shakes, let me know. I think I can help translate."

He couldn't help but grin.

She stepped closer, bringing the door with her so that it pressed against her back. "Max told me he was excited to see his mom, but the closer it came to today, the more nervous he seemed. I didn't think it was humanly possible but he got quieter and quieter as the day went on, more withdrawn."

"When they walked away," Eddie said slowly, "hand in hand, Max glanced back at me. He looked so little…lost and scared…I wanted to grab him and race away, drive like a bat out of hell somewhere secluded. Safe. Where no one could ever take him away from me."

Not even his mother.

"Does your ex-wife want custody of Max?" Harper asked.

"She's always been happy sharing custody. Seeing Max a few times a year used to be enough for her."

"Used to be?"

"She's changed." He understood the reasons behind it and he found himself wanting to share those reasons with Harper. Wanted to tell her about Lena's illness, to share his worries, to get Harper's take on it all.

"But isn't her wanting to see Max more often, to be a bigger part of his life, a change for the better?"

"I'm not sure. I'm afraid," he said, choosing his words, his confession, carefully, "that she'll want Max with her all the time."

It was his great fear, one he'd lived with every moment since she had walked out of their house, out of their marriage, leaving their son behind.

Harper laid her hand on his forearm, her fingers cool. "It doesn't do anyone any good to worry about things that might not happen."

He liked how her pale hand looked against his tanned skin. How delicate and feminine it was with her long, slender fingers and pale pink nails.

As if realizing she was touching him, Harper

curled her fingers, her nails scraping his skin lightly as she pulled her hand away.

She stepped back. "I…I'd better get Cass up or she won't sleep tonight."

He wanted to touch her. Badly. He shoved his hands into his pockets. "I'll see you Tuesday."

"Hmm? Oh, right. Yes. See you then."

She slammed the door in his face.

Slapping the folder against his thigh, he walked to his truck, the rain dotting his shirt, wetting his hair. He opened the door and tossed the folder onto the seat. On top of a tinfoil-covered plate.

Harper's plate.

He tapped his forehead against the truck's door frame a few times but when he straightened, the plate was still there.

Shit.

Grabbing it, he stormed up the porch steps, pounded on the door.

It opened almost immediately—had she been standing there this whole time?

"Did you forget something?" Harper asked, looking confused, sounding flustered.

"I wanted to give this back to you," he said, practically shoving the plate into her stomach.

She lifted a corner of the tinfoil, frowned and then ripped it off entirely to stare at the plate. "These are brownies."

The back of his neck heated. "My mom always said you shouldn't return a plate empty."

"So she made me brownies?"

"I made them. Max and I made them," he corrected.

She stared at him as if he'd admitted they'd added marijuana to the batter. "You made brownies? For me?"

"For you and Cassidy. Mostly Cass."

She studied him as if trying to figure him out. "You keep surprising me," she said softly.

She was so close, he noticed a sprinkling of freckles on her nose. He dropped his gaze to the deep dip in her top lip. His body tightened, his head spun.

It wasn't an entirely bad feeling.

He just wasn't sure if it was a good one, either. He couldn't remember the last time a woman had captured his thoughts. Had slipped into his dreams.

He edged closer, gratified and relieved when she didn't retreat. "You like surprises?" he murmured.

She visibly swallowed, seemed to have trouble finding her voice. "Love them."

"Good."

Holding her gaze, keeping his hands to himself, he leaned in and brushed his mouth against hers. Her breath stuttered out, warm and minty across his chin. She held the plate between them and with each inhale he breathed in chocolate and Harper. A nice combination. Tasty. Intoxicating.

Wanting, needing another sample, he settled his mouth on hers.

HOLY CRAP, EDDIE MONTESANO was kissing her.

Harper's eyes widened, her fingers clenched the plate. Still, she stood frozen, numb, as Eddie's mouth moved gently over hers. Gently and expertly.

The man knew how to kiss. His lips were warm. Dry and firm. He took his time, explored her mouth as if there was nothing he'd rather do, nowhere he'd rather be than on her porch, a plate of brownies digging into his sternum, kissing her.

Kissing. Her.

He stroked his tongue, just the tip, over the cupid's bow of her top lip.

She jerked back, shoving against him at the same time so that they both stumbled. He reached out to steady her but she slapped his hand away then raised her fingers to her mouth.

"What was that?" But her words came out a croak, muffling her outrage. Her fear. She cleared her throat, forced her hand to her side. "What the *hell* was that?"

That had been better. Or at least, louder. Much louder.

"Harper." His voice was low and soothing, as if she was a wild animal in need of calming. "I—"

"You what?" Now she was shrieking. She was literally shrieking at the man and she couldn't seem to stop. "Tripped and just happened to land on my mouth? Were telling my lips a secret? Thought I was having a heart attack and jumped right into mouth-to-mouth resuscitation?"

"I kissed you. I want to kiss you again."

She held up the plate, though he hadn't made a move toward her, had actually moved to stand at the edge of the porch where he watched her from hooded eyes. Where did he get off, dropping that little bomb on her? And if he kept up with that soothing tone, she was going to hit him.

Her heart beat hard. Fast. Too hard. Too fast. Good Lord, maybe she *was* having a heart attack.

"No. No," she repeated, shaking a brownie at him. Crumbs flew, scattered on the porch floor. "You can't kiss me. You…can…not…kiss…me!"

He nodded, his mouth tight. "Got it."

"I don't think you do." How could he when he was the one who had kissed her in the first place? "What were you thinking? You weren't thinking," she continued when he opened his mouth. "That's obvious. Or maybe this was all part of your plan?"

"Plan?" he asked with that damn scowl of his.

"Oh, it's all so clear now." She waved the brownie. A piece flew off, hitting the window. She tossed the rest aside, picked up another one. "You and that whole aw-shucks, bashful act. Telling me I'm pretty, that you…that you dream about my mouth. For God's sake, you can't dream about my mouth."

The more she thought about it, the angrier she got. How dare he say those things to her, things she wasn't ready to hear? How could he kiss her? She wasn't free.

Without even realizing it, she threw the brownie. It hit him square in the chest.

He looked down at the chocolate on his sweatshirt, then to the porch where it landed, then, finally, to her. "I didn't mean to upset you."

His words, so quiet, so honest, and filled with compassion, with concern, had tears pricking her eyes. But she wouldn't cry. She'd cried enough for one year, had sobbed out her heartbreak over losing her husband. Now was the time for healing.

But not the time for moving on.

She threw another brownie at him, this time missing his head by inches. "I'm not upset. I'm mad." Another throw, this one he caught neatly before it smacked his face. "What did you think, that because I'm...alone...I'd be...easy?"

The next brownie bounced off his shoulder.

"Harper," he grumbled, "there is nothing easy about you."

"Damn right there's not." She threw another one. And another, pelting him again and again while he silently stood there. "I'm not some lonely, pathetic, needy widow."

He strode up to her, took the last brownie from her hand and threw it out into the yard. His face was red, whether from anger or because he was embarrassed, she didn't know. Didn't want to know because if he was blushing, she might start feeling guilty. Might soften toward him.

As if sensing she wasn't above using the plate to

coldcock him, he snatched that away, too, tucked it under his arm. "I'm sorry," he said, his voice incredibly gentle despite his hard expression. "Go on inside now. Cassidy's calling you."

Only then did she hear Cass's voice.

"Mommy! Mama! Someone get me out of here!"

Here being her crib. If Harper knew her daughter, Cass was holding onto the rail, bouncing like Winnie-the-Pooh's buddy Tigger trying to get enough height to reach blessed freedom.

"Cass," Harper breathed with a frantic glance into her house. She turned, winced at the chocolate crumbs on Eddie's shirt, the smear of it on the side of his neck. Blinking furiously to contain the tears she'd promised herself she wouldn't let fall, she swallowed. Swallowed again. "Could we…could we forget any of this…all of this…ever happened?"

"Believe me," he said, handing her the plate, "I wish it never had."

She didn't move as he walked down the sidewalk, climbed into his truck. Forced herself to stay rooted to her spot as he drove away.

Inside her house, she leaned against the door and slid to the floor, let the plate fall with a clatter. Her legs were weak, her knees shaking. She'd yelled at him. Yelled and screamed, accused him of thinking she was some sort of…of…harlot, and then, as if that hadn't proved she was, indeed, a raving lunatic, she'd thrown an entire batch of brownies at him.

All because he'd kissed her.

"Mommy! You coming?"

"One minute, baby," Harper managed to say, though it felt as if she had a marble stuck in her throat. "Hang on. And no bouncing."

"Okay!"

Her reaction hadn't been that overboard, had it? Not considering her circumstances. For one thing, she'd been taken by surprise.

She nibbled on her lower lip. Okay, maybe she hadn't been that shocked when he'd made his move. It hadn't exactly come out of nowhere. And she had touched him first. Sure, it was just a hand to the arm but some could construe that as flirting.

With a groan, Harper brought her knees up and laid her head on them, covered her face with her arms. She really, really wished she hadn't whipped those brownies at him.

She could use some chocolate right now.

She'd flirted with him. Had encouraged him by not putting a stop to it before his mouth had touched hers.

Because she'd been stunned. She pressed the palms of her hands against her temples. Hard. Oh, who was she kidding? She'd wanted him to kiss her. Was attracted to him.

She didn't want to be.

She hadn't been kissed by a man in almost a year. The last time Beau kissed her, had been the morning he'd died. He'd been running late and hadn't had time for breakfast. He'd poured coffee into his travel mug, rubbed Cass's head, given Harper a quick peck on the cheek and hurried out the door.

A sob broke free. Then another. She pressed her fist against her mouth to muffle the sound, bit down hard on her knuckle. How she wished she'd pulled him into a hug, had kissed him properly, held on to him for as long as possible. But she'd been distracted trying to get ready for an early morning meeting, had been irritated he couldn't help get Cass fed or drop her off at day care.

Now he was gone and she could no longer smell him on his pillow. Didn't expect him to be there, next to her, when she awoke. She'd stopped listening for his car to pull into the drive at the end of the day. Couldn't clearly remember the sound of his laugh.

Rocking back and forth, she lost her battle against the tears. They coursed down her cheeks, her shoulders shaking with the effort to keep from crying out. From calling her husband's name aloud.

"Maaamaaa!"

Harper lurched to her feet, staggered before regaining her balance. "Coming." Her voice was a croak. She sniffed, wiped the wetness from her face and tried again. "Coming, honey."

It was okay, she assured herself. She had no reason to feel guilty, no reason to feel as if she'd cheated on Beau. Yes, Eddie kissed her, but there was one thing she needed to remember, one very important fact.

She hadn't kissed him back.

"You ready?" Eddie asked Maddie when he stepped into her kitchen.

She looked up from the laptop she had set up on the island. "Come on in," she said dryly. "You know I love nothing more than when one of my brothers lets himself into my house."

He scowled at her. Ornery, contrary cuss that she was, she grinned.

"I need a beer," he muttered.

A beer, ten beers, maybe a couple shots of whiskey. Would that be enough to wash away the taste of Harper? To deaden the humiliation he'd endured?

He twisted the lid off a beer, drank deeply. If he didn't have to be present and responsible for his kid in approximately three hours, he just might find out.

He'd been rejected before, more than once, but not since he was a kid. He'd gotten better at reading the signals, of knowing whether or not a woman would welcome his kiss.

Christ, he'd been wrong on all counts with Harper.

It was humiliating. And disappointing.

He lowered the bottle, tipped it toward his sister. "You ready or not?"

"So charming. That must be why I agreed to spend my Friday night with you."

"You want charming, go to dinner with Leo."

"Please, Leo never buys."

True. Thirty years old and the man was still a mooch.

She shut the laptop lid. "What's the hurry?"

"I'm hungry."

"So get a snack."

"Here?" Maddie was even worse than he was at keeping food in the house. "I told you I'd pick you up at six. It's six."

And she still had on her work clothes—faded jeans and a T-shirt, her long, dark hair pulled back in a messy ponytail.

"Hey, some of us worked a full day instead of taking off at two."

"You know I had to leave early to go to Max's school."

"Yeah, I know. And you should know that when I finished work at four-thirty, I had to come home, get Bree, then take her across town to her friend Claire's house where, on the way, my darling daughter informed me that this wasn't just a sleepover. It was a slumber party."

"What's the difference?"

"In this case, the difference is that the slumber party is in celebration of Claire's birthday."

He nodded. He'd been there. "You had to stop and get a gift."

"It took your niece half an hour just to pick out the card. When I got home, Neil called and wanted to video chat before his game."

Neil played for the Seattle Knights, the reigning Stanley Cup champions, though he was looking to get traded to a team closer to Maddie and their daughter.

"How'd it go with Lena?" Maddie asked.

"Fine," he said into the bottle.

"I'm still surprised you agreed to let her see him on relatively short notice. Usually you make her put in a request a month in advance."

He wasn't as bad as all that. Was he? "She wanted to see him."

Maddie raised her eyebrows. "Wow. Did hell freeze over and I missed it on the news?"

"She's his mother."

"Yes, but that doesn't usually matter to you."

"Did it matter to you when Neil wanted to see Bree before the two of you got back together?"

She pursed her lips. "Sometimes," she admitted. "This is good, right? Max needs his mother in his life."

Eddie gripped the bottle so hard, he was surprised he didn't crush it. "He has me. He has Mom and Dad and Pops and you and his uncles and Bree."

Maddie patted his arm, reminding him of Harper doing the same thing not twenty minutes ago. "He does have all of us but sometimes, kids need more. That's what I've learned since Neil came back. I thought I was enough for Bree, wanted to be all that she needed but it turned out, she needed her dad in her life. And funny enough, he needed her. Maybe even more so."

"Lena left." He couldn't help pointing out that fact, wanting to throw the bottle. He drank more instead. "She walked. Doesn't that count for something?"

"Weren't you the one who said Neil had rights when he first came back?"

"Fathers do have rights."

"Sorry, but you can't have it both ways. You can't say that Neil could come back simply because he has a di—"

"Watch it."

"Divine right as a father." She batted her eyelashes at him. She couldn't pull sweet off, though. She was too strong. Too self-assured for anyone to believe she didn't know exactly what she was doing or saying at any given moment.

"Lena's here, isn't she? She's with Max."

Even if part of the reason he'd given in was a secret hope that if he did, she'd return to Chicago satisfied with her time with Max and leave it at that.

That she'd leave them alone.

"You have a double standard," Maddie said, "when it comes to father's rights and Lena's rights as a mother."

He bristled. "I just don't want my kid to get hurt."

She rolled her eyes. "No one wants that, bonehead. But kids are resilient. And maybe Lena's changed."

"Why? Because Neil did?"

"I'm not sure he changed so much as finally figured out what's really important. And luckily he realized that being in his daughter's life was way more important than throwing money at her. But he had his reasons for acting the way he did. Maybe Lena does, too."

"Maybe." Though he didn't want to consider that possibility. He scratched his neck, frowned at the chocolate on his finger. He'd stopped at his place, changed into a clean shirt before coming here but he hadn't checked his reflection in the mirror. "Are we getting something to eat or not?"

"How could I refuse when you're so charming and guaranteed to be such scintillating company?"

"You want entertained? Go out with Pops."

"That's all right. I've heard all of Pops's stories anyway. Besides, you know how much I enjoy trying to decode your grunts and one-word responses. Let me change real quick and we'll head out." She grinned, fast and wicked. "I'm starving. And in the mood for steak. Really expensive steak."

Glowering at her back as she left, Eddie finished his beer. And prepared to pay through the nose for their dinner.

CHAPTER TEN

"I DIDN'T KNOW where else to go," Harper blurted, still frazzled and overwrought an hour after her meltdown with Eddie.

Sadie raised her eyebrows. "You have no idea how warm and fuzzy that makes me feel," she said, stepping aside to let Harper and Cass in the log-style home she shared with James. "Especially since you blew off my dinner invitation."

"Glad I could make your night," Harper said, hefting Cass higher onto her hip. Cass stared wide-eyed at Sadie. Well, she did make a statement in a bright lime-green sweater that fell off the shoulder to reveal the strap of a white tank top, and faded, ripped jeans. "Where'd you get those jeans? The 1984 store?"

"The retro look is in," her cousin informed her haughtily. "Is that why you're here? To critique my outfit?"

"Sorry, it's just…I'm freaking out. Seriously freaking out." She thought about Eddie's kiss. And her horrible reaction. She started breathing faster. And faster. "Quick," she wheezed, "get me a paper bag to breathe in."

"Hey, it's okay." Sadie shut the door and wrapped

one arm around Harper's shoulder, guiding them into the huge living room. "You don't need a paper bag. You need a glass of wine."

"I haven't even told you what happened. How do you know I need a glass of wine?"

"Because all problems can be solved with a glass of wine. It's a rule."

Sounded like a good one to Harper.

"I got chicken," Cass told Sadie, holding up the fast food bag containing her dinner. "And French fries."

"My favorites," Sadie said. "You want to eat them now?"

"No," Cass said as Harper set her down. "I want Zoe and Prince."

"They're out back playing. I'll call them in." Sadie took Cass's dinner into the kitchen while Cass waited, her nose pressed against one of the floor-to-ceiling windows. A moment later, Sadie opened the kitchen door and whistled sharply.

Cass puckered her lips. "Whoo wee!"

Zoe, James's German shepherd/Husky mix, ran onto the wide deck followed by Sadie's new puppy, Prince, a little black puffball with a white patch on its nose. Cass jumped up and down, clapping her hands.

Zoe raced in, sniffed Cass's feet while Sadie carried in Prince. Crouching by Cass, she held up the puppy. "Look. Cass came to play with you."

"Hi, Prince!" Cass cried, hugging him hard

around the neck. The puppy, all too-big feet and floppy ears, wriggled—probably trying to save itself from being choked to death. "Hi! Did you miss me?"

"Cassidy, be gentle," Harper admonished, reaching down to loosen her daughter's hold.

"I want him," Cass said, her face puckering into a frown. Which only made her look even more adorable.

Harper could not win here.

"She's fine." Sadie put the puppy into Cass's outstretched arms then patted Zoe's head when the older dog nudged her leg. "If she holds him too tightly or if he wants down, he'll let her know."

Amazingly, Prince went limp once in Cass's clutches.

Probably some instinctive sense told him he'd be better off playing dead.

Cass flopped onto the floor. Prince raised his head and licked her cheek. She gave a rolling belly laugh that made Harper smile.

"He licked me."

"He's kissing you."

And kissing brought her thoughts right back to Eddie. Her smile faded, her stomach cramped. Crap.

"Sit down," Sadie said. "I'll get that wine."

Harper sat on the edge of the leather sofa only to jump to her feet again. She paced the length of the room, then, to change things up, the width. Zoe, lying on the rug, lifted her head then, giving a doggie version of a shrug, put it down and shut her eyes.

James's house had vaulted ceilings and an entire wall of floor-to-ceiling windows. She wasn't sure she'd like to live with "all wood, all the time," but for a log home, it was cozy and warm. Russet-colored pillows softened the brown of the couch, a sage-green rug added warmth to the room, as did the fire burning in the stone fireplace.

"Here you go," Sadie said, returning with two glasses of white wine.

Harper debated. She was driving and she had the most precious thing in her life with her, but if she had only one glass and didn't leave for a while, she'd be okay.

Still, she allowed herself only a small sip.

She resumed her perch on the sofa, maintained a ready position in case Cassidy decided to test Harper's theory about fire being hot.

"All right," Sadie said, dropping next to Harper with the grace of a prima ballerina. "What happened?"

"Eddie Montesano kissed me," Harper said in a breathless rush at the same moment James stepped into the room from the kitchen, his hair windblown, his hands in his jacket pockets. A look of surprise, and some sort of horrible glee, was on his handsome face.

Her face heating, she glanced at her wine. Wondered if there was enough liquid in there to drown herself. Since there wasn't, she tossed aside her earlier vow to sip, to savor, and took a large gulp.

"Is there any way you could pretend you didn't hear that?"

"Afraid not," he said with a grin. He was taller than Eddie, handsome with his dark eyes and neatly trimmed goatee. But the wicked gleam in his eyes made her nervous. Oh, God, he wouldn't tell Eddie he knew, would he?

Double crap.

Hearing a male voice, Cassidy scrambled to her feet and ran over to James, the puppy at her heels. "Hi. Hold me."

"I think I can handle that." He lifted Cass, held her with the same natural ease Eddie did. "There. I can't resist a pretty blonde."

"I hungry. Let's eat chicken."

"Her dinner's on the counter," Sadie told him. "Would you mind…?"

He looked from Sadie to Harper then nodded. "Got it. Girl talk."

"His mother taught him well," Sadie told Harper as James carried a delighted Cass into the kitchen. "Now, let's get back to this kiss." Crossing her legs under her, she leaned forward. "Start from the beginning. First kisses are the best."

"I didn't kiss him back."

Sadie's eyes widened. "You denied him? Ouch."

"Well, I couldn't just let him kiss me, could I?"

"Why not?"

"Because…because…" Harper finished her wine in one long swallow. Nodded firmly. "Because."

"Glad we got that cleared up."

"I can't go around…kissing…the fathers of the kids in my class. No matter if those fathers are single or not."

"So you didn't want to kiss him at all? Didn't feel anything when he kissed you?"

Harper lifted her glass, cursed when she remembered it was empty. "No." The lie felt heavy on her tongue. Clumsy. She sighed. "I didn't *want* to want to. But maybe I did. Just a teeny, tiny bit."

"And?"

"And? And?" she repeated, sounding slightly hysterical. "I'm a married woman."

Sadie's expression softened. "Oh, honey…"

Harper's eyes stung with tears. "What about Beau?" she whispered.

"You felt guilty?"

"Guilty. Dirty. It's…wrong. It's wrong of me to even look at another man, let alone seriously consider kissing one." Thinking of one when her guard was down, letting some broad-shouldered, hooded-eyed man sneak into her thoughts. Her dreams.

Those both belonged to her husband still.

Sadie scooted closer so that her knee touched the outside of Harper's thigh. "Do you really think Beau wouldn't want you to move on with your life?"

"He would." He'd want her to find someone to spend her life with. He wouldn't want her to be alone. "That's not what this is about. I'm not against dating again or eventually meeting a man I can share

my life, my heart and my daughter with. It's just…
I loved Beau, so much. Fully. If he was still alive,
there's no way I'd be having these thoughts about
Eddie—"

"You're having thoughts about him?"

"I guess. I mean, he's handsome and a good father and thoughtful, if a bit reserved." Harper's blood
went cold, her face numb. "Oh, my God, you don't…
you don't think I'd have this attraction to Eddie if
Beau was still alive, do you?"

"Absolutely not. You might have appreciated
Eddie's looks but I doubt very much you'd spend
much time thinking about him." Sadie rubbed Harper's upper arm. "Everyone knows you adored Beau,
and he adored you." Her voice lowered. Gentled.
"But he's gone."

"I know. And I'm getting over losing him." She'd
never get over him. Never forget him. "I guess I assumed it'd be a while before I was ready to move
on—and I'm not even sure I am ready. Beau hasn't
been gone a whole year. Don't I owe him, and what
we had together, the respect of waiting a little longer?"

"There's no set time limit. The grieving process
is different for everyone. It's a matter of meeting the
right person, not the right time. Look at my mom
and Will. Mom loved Dad, but by the first anniversary of his death, she was married to Will and had
just found out she was pregnant."

"Weren't you upset?"

"I was. But I was also happy for her. For us." She shook her head. "I guess mostly I was conflicted. Looking back, I think Mom was, too. I don't think she set out to find someone, she wasn't trying to replace my dad. She just happened to meet a very nice man and fell in love."

Love.

Just the thought of it sent panic skittering through Harper. She wasn't ready to have those kinds of feelings for another man. She still loved her husband.

"Maybe it's just physical. It could be. I haven't had—" she glanced into the kitchen where Cass sat on James's lap at the center island "—sex in almost a year."

"Let's say it is only sex," Sadie said, mimicking Harper's low tone on the last word. "Is that so bad? You're a grown woman. You have needs. You're single. Eddie's single. There's nothing wrong with two unattached adults enjoying each other's company."

Nothing except that he was Max's father and Max was one of her students.

She rubbed her fingertip around the edge of her wineglass. "I sort of yelled at him."

"You couldn't have just given him the Heisman?"

"You mean the Heimlich? He wasn't choking. He was making a move."

"The Heisman is a move. Well, technically it's a football trophy." Picking up a pillow, Sadie stood and tucked it under one arm while lifting a knee

and holding her other arm out straight. "You know…
the Heisman."

"I panicked. Even if I was the type of woman
who could have a physical-only type relationship—"
which sounded so much better than affair "—I doubt
he's interested after I made a fool of myself and
embarrassed him, accused him of thinking I was a
woman of loose morals."

Sadie's lips twitched. "Poor Eddie. He must've
been horrified."

"No, I'd say the horror didn't happen until I started
throwing brownies at him."

There was a moment of blessed, stunned silence.
Then Sadie burst into laughter. "Oh, that is priceless. Priceless, I tell you."

Harper let her head fall to the back of the sofa.
Squeezed her eyes shut. "Oh, God, I made such a
mess of things."

Still chuckling, Sadie patted Harper's knee. "So
you made a mess. You'll clean it up. Or not. Either
way, you'll both survive. You just need to decide
what you want."

That was the problem. Harper was afraid she already knew what she wanted. *Who* she wanted.

She was too terrified to admit it. Even to herself.

THREE HUNDRED AND SIX DAYS.

Joan's entire body ached, each move, every breath
painful. Her eyes were red-rimmed, gritty and raw.

Exhaustion weighted her limbs, flowed through her veins like a drug.

She was tired, so very tired of pretending everything was all right, that she was happy and whole. But she had to keep up the pretense. People counted on her, relied on her to be strong.

She couldn't show any weakness.

She shivered, couldn't seem to stop, though she wore a jacket over a heavy sweater. She'd been to countless youth hockey games, had been in the ice rink plenty of times and had never before felt this cold. So cold.

Sitting next to her on the bleachers, Steve glanced her way. "You okay?"

He sounded concerned. Like he used to right after Beau died. Back then it had seemed as if he'd been constantly questioning her about how she felt, what she was thinking. She ground her teeth together to stop them from chattering, to stop from snapping at him to leave her alone. That his concern, his worry was a burden, a rope around her neck that grew tighter and tighter with each passing day.

She smiled in case anyone around them was watching. "Fine."

He turned to the game.

She stared at the ice but the boys and girls were nothing more than moving shadows, the puck a sliding black blur.

Why did these games have to start so early? These kids should be at home sleeping in or watching cartoons, not forced to play a game at nine in the morning.

The visiting team scored, the referee blowing his whistle to indicate a good goal. Parents and grandparents leaped to their feet, cheering and waving their arms, high-fiving each other.

She wished she was at home, in bed, had considered staying home, curled up in a ball under the covers, the blinds drawn against the brilliant sunlight. The silence. The darkness. They were luxuries she couldn't afford.

Instead, she'd forced herself to get dressed, as she did every day. Had gone into the kitchen for coffee and toast, found Steve there reading the morning paper. They hadn't spoken.

She glanced at her husband. His four-year-old granddaughter, Allie, now sat on his lap, her head leaning against Steve's chest. His hair was swept back from his forehead, making his hawkish nose more pronounced. He looked tired, she thought, wanting to reach for him. To smooth away the worry lines on his forehead, to lay her hand on his arm if only to let him know she cared.

She kept her hands in her lap. Stared at the time left on the game clock, willing it to go faster. Next to Steve, his daughter, Miranda, chatted happily about the game, only pausing her never-ending commentary about her kids, her husband, her job…her life… to call out encouragement to her eight-year-old son, Gabe, and his teammates.

Finally, thankfully, the ref blew his whistle as the digital clock reached zero. Clutching her purse to her chest, Joan leaped to her feet, glanced at the exit.

"Jeremy and I promised the kids we'd take them out to breakfast," Miranda said as she gathered her coat and purse. "Would you two like to join us?"

Spend another hour, possibly more, with Miranda and her very nice husband? An hour of being reminded what she no longer had?

No. She couldn't.

"I would love to," Joan lied, "and I appreciate the offer, but I have a bit of a headache." She touched her fingertips to her temple as if to reinforce her words. "I think I'll pop into the grocery store, then head home."

"Oh," Miranda said, obviously disappointed. "Maybe next weekend."

"Of course." She'd have to make sure she was too busy to come to the game next week. And the week after that.

"Are you ready?" Joan asked Steve.

"You go on ahead." He didn't look up from buttoning Allie's coat. "I'm going to breakfast with my family. You can drop me off home later?" he asked Miranda.

She glanced between them. "Uh, sure. Come on, Allie," she said, taking her daughter's hand. "Let's wait for Daddy and Gabe in the hall."

Joan held out her hand. "I'll need the car keys."

He pulled them from his pocket, clenched them in his hand. "I want you to come to breakfast with us."

She bristled. Why was he pressuring her? He hadn't before. He'd never tried to push her into doing something she didn't want to do, something she wasn't ready for. "No."

He edged closer, reached for her with his free hand. She flinched then glanced around to make sure no one noticed.

His expression darkening, he slowly lowered his arm. "You've been blowing off Miranda and the kids for months. You're always too busy or not feeling well. Do you know how badly you've hurt her?"

Joan hardened her heart against his words, against the truth of them. She refused to be responsible for other people's feelings. She had all she could handle getting through each day. Didn't he see that? Didn't he know? Coming here, pretending to be happy watching other people's children, was torture when she had so much inside of her. So much sadness. So much anger. So much bitterness. It constantly coated her throat, her mouth, she had to fight to keep it under control, to not let it affect her actions, to not simply open her mouth and let all the toxicity inside of her spew out. To swallow it down.

"She'll get over it."

Joan hadn't meant to say that, hadn't meant to sound so harsh, so heartless. But she wouldn't take it back. Miranda was a grown woman, an intelligent, capable adult. Surely she could move past a few injured feelings.

Steve looked at her as if he'd never seen her before. "If you keep pushing her away, it'll only be a matter of time before she gets tired of being rejected."

It couldn't come soon enough.

"That's what you want, isn't it?" he asked softly. Incredulously. "You want Miranda to leave you alone. For all of us to leave you alone."

"Don't be ridiculous," she snapped, crossing her arms. "I have a headache and a lot to do today. That's all."

He shook the car keys in his hand and the soft jingle of them seemed to echo in her ears. She wanted to snatch them from him, run out of the building and go home.

She didn't have to. He set them on the bench and silently walked away.

She inhaled a shaky breath, her eyes painfully dry. Turning, she watched his back as he climbed the bleacher steps two at a time, joined his family at the top.

He didn't look back.

"Nana Jo!"

At the sound of her granddaughter's delighted cry, Joan turned to see Cassidy racing toward her.

"Slow up, Cass," Harper said, holding Cassidy's hand as they descended the wide steps. "Nana's not going to disappear."

Joan swayed, had to reach out to steady herself

against the upper bleacher. That was what it felt like. That Beau had disappeared. Vanished. There one day and gone the next.

"Hi, Nana," Cass said when she reached Joan.

Her knees weak, Joan bent and lifted her granddaughter. "What brings you two out?" she asked, sounding normal and sane when she felt neither. "Gabe's game just got done."

Harper frowned. "Gabe played already? Shoot. We were hoping to watch him, too."

"Too?"

"Sadie—you remember my cousin, Sadie Nixon? She invited us to watch Max Montesano, who also happens to be her nephew—well, I guess it'd be her boyfriend's nephew—play."

Joan frowned. That had been one long explanation given almost breathlessly. As if Harper was nervous. Or lying. Plus, Joan didn't think it was a good idea for Harper to attend one of her student's games. It might seem like favoritism.

But she didn't have the energy to question her daughter-in-law. Not when she felt so claustrophobic with all these people milling about, the noise of their constant chatter echoing in her head. Her breathing grew ragged. Cold, clammy sweat formed at the back of her neck. They were all staring at her, watching her to see if she was going to break down. Testing her strength, her resolve all because they were happy and content with their lives.

It wasn't fair.

And she wasn't sure how much longer she could act as if it was.

Cassidy squirmed and pushed against her chest. "Ow, Nana. Too tight."

Joan blinked. She had Cass in a viselike grip, holding on as if afraid to let go. She forced herself to loosen her embrace and ran a trembling hand over Cass's fluffy hair. "Sorry," she whispered.

"Joan?" Harper asked, the concern in her eyes, the question in her voice making it clear it wasn't the first time she'd called her name.

Joan opened her mouth to tell her everything was fine, but the lie wouldn't come. "I have to go." It was all too much, too overwhelming. Her grief. Her anger. She practically shoved Cassidy at Harper, ignoring her granddaughter's cries that she wanted her nana. "I'm sorry," she said again.

Sorry she wasn't stronger. Sorry she couldn't get past her loss. Sorry she wasn't the woman she wanted so desperately to be.

She bolted. Kept her head down, her stride brisk as she exited the rink and rushed out the double doors into a cold, light rain. She jogged down the concrete steps, raced across the short bridge that connected the park to the parking lot, her feet slipping on the wet wood. At Steve's car, she fumbled with his key chain, pressed the unlock button. The alarm blared, the lights flashing as it beeped.

A sob escaped her throat and she clamped her lips together. She shut off the alarm and got behind the wheel, cranking up the radio after turning on the ignition. Peeling out of the lot, her tires squealing, her hands clenched on the wheel, she screamed.

And screamed. And screamed.

HAIL, HAIL, THE whole damn gang was here.

Almost the whole gang, Eddie thought, sitting between his dad and Pops. Only Bree and James were missing the start of Max's first hockey game of the season. But the rest? All accounted for. Pops sat to Eddie's right, Frank to his left then Rose and Maddie. Leo was behind him, his bony knees digging into Eddie's back.

More than likely on purpose.

The best part about his family was how they supported each other. They attended every game or event Max had, banded together in times of turmoil and celebration. They were always there.

He could count on them.

Pops nudged Eddie's ribs with his elbow—between his grandfather and his brother, he was going to be black-and-blue tomorrow. "How did it go last night?" Pops asked as the teams warmed up.

Eddie whirled toward him. "What do you mean?"

Pops couldn't possibly know that he'd kissed Harper. Could he?

Pops raised his bushy eyebrows. "I mean how did Max's evening with his mother go?"

Right. That. Eddie shrugged. "Okay."

"Okay? That's all you've got to say?"

What else was there? "That's a direct quote from Max.

"I don't want him to get confused. Or be disappointed when Lena goes back to ignoring him."

"Kids are resilient," Frank said, leaning forward to see his father past Eddie. "Max will be fine. It's good that he knows his mother wants to spend time with him. Maybe this time she'll follow through."

"Why don't you ask Max what he wants?" Leo piped in, as if this had anything to do with him. "He's big enough to make the decision whether he wants to spend time with her or not."

Pops snorted, scowled at his youngest grandson. "Seven's not old enough for that. Eddie is the one who has to decide what's best for that boy."

"Eddie has to decide what's best for Max," Frank agreed, "but that doesn't mean he shouldn't take Max's wishes into consideration."

Eddie squeezed the back of his neck. Had he really thought having his family around was a good thing?

"It's under control," he told them, before they could continue discussing his life as if they had every right to put in their two cents.

Yeah, they were worried about Max. Eddie got that. But his son was fine. Lena had dropped him off when she'd said she would, and by ten-thirty, Max was bathed and in bed. He'd been where he belonged. At home with Eddie.

Today, Eddie was letting Lena take Max after

lunch until this evening but then, by this time to-morrow, Lena would be on her way back to Chicago.

And things could return to normal.

"Hey, Pops," Leo said, tapping their grandfather's shoulder, "Mr. Swanson is waving at you."

Returning his old friend's wave, Pops stood. "I didn't realize he was out of the hospital. I'll go see how he's doing."

"Tell him we're all thinking of him," Frank said.

Pops nodded and walked down the narrow row. When he turned to go down the steps, Eddie spotted James and Sadie making their way toward them.

Followed by Harper.

Eddie slouched, caught his mother giving him an arch look and immediately straightened. Couldn't help but glance Harper's way again. They made solid eye contact. She slowed but kept putting one foot in front of the other, her gaze wary, the lift of her chin determined.

What fresh hell was this?

"Did we miss anything?" James asked.

"They're getting ready for the face-off," Leo said.

"Great." James sat next to Leo while Sadie took a seat next to Maddie.

Leaving Harper standing next to Eddie. Shit.

His family greeted Harper warmly, all of them knowing she was Max's teacher this year. Then came the inquiries: How was she? How was her family? How old was Cassidy? How was Max be-having in school?

On and on and on they went. His family loved to talk.

Still standing, Cassidy's face buried against her neck in an uncharacteristic show of shyness, Harper responded politely. Finally, the game started, the questions died down.

And Harper sat in Pops's recently vacated spot.

Cass lifted her head, caught sight of Leo behind them and stared, mesmerized by his too-pretty face.

Grinning, he winked at her. "Hey, there, beautiful. What's your name?"

"I Cassidy," she said, just short of batting her eyelashes. Must be something girls were born knowing how to do. "I—" Spotting Eddie, she squealed in delight. "Hi, Deddie! Hi!"

She lunged at him, easily breaking her mother's hold. What choice did he have but to catch her?

As he settled her on his lap, the rink went silent. Or maybe it was just his family that'd been stunned into silence. If he knew them—and he did—when the game was over, they would badger him with their nosy questions and endless comments.

"Hi," he said, unable to stop himself from returning Cassidy's guileless smile. She was too freaking cute with her messy hair and those big blue eyes.

"Do you have any candy?" she asked, all innocent and hopeful.

"Cassidy," Harper said, "what have I told you about asking men for candy?"

Cass gave a resigned, heartfelt sigh and slumped against Eddie's chest. "I not 'posed to."

"Yet you continue to do it." Harper dug into her purse. "Here, come sit with Mommy and I'll give you a banana."

"No," Cass cried, as if that was a fate worse than a thousand deaths. Whirling, she flung her arms around Eddie's neck, held on tight enough to choke him.

Leo slapped Eddie's free shoulder. "You finally got a female to fall all over you. It's a banner day."

"Shut it," he grumbled. He patted Cass's back. She was so small, and the scent of her hair reminded him of the baby shampoo he'd used on Max when he'd been her age.

"I want candy," Cass wailed.

"No candy," Harper said, using a tone that must keep the kids in her class in line. "You didn't eat your breakfast."

Cass raised her head, her eyes dry. "I eat it now."

Harper held out the banana, waved it. "Too late, kiddo. Your breakfast is in the garbage at home so now you can eat a banana or nothing."

Cassidy shoved it away. "No." She laid her small, warm hands on either side of Eddie's face as if to ensure she had his full attention. "Will you get me candy? Please?"

How the hell was he supposed to hold out against that? "You're going to get me into trouble," he whispered to her.

"No, I not," she whispered back. Then she smiled like a little angel.

Harper huffed out a breath. "Don't let the helpless routine fool you. She may only be two—"

"I tree!"

"But she's an expert at getting what she wants. She takes after her daddy."

"Daddy's in heaven," Cass told Eddie solemnly. "He likes candy."

Eddie's arms tightened on her a bit, wanting to shield her from her loss. But it wasn't up to him to protect her from anything. "No candy until you eat your banana."

"Okay, Deddie." She took the peeled banana and started chomping away.

"Well, that was relatively painless," Harper said as if surprised. "Thank you."

He looked away. She was too close, too pretty with her gray eyes and prominent cheekbones. Too tempting with her nearness and that unpainted mouth.

Giving in to that temptation yesterday had been a mistake. A big one.

He wouldn't make it again.

But he couldn't focus on the game. He was too aware of her next to him, of her daughter's warm weight in his arms. Of the curious glances his family shot them.

And he had to know the answer to the question burning on the tip of his tongue.

"Why are you here?"

CHAPTER ELEVEN

"HERE AS IN the ice rink," Harper hedged, her voice high and thin, "or *here* as in life as we know it? Because I don't usually have deep, philosophical discussions until after noon and at least three cups of coffee. I've only had two so far today—okay, two and a half if you want to count that last one, which I'm not sure should be counted so—"

She inhaled, stopping the flow of words flying from her mouth. She was babbling like a loon, saying whatever popped into her head without giving more than a passing thought as to whether or not it should actually be shared with the world.

Eddie did not care to hear how much caffeine she'd ingested so far today. That much was clear from the hard expression on his face.

Well, she wouldn't be so nervous if he'd stop looking at her with such…intensity. As if *he* had reason to be worried about *her* instead of the other way around.

Then again, he was the one who'd been pelted with brownies last night.

Her face heated, her palms grew damp. She

rubbed them down the front of her thighs to dry them. "What was the question?" she asked weakly.

"Why are you here?"

"Sadie invited me."

Sort of.

When Sadie had mentioned last night that she and James were going to attend this game today, Harper had asked if she could tag along.

She'd wanted to see Eddie. To apologize for flipping out on him like some recently lobotomized shrew. To clear the air between them so things wouldn't be awkward when he came into her classroom Tuesday.

She'd planned to come in here, set things right as quickly as possible, then head out again. What she hadn't counted on was being surrounded by Eddie's family and what seemed like half the population of Shady Grove.

She hadn't counted on running smack-dab into her mother-in-law.

Had Joan somehow figured out that Harper had been kissed by another man? Was that why she'd been so pale? So upset?

Harper's stomach turned. No, that was ridiculous. Joan was a psychologist, not a mind reader. Though they were fairly similar professions. Harper would swing by Joan's place on her way home, check that she was all right.

"All done," Cass said, tossing the banana peel

aside as if it had tried to rear up and bite her. "I want candy now."

Right. Back to the candy thing again. Cass never forgot anything.

"Why don't we go up to the concession stand?" Harper asked.

She held her arms out but Cass shook her head and hugged Eddie. Poor guy was lucky he could still breathe the way her daughter latched on to him.

"I don't want you, Mommy," her sweet baby, the light of her life said before leaning back and sending Eddie a look that was pure adoration. "You take me, Deddie."

"Cass, give the man a few minutes peace," Harper said.

"Why?" Eddie said in his low voice as he stood and shifted Cass to his hip. "You don't."

Crossing her arms, Harper followed him up the stairs to the upper level of the rink and into the small, thankfully empty concession stand. So she'd jabbered on a bit. What was he, allergic to talking?

Cass bounced in Eddie's arms and pointed at a picture of steaming cocoa. "Hot chocolate!"

"That okay?" Eddie asked Harper. She nodded. "Small hot chocolate," Eddie told the preteen boy working behind the counter. "Could you use half the regular amount of hot water? Then add cold?"

"No problem."

Digging out his wallet, Eddie turned to Harper.

"You want anything? Half a cup of coffee to make it an even three for the day?"

Harper's lips twitched. "No thanks. And you don't have to pay for it, I—"

"I've got it." He handed the kid ten dollars, told him to keep the change for the hockey league. Carrying the drink, Eddie crossed to the corner. He set Cass on a tall, round table, bent slightly and looked her dead in the eye. "Don't. Move."

Cassidy sat completely still—the child didn't even blink. Harper had to stare at her chest just to make sure it was rising and falling and that she was, indeed, still breathing.

"If I'd put her on there and told her not to move," Harper grumbled, "she'd be doing a tap dance along with a few cartwheels just to keep my heart rate up."

"Max listens to James before he listens to me," Eddie said, taking the plastic lid off the cocoa. "Guess it's their way of proving their independence."

He took a cautious sip, making sure it wasn't too hot for her baby.

Something inside Harper, something she could've sworn died along with Beau, warmed. She rubbed a hand over her aching heart.

Oh, this man was such trouble for her.

Cassidy didn't try to grab the cocoa or say, *I do it myself!* A popular refrain at Harper's house. No, her daughter sat there, well behaved and obedient, and sipped delicately from the cup in Eddie's hands.

She lifted her head and smiled—all the better to show off her chocolate mustache. "Thank you."

"You're welcome," he said, using the pad of his thumb to wipe the cocoa from Cass's lip.

His hands were large, tan and riddled with scars, cuts and scrapes. Harper wondered what it would be like to have those hands on her. Hands that belonged to a man who wasn't her husband.

Guilt swamped her, threatened to drag her under. She couldn't let it. Not now. It'd have to wait until later, when she was alone and could wallow in it, could sit in silence and analyze her mixed-up feelings for the man in front of her. Could decide what to do about them. How to stop them.

She moved closer to Eddie. Ran the tip of her finger over a scratch on the table. "I'm sorry," she said softly. "About last night. The yelling and the…the… brownies. Everything. I overreacted."

He stiffened but when he spoke, his voice was mild. "You have a right to react any way you want."

He was letting her off the hook. She should take this reprieve, snatch up her daughter and get away from him, as fast and as soon as she could.

She didn't want to go anywhere.

"It's not you," she said, needing him to understand, "it's me."

He snorted. "That's a new one."

"It may not be a new sentiment, but it's an honest one. I reacted badly. I'm not sure what came over me but I want to say I'm sorry. I'm really sorry and I hope what happened didn't change your mind about continuing to volunteer as a room parent."

"It didn't."

"Good. That's good. I mean, Max enjoys having you in class and I know the other kids do as well, and I really appreciate you taking the time to help out and, well, I hope that the whole thing—" she gestured between them "—that happened won't make you uncomfortable," she finished, sounding like an idiot.

Which made sense seeing as how she felt like a top-notch one.

"I'm comfortable," he said, looking and sounding as if that was true. "Unless you have a problem with me being in your room?"

She had a flash of him in her bedroom, on her bed, his hair swept back from his forehead, his handsome face unsmiling as he looked up at her, his eyes darkening as she smoothed her fingertips across his cheeks, her nail lightly scraping his upper lip.

And it hit her that he'd meant her classroom.

Dear Lord, she was losing her mind.

"Of course not," she squeaked, her voice not working properly.

"Then we're square," he said, picking up Cassidy when she lifted her arms toward him.

"Square. Yes." But seeing how good he was with Cass, how much her daughter adored him, made Harper uneasy. "Why don't I take Cass and—"

"Eddie."

Harper turned as a woman with close-cropped dark hair walked toward them. Maybe walked wasn't quite the right word. More like she slunk. She was leggy, thin and tall, her heels bringing her to at least five-ten so that she was head to head with Eddie.

"Lena," he said gruffly. "What are you doing here?"

Harper's eyebrows crept up. Lena? As in Max's mother, Lena?

Lena smiled uncertainly. "Watching Max."

"Does he know you're here?"

"He invited me. I don't know much about hockey but I'm enjoying watching him. And this way, I can take Max from here instead of driving out to your house." She turned to Harper. "Hello. I'm Lena Adams."

"It's nice to meet you. I'm Harper Kavanagh, Max's teacher. He's such a sweet boy."

"Thank you," Lena said, glancing at Eddie. "I'm afraid I can't take credit for any of that, though."

Tension filled the air.

If that wasn't Harper's cue to leave, nothing was.

"Come on, Cass," she said, pulling her kid from Eddie's arms. "Let's go home."

"No!" Cass wriggled and squirmed.

"Thanks for buying her the cocoa," she said to Eddie over her daughter's high-pitched cries.

She walked away.

"Deddie!" Cass called, reaching for him as if

Harper was some deranged stranger dragging her to work a chain gang. "I want Deddie!"

"I know you do," Harper snapped, struggling to hold on to her daughter. "That's part of the problem."

Neither one of them had any business wanting him.

The sooner they both realized that, the better off they'd be.

"SOMEONE'S TEACHER'S PET," Leo said when Eddie returned to his seat.

Eddie ignored him. If you gave Leo attention, he'd never shut up.

"Where's Harper?" James asked.

"She went home."

Thank God. He wasn't sure which was worse, having her there or Lena. At least his ex-wife kept to her side of the rink. He'd agreed to let her take Max after the game. He hoped that wasn't a mistake. But he hadn't been able to refuse her, not when she was making a real effort for the first time.

It scared the hell out of him.

"Never would've pictured you with Harper," Leo said, clapping both hands on Eddie's shoulders. "But I think it's great. About time you got back on the horse and all that."

Eddie glanced at James, who was typing something into his phone. "Did he compare Harper to a horse?"

"He's an idiot," James said without looking up. "We all know that."

"Harper's not a horse," Leo said. "So don't go telling her I said any such thing. She's pretty enough."

"But?" James said, finally putting his phone away.

"But she's a mom."

"So?" Eddie asked.

"So, her being a mom is fine for you. You've got a kid."

"You never cease to amaze me," James said.

Leo grinned. "That's what I'm here for. Amazement. Awesomeness."

James cuffed him upside his head. "It wasn't a compliment."

Leo frowned and rubbed his head. "It should be. Seeing as how I have such great luck with the ladies."

That was true. Women loved Leo.

There was no accounting for taste.

"Harper is Max's teacher," Eddie said, as Max's line got buzzed in to go out on the ice. "That's all."

"You two looked pretty damn cozy for her being just Max's teacher." Leo turned to James. "Back me up here."

"It's okay if you like her," James told Eddie.

"Great. I'll pass her a note in study hall."

"I'm just saying she's a very nice woman. And Cass is a kick. They were over last night and—"

"She was at your house?" Eddie asked as everything inside of him stilled. "Last night?"

She must've gone there after he kissed her.

He forced his eyes up to his brother's face. Ground his back teeth together. "You know."

James's expression was a cross between sympathy and amusement, with amusement winning out in the end. "I overheard her telling Sadie. Tough break, man."

"What's a tough break?" Leo wanted to know, just like when they'd been kids and he'd followed James and Eddie everywhere.

"We've all been there," James said, as if that was supposed to make Eddie feel better. "When I first told Sadie I loved her, I thought her head was going to explode."

"You told Harper you loved her?" Leo asked. "I didn't even realize you two were dating."

Eddie whirled around, lowered his voice. "No and we're not."

"Then what…" Leo frowned, studied both his brothers' faces. Then the son of a bitch smiled. Laughed. "Oh, I get it. She shot you down. What'd you do? Try to ask her to dinner using as few words as humanly possible? Grunt at her and expect her to realize that in Eddie-eze that means you think she's hot?"

"It's no big deal," Eddie said. "I kissed her. She wasn't into it. End of story."

But saying the words out loud seemed to have the same effect on both his brothers. They burst out laughing, causing the rest of the family to look at them curiously.

"Sorry, sorry," Leo said, holding a hand up. But he kept right on chortling. "James is right, though. It happens to the best of us. I mean, not me, of course. But then, I'm a lot prettier than either of you two."

Because it was true, and because Eddie was frustrated with his thoughts about Harper and worried about his kid spending so much time with Lena, he couldn't let Leo's teasing slide off his back.

"Not in the mood for you or your mouth right now," he warned, knowing full well Leo didn't take warnings seriously. He saw them as a red flag, one waving in the wind.

As Eddie had hoped, Leo's grin slid from amused to cocky. "What are you going to do about it?"

Leo thought he could beat Eddie. It was an idea that'd first taken hold when they'd been seventeen and fifteen and Leo had shot past him in height.

Eddie had quickly disabused him of that notion. And he didn't mind continuing that lesson as many times as his fatheaded brother needed. "I'm going to kick your ass."

"No one is going to do any such thing," Rose warned, leaning across her husband to give her sons a stern glare.

"How'd you even hear that?" Leo asked, since their mother had seemed to be in deep conversation with Maddie.

"Mothers are trained to pick up certain words no matter how softly they're uttered. Now act like the responsible, mature men I like to pretend you are and watch the game."

"Yes, ma'am," Eddie and Leo said at the same time.

Eddie faced forward, watched the kids on the ice. What a crap morning. Harper had shown up and given him the *it's not you, it's me* bullshit speech, Max was spending the rest of the day with Lena and now Eddie couldn't even take his frustrations out on Leo's hide.

Leaning forward, his knees digging into the back of Eddie's ribs, Leo sang Van Halen's "Hot for Teacher" under his breath.

Eddie exhaled heavily. Then, in one smooth motion, stood and raised his elbow—connecting sharply with his brother's nose.

"Ow." Leo cupped his hands under the blood dripping from his nostrils. Glared at Eddie.

Eddie pursed his lips. "Oops. My bad."

Then he sat again, fighting to hide a grin. Maybe his day was looking up after all.

EDDIE MONTESANO WAS a man of his word.

For the past two weeks when he'd come in to help with the kids, he'd seemed comfortable and completely at ease.

Guess their kiss—and her rejection—hadn't meant much to him.

He'd probably already moved on, Harper thought, looking for a pen in her desk drawer. Was probably pursuing another woman. Someone who didn't overreact to a simple kiss. Who wasn't stuck in the past. Some long-legged brunette like the woman he'd loved enough to marry.

Harper slammed the drawer shut, almost taking her fingers off in the process.

"You okay?" Eddie asked from his seat on the other side of her desk.

"Fine. Just fine." Giving up on the pen idea, she smiled tightly at him. "Was there anything else you wanted to discuss?"

After the whole kiss/brownie-throwing debacle at her house, Harper had decided it was better, safer, for them to discuss Max's progress right here in her classroom, gossip or any worries about her playing favorites with a student be damned.

"No," Eddie said, getting to his feet. He slapped the folder against his thigh. "From now on, you can send the reports home with Max. If I have any questions, I'll let you know."

He didn't want to meet with her, had no reason to even see her again since Lydia was to return as room mother Tuesday. Harper shouldn't be surprised Eddie didn't want to be around her anymore. Shouldn't be hurt.

But she was.

"I hope we can at least meet face-to-face at the end of the next marking period," she said, standing. "Unless you plan on reneging on your promise?"

As per the agreement she'd dragged out of him, if

Max didn't improve by the end of next month, Eddie would let Joan observe Max in the classroom and have him evaluated for ADHD by his pediatrician. Though a few of the techniques she'd implemented were helping Max, he was still behind on all subjects—a fact recorded in his report card last week.

"I keep my word," Eddie said so simply, she felt about two inches tall for being snide.

Damn him.

She nodded as if she'd had no doubt of that. Straightening the already straight piles of papers on her desk, she searched for something to say to keep him here. To keep him talking to her.

Or, as the case may be, responding to her in as few words as possible.

"Max is excited about spending the night with his mother," Harper blurted when Eddie started turning as if to leave.

"He's looking forward to it."

From the flat tone of his voice, Eddie wasn't too happy about that.

"I think it's really nice," Harper said, "the way you're letting your ex-wife have time with Max."

"After Lena was here last time, I spoke with my attorney. She feels it's best I let Lena see Max as often as possible. In case Lena decides to sue for more custody."

"Is that what Lena wants?"

He lifted a shoulder.

Harper couldn't help but heave a soft sigh of exasperation. "If you're unsure and obviously worried about it, why don't you just ask her?"

He looked away for a second, his mouth a thin line. "Because," he said, his voice low, his eyes on hers again, "I'm afraid I won't like the answer."

"Sometimes, those are the questions that need asking the most."

"Sometimes, they need to be left unsaid."

He walked toward the door and she hurried around the desk. "I guess we're both on our own for the night," she said then slapped a hand over her mouth. Oh, dear God, that had sounded like a hint, a broad one letting him know she was free for the evening.

He faced her and she quickly dropped her hand. His eyes narrowed slightly. "Where's Cass?"

"She's spending the night with my in-laws." Harper forced a smile. "When I have the house to myself I always plan on getting a ton of work done—cleaning out dresser drawers and the refrigerator, painting walls, maybe even cooking meals ahead to freeze…" She rolled her eyes at her own delusions of grandeur. "Then I end up eating a bowl of cereal for dinner and curling up with a good book for hours on end." She linked her hands together in front of her at her waist. "What about you?"

"I don't often curl up with a book. Good or otherwise."

"No." She swallowed. "I mean, do you have plans? For tonight."

"Plans?"

Did he have to repeat what she said? It drove her nuts. "Plans. Dinner plans with your family or… or…a…" She could barely even think it, let alone say it. "A date," she said, spitting the offensive word out.

He stood in the doorway, looking big and broad and handsome. "I don't have a date."

Relief rushed through her, made her knees weak. "No?"

He gave one slow shake of his head, his eyes never leaving hers. "No."

"So you plan on staying home tonight, too?"

Another of those head shakes. "I'm going to eat dinner at O'Riley's at seven." He turned only to face her again and murmur, "Maybe I'll see you there."

CHAPTER TWELVE

TWO HOURS LATER, Harper let herself into her house, tossed her keys onto the small table in the foyer, Eddie's words echoing in her head.

Maybe I'll see you there.

Did that mean what she thought it meant? He wanted to see her there?

But he hadn't asked her to dinner. He was leaving it, the decision, up to her.

Was that supposed to make her feel in control? She snorted, shoving a Barbie doll aside with her foot. How could it when she'd never felt so out of control in her life? So confused. Conflicted.

She'd thought of him. During times when she used to think of Beau, when she used to remember how they were together, how he'd been, Eddie had slipped into her head instead.

She paced the confines of her living room, bumped into the coffee table, skirted it and made the trek toward the television.

She glanced at the clock. Six-thirty. She wasn't going. She couldn't. O'Riley's was a popular bar, a place where many people went for drinks or a casual dinner.

Someone, possibly many someones, would see her there. With Eddie.

Beau had only been gone eleven months. It was too soon to date. Too soon to even think about letting another man kiss her. Touch her. Make love to her.

Except she was thinking about it. Had thought of it over and over again since Eddie had kissed her on her porch two weeks ago.

But that's all she'd do, she assured herself. Think about it. About Eddie.

She'd just stay home tonight. Maybe she'd order Chinese, watch a romantic comedy. She had the house to herself. Her time was hers, all hers. She could do anything she wanted. Or nothing at all.

That's what she'd do, Harper thought with a nod as she plopped down onto the couch and picked up the TV remote, pushed the on button. She'd hang out here. By herself.

Alone.

There was nothing, absolutely nothing wrong with being alone. She'd been a single woman way before she'd met Beau. There had been plenty of weekends where she'd curled up on her couch with a good book or small stack of DVDs. She'd been fine then and she'd be fine now.

But as the TV came to life, she didn't see a commercial for car insurance, she saw Eddie's face, heard his voice again. She saw him sitting at O'Riley's by himself. Waiting for her.

How long would he wait?

What if he decided she wasn't worth waiting for?

She clicked off the TV and jumped to her feet, searched frantically for her car keys—which she knew darn well were on the table where she'd tossed them. Luckily, she glanced down, saw she was in just her socks and she still had on her god-awful Shady Grove Elementary shirt and horribly wrinkled khakis.

She checked the time again. Six-forty. Ugh. Peeling the shirt off, she hurried to her bedroom. Yes, she could be alone. Had been alone, had been lonely a few times. But tonight she didn't have to be. Tonight she could be with Eddie.

IT WAS SEVEN-TWENTY.

The waitress came up to Eddie's table yet again. In the past few months, O'Riley's had grown quickly from a popular bar to a popular restaurant. The tables and booths were filled with the dinner crowd. It would shift eventually as the diners left. People would come in wanting a drink or two instead of a meal, they'd crowd onto the tiny dance floor or play pool, maybe throw some darts.

But right now, he was smack dab in the dinner rush, taking a table on a busy night and he hadn't ordered anything other than a beer.

He was lucky the waitress with the funny crooked hair and neck tattoo didn't stab him in the throat with a fork.

He couldn't wait for Harper any longer.

Shouldn't have waited this long, wasn't sure why he had.

He'd been hopeful. After two weeks of keeping his distance, of trying to convince himself that he had little interest left for her, his damn hopes had soared simply because she'd asked about his plans for the night. Had told him she was going to be alone.

He thought she'd wanted to be with him.

Stupid.

"I'll have the fish fry," he told the waitress. "And an order of sausage bread to start."

He doubted it would come even close to Pops's bread but he wanted to make sure his bill covered the time he'd sat there not eating. He handed the laminated menu to her. "And another beer when you get a minute."

"Hi."

He glanced up to see Harper, her cheeks pink, her breathing fast. She swallowed. Searched his gaze. "I'm not too late, am I?" she asked, and he wasn't sure what she meant, but it seemed to be more than just if she was too late for dinner.

Christ, but he was glad—really glad—to see her.

He just wasn't sure if he should be.

Standing, he reached around to pull out her chair, and she sat and hung her purse over the back of it. Harper had changed into dark jeans that cupped her hips and ass and a V-neck sweater that showed the pale, delicate skin of her chest, the curve of her breasts.

Leo's voice floated through Eddie's mind. Hot for teacher, indeed.

The waitress took Harper's order and Eddie sipped his beer to soothe his dry throat. He wanted to tell her he was happy she'd come, that she looked pretty in that peach sweater, that he was looking forward to getting to know her better.

He kept silent. It was safer. And, if he was being honest with himself, easier.

When they were alone, Harper smiled at him, seemed more at ease as she looked around. Eddie gave himself a mental pat on the back for choosing a table in the far corner where the lighting was dim, the sounds somewhat muted. Where fewer people could see them.

"Not much has changed about this place since I was here last," Harper said. She shifted. Their table was small, so small that her knee bumped his. He didn't move away.

"When was that?" he asked.

He liked how her forehead crinkled when she was thinking, as if she had to get it just right. As if they were the students in class and the teacher had called on her.

"Five years…no, more like six." She brushed her hair aside, smiled at the waitress when she brought Harper's glass of wine. "Beau and I came here after his stepbrother's wedding and…" She shook her head. "And I doubt you want to hear about ancient history."

He had a feeling she thought he didn't want to hear about her husband. Looked as if he was going to have to figure out the right thing to say. Never an easy or comfortable task for him. But he'd give it a shot.

"I want to hear about you," he finally said.

She sipped her wine, averted her gaze. "I'm an open book. A boring one."

"I don't think so."

"No?"

He thought she was fascinating. He had firsthand insight into her as a teacher. Had seen her with the kids in her class, how good she was with them, how much she cared about them. He'd seen her with her daughter, knew she was an excellent mother. She was smart, pretty, friendly and way too open.

"No," he said gruffly. "There's nothing boring about you."

She reached over, laid her hand on his, her fingers warm and soft. "That's one of the nicest things anyone's ever said to me."

He wanted to turn his hand, capture hers with his, link their fingers together. Because he did, too much, he waited a moment and then slid his hand away on the pretense of lifting his beer. "I doubt that."

She'd been married to a lawyer. A trial attorney who used words for a living. Beau Kavanagh had probably told her daily how special she was. How beautiful. Things that Eddie thought to say but for some reason, couldn't get out.

"I'm being serious," Harper said. "It is one of the nicest things anyone's said about me because I know you mean it."

"I'm that easy to read?"

She laughed, the sound drawing attention from the table next to them, had the other diners smiling. "No, because you don't say anything you don't mean. Anyone who speaks as infrequently as you do usually means what they say. Why waste those precious words on lies?"

"Exactly." He wasn't sure how he felt about her knowing him that well, though. "Tell me about the last time you were here."

She hesitated but then nodded. "Like I said, it was after Michael's wedding. We all came here after the venue in Pittsburgh shut down for the night, and a couple of college kids hit on one of the bridesmaids. She wasn't interested but they weren't too eager to take no for an answer. Her boyfriend got involved and—" She shrugged. "One thing led to another and the next thing I know, guys are pushing each other, yelling. I thought for sure a riot was about to erupt but Beau talked everyone down, had them buying each other drinks by the end of the night."

"He was a mediator?"

"He was a charmer. And, yes, a peacekeeper. I

think he came into that role naturally, playing it between his parents until they divorced. He then took those two natural abilities—that charm and the ability to talk anyone into anything, and his wanting peace between all parties—and decided to make a career out of them. Then again, I guess that's what a lot of people do."

"Did you?"

"I loved kids, always knew I wanted to be a teacher. What about you?"

"I knew I wasn't cut out for college—obviously."

She frowned. "What does that mean?"

"You know what it means."

"Just because you had some struggles, doesn't mean you can't get a college degree. I just figured you didn't want one. Not everyone does."

That was true and had been for him. Even if he had been able to get better grades, the idea of sitting in classrooms for another four years had made him break out in a cold sweat. It still did.

The waitress brought their appetizer, set it on the table between them.

Harper groaned and the thought of her making that sound for him, because of what he was doing to her, had his body stirring.

"Oh, that smells so good," she said.

"Help yourself."

She looked at him as if he'd just suggested she crawl on top of the table and nibble on his neck.

Which wasn't the worst idea he'd ever heard.

"Do you know how many carbs are in this? Not to mention fat. And the calories. Oh, the calories."

She was so earnest, his lips twitched. "No. Not calories."

"Sure, jest. You're not the one trying to lose ten... okay, okay...fifteen pounds."

"Why?"

"Why what?"

"Why would you want to lose weight?" Lena had been always moaning about calories and carbs and working out. When she'd been pregnant, every bite of food had to be measured, weighed and carefully calculated so she could achieve her goal of being back to her pre-baby weight within four weeks of giving birth.

"You do remember what I looked like in high school, right?"

He helped himself to a huge slice of the sausage bread. A long string of mozzarella stretched from the loaf.

"Now you're just torturing me," she muttered, pouting.

"Do you want some?"

"Am I sitting here, living and breathing and smelling how good it smells? Of course I want some."

He cut her a small slice. "Then you should have it. Why deny yourself? So you were skinny in high school. You ask me, you look better now." He set the plate in front of her. "You've blossomed. You were cute back then. Now you're beautiful."

She blinked. Blinked again. Her mouth opened and shut.

He'd made her speechless. Just by telling her the truth. Just by telling her his thoughts.

He'd have to try it more often.

"I'm going to eat this," she said, picking up her fork. "But only in celebration of you stringing together that many words. Who knows when a miracle like that will happen again?" She bit into the bread. "So," she said around her mouthful, "tell me why you chose to become a carpenter."

"It wasn't a choice," he said. "It just…was. I never even thought of doing anything else. From the first time I made something with my dad, I just knew."

"It must be nice, being able to make…to build… something out of nothing. To see it in your head and make it a reality. It takes a lot of creativity, doesn't it? And math skills—never my strong suit."

"Weren't you in the top twenty percent of our graduating class?"

"Ten."

Ten percent. Of course. "I'm betting your math is fine."

"Only because I worked my butt off to keep my grades up. Calc about did me in."

"I don't use much calculus in my work. Just regular addition and subtraction. The basics."

"Please. I'm sure you have to work with percentages, fractions, volume and square footage. Right?"

What could he do but nod?

"See. Just the idea of all that figuring makes my head hurt."

"At least I don't have to read Shakespeare anymore."

She grinned. "Me either."

Their dinners arrived and they dug in. She even helped herself to a second slice of sausage bread.

"Did you travel after school?" Harper asked him.

"I did the summer thing, went down South—which was a mistake. Never go to the deep South in the summer."

"I bet."

"What about you?"

"I worked at Cass's day care center the summer after graduation and went to Clarion University. It's a small university about an hour and a half away from here."

"You stayed close to home."

"Relatively speaking. I thought I wanted to get as far away from Shady Grove as possible but it wasn't meant to be."

"You got homesick?"

"Nah. Although that may have played a part in it. Only child, doting parents. I'm not sure how any of us would've done if I'd been too far away. I applied to Georgetown. It was perfect. Far but not too far."

"What made you decide not to go there?"

"They decided for me. I didn't get in."

"But you were in the top ten percent of our class."

"Actually, I was in the top five percent. I didn't

want to brag," she said, blushing. "It didn't matter
to them that I was smart and in the top of my class.
I was upset at first, for months actually, but it was a
great lesson to be learned. There are always people
smarter than you. There will always be someone
who has more success, someone who has less. You
can't get picked for every club, school or organization. Not everyone is going to like you. I didn't like
learning those lessons at the time but I've come to realize how important they were to me. I went to Clarion, I got a great education, I became a teacher like I
always wanted and I made some lifelong friends in
the process. I got a job in my hometown, met Joan
who introduced me to her son and fell in love with
a good man. I married him. Had his daughter." She
smiled softly. "All in all, it wasn't such a bad deal.
And I can't help but believe things worked out exactly as they were meant to."

"You can say that even after what happened
to your husband?" he asked quietly, awed by her
strength. Her faith.

"You know, when I didn't get into Georgetown, it
was the worst thing that had ever happened to me.
But a few months after Beau died, I realized how
incredibly blessed I'd been all these years—was still
blessed. Because even though I didn't have him in
my life anymore, even though I still miss him every
day, I can't help but be grateful for the time we did
have together. Both as a couple and as a family. He
loved me. That makes it easier to get through each

day. But I hate that Cassidy doesn't remember him, that she'll never know what a truly wonderful man he was, how much he loved her."

"She'll know."

"How can you be so sure?"

"Cass will know her dad loved her, that he was proud of her, that her parents loved each other and were happy together. She'll know," Eddie repeated, wishing he'd kept his mouth shut, afraid he'd say the wrong thing, "because you'll tell her. But more importantly, because your memories of Beau will keep him alive for her. Will help her know *him*."

She smiled, as if he'd given her so much more than a few of his thoughts put into words, and squeezed his hand again.

Maybe he was better at this whole talking thing than he'd realized.

She'd had fun.

Harper wasn't sure what she'd expected. If she hadn't thought she would have a good time, why would she have shown up in the first place? Eddie hadn't talked much but he *had* talked and, better yet, he'd said exactly what she'd needed to feel better about Beau.

Your memories of Beau will keep him alive for her. Will help her know him.

Eddie was direct and insightful—more than she'd realized, and she'd enjoyed getting to know him better. They'd discussed mutual acquaintances and friends, their parents, his family and their work.

They hadn't talked about Max or his issues at school. They hadn't talked about their pasts—when they'd been in school or his marriage.

The parking lot was packed but, fortunately, empty of people. Music floated out from the bar, a classic rock song with a fast beat and heavy bass, perfect for dancing.

Harper couldn't remember the last time she went dancing. "Do you like to dance?" she asked, wondering if she could talk him into going into Pittsburgh—far from prying eyes. They could go to a bar like O'Riley's where the music was provided by a jukebox or a DJ who played rock and roll. She had a feeling Eddie Montesano didn't do dance music, strobe lights or techno-anything.

He glanced at her. "I don't dance."

"You don't dance? Or you can't dance?"

"Does it matter?"

"Sure. The first is a choice. The second is a matter of opinion."

"I choose not to dance."

She dug her keys from her purse. The wind picked up, chilled her arms as she'd been running late and hadn't bothered to grab a jacket. "Too bad. I love to dance. Don't get me wrong, I'm a horrible dancer. But I still like it."

"What makes you think you're so horrible?"

She laughed. "My own father told me it looked

as if I'd been electrocuted. And believe me, my dad thinks I can do no wrong. Plus, I've seen the video of my wedding day. Not pretty. But I still like to dance."

"I won't take you dancing."

She grinned up at him. "Yeah. I got that. What if I invited you?"

Again, it'd have to be somewhere other than Shady Grove. She might be able to explain away them having dinner together tonight. It wasn't as if he'd been flirting—she wasn't sure he knew how to flirt, and it'd been so long since she'd been eligible, her own skills were mighty rusty. So they could play tonight off as the casual dinner it'd been.

But she didn't want people to get the wrong idea about them. Especially when she wasn't sure what the right idea was. Keeping their…whatever name you wanted to put on this fledgling relationship… to themselves seemed the best idea.

They stopped by her car and she pushed the button to unlock it. Opened the door and tossed her purse inside.

"If you asked me to go dancing, I'd tell you no," Eddie said, edging forward to trap her between his hard body and the door. "But if you asked me to go to a Steelers game, I'd say yes."

"I've been known to dance at a Steelers game," she warned him. "I've even been on TV."

"Sounds as if we'd both get what we wanted."

You have to decide what you want, wasn't that what Sadie had told her? Harper still wasn't sure but she was weakening, her feelings growing for this man before her.

He came even closer. Lifted a hand slowly, giving her plenty of time to back away. She didn't. She barely breathed as he touched her hair, just the ends of it, then let his hand drop.

"You and Cassidy could come over Sunday," he said. "Watch the game with me and Max. I'll even let you dance."

She opened her mouth to invite him to her house on Sunday. The Steelers were playing Baltimore; it was a fierce rivalry, and she and Beau always hosted a party when the two teams played.

But she couldn't ask Eddie to come. The party was something she'd done with her husband, something it'd taken her weeks to decide she was ready to do on her own. Her family and his would be there along with their mutual friends.

She wasn't ready to go public with this. Not yet.

Maybe not ever.

"Actually, I have a few people coming over to my place." She smiled to soften her rejection. "My parents, and Joan and Steve, and Beau's stepsister and her family." Sadie and James and Sadie's sister, Charlotte, and their parents.

Crap.

He was watching her steadily. Not expectant, really, and that was what got to her. He didn't expect her to invite him to join them.

"Why don't you and Max come?" she asked.

"There'll be plenty of food and you know just about everyone who'll be there."

"That going to be a problem for you?"

"What?"

"Having so many people there that know us?"

She narrowed her eyes. What was he? A mind reader? "It won't be a problem for me."

But she wasn't so sure.

"I'm not sure what Max and I will end up doing."

She hoped he couldn't tell how relieved she was, but then again, he seemed more observant than any man should be.

"Thank you for dinner," she said, feeling sulky—sounding it, too. She brushed it aside; life was too short to be anything other than happy. "I had a good time."

"Me, too."

"And you don't even sound shocked," she teased.

"I'm not. Much."

She raised her eyebrows. "A joke. Wow. A couple of beers and you turn into quite the charmer."

"You okay to drive home?"

They'd both had alcohol but they'd switched to water over two hours ago. They'd spent quite a bit of time lingering over their dinners. Not because the food was delicious—though it was pretty good—but because they'd been talking. Or she'd been doing most of the talking but he'd been listening.

She hadn't realized how nice it was to have a man simply listen to her.

Oh, Beau had listened. But he'd also given his opinion, his advice on everything. Not that she wasn't grateful for his input, but sometimes it was nice just to vent and to figure things out on your own.

"I'm fine," she said. "That piece of cake you talked me into absorbed the last of the alcohol."

"Didn't take much talking."

"That was a lucky break for all involved." She liked when he teased her, that he was obviously growing more comfortable with her. She liked him. She wasn't surprised she'd had a good time with him, but that she'd been able to spend so much time with another man and not constantly compare him to Beau—although there had been moments. But that was perfectly normal. It had to be.

She felt normal. Like a single woman enjoying an evening with a good-looking man. She just wished she didn't feel so happy about that. So guilty.

Still, she wasn't in any hurry for the night to end but short of asking him back to her house—not going to happen—she knew she'd have to say good-night any second now. "So much for your lone wolf status."

"How do you figure?"

"Well, after that dinner, I'd say we're officially friends. I'm thinking of getting us matching ball caps."

She'd meant it as a joke, as a way to keep things light between them. Maybe even a reminder, for both of them, that friendship was the best course of action for them. But Eddie's mouth tightened. Under the harsh glare of the parking lot lights, he looked dark and foreboding. "We're not friends."

Disappointment settled heavily on her shoulders, weighed her down. She tried to ignore it. "No? Well, you're missing out because I am a terrific friend. I never forget a birthday or anniversary. I keep in touch regularly, and am a really good listener. Oh, and I give excellent advice on all situations from parenting to elderly parents to your love life."

"I can handle all those situations on my own."

"Ah. I can see the headlines now—The Lone Wolf Returns."

"You think I kissed you because I want to be your buddy?" he asked quietly and, if she wasn't mistaken, amusedly.

She'd amused him. And he was scaring her to death, making her palms sweat, her fingers tingle. "I—"

"Because I already told you. I wanted to kiss you because you're beautiful. And sexy."

"You want to have sex with me?"

Her question, a high-pitched squawk, caught him by surprise. It caught her by surprise, as well. She usually said what was on her mind but at times, not having a filter made for some interesting—and humiliating—situations.

"I want to spend time with you," he said in answer. "I enjoy being with you."

"You sound shocked."

"I didn't think we'd have anything in common."

"We went to school together, grew up, live and work in the same town, know most of the same people, are both raising kids on our own.... How much more in common do you need?"

A truck pulled into the lot. They waited while it parked, the driver and a passenger getting out and making their way to the bar's door. After they were alone again, Eddie said, "We didn't exactly run around in the same crowd in high school."

"I was friends with everyone," she pointed out. "It's called being friendly."

He was so close she could see the dark stubble on his face. "I don't want to be a part of the crowd that you call friends. I'm attracted to you."

But he didn't touch her and she wished, oh, how she wished, he would. That he'd take the initiative with his actions as well as his words, words that he was so stingy with but that somehow warmed her heart anyway.

He wouldn't make any move on her, she knew. Not after she'd already rejected him. If he did, she could claim that he'd taken the decision away from her. If he grabbed her and yanked her against him, kissed the living daylights out of her, she could pretend she'd had no choice. That he'd taken away her ability to think, along with her ability to refuse him, with his actions.

He was a man of actions, that much was certain. She was a woman of words. But she had no idea what to say to get him to do what she so desperately wanted.

She'd have to show him. Would have to make the first move.

Oh, God.

CHAPTER THIRTEEN

ANTICIPATION BUILT INSIDE Harper, mixed with a hefty dose of fear to make her knees weak even as her resolve strengthened.

Why deny yourself?

He'd asked her that a few hours ago but it seemed more appropriate now, even if the hunger she felt was for something much more enticing and dangerous than extra carbs.

She slowly laid her hands on his chest. He was solid. Warm. She wished he didn't have on a jacket, that she could feel his heart under her hand to see if it beat as erratically as hers. But he didn't pull away, didn't reject her as she'd done to him. She'd take those as good signs.

She edged closer to him so that the front of their thighs touched. "Be patient with me," she said on barely a sound as she rose onto her toes and slid her hands to his shoulders.

Holding his gaze, she brushed her mouth against his. His breath shuddered out, the shakiness of the action giving her courage. Confidence.

"Okay?" she asked.

He nodded, settled his hands on her hips. But he

didn't tug her close, didn't close the distance between their mouths. This was entirely up to her, every move, every decision.

It was intoxicating, the power and freedom. It was also terrifying.

But she couldn't stop now. Didn't want to stop.

She kissed him again. And again. Soft kisses as she learned the shape and texture of his mouth. The stubble on his chin lightly scraped against her upper lip but that, too, was exciting. Different. Every time a thought entered her head, one reminding her she was standing in the middle of a parking lot where anyone could see her, that she was kissing the father of one of her students, that this man—this quiet, reserved man—was not her husband, she pushed it aside.

No, Eddie wasn't Beau. She didn't want him to be anyone other than who he was, and she wouldn't disrespect either of them by thinking of her husband now.

She let her fingers drift into the thick hair curling at Eddie's nape. Slowed down so that each kiss was longer, deeper. Unable to help herself, she swept her tongue against his mouth and he groaned, his fingers tightening on her hips.

Still, he didn't take over, he let her set the pace. Let her give him as much as she was able without pushing her or asking for more.

She touched the tip of her tongue to his and, at the taste of him, was lost. Time seemed to stop until she had no idea how long they stood there, mouths clinging, bodies separated by mere inches. Slowly, faintly, sanity and reason returned. The sound of the Eagles' "Take it Easy" reached her. Someone hailed a friend then laughed. Then it all muted again.

Breaking the kiss, Harper lowered to her heels but kept her hands on his shoulders. She liked touching him. Liked knowing she could touch him, that he wanted her to.

Was glad he kept his hands on her, as well.

Her head spun, her entire body tingled painfully as if her limbs had gone to sleep and were now waking. As if she'd been in hibernation all these months. Warmth pooled low in her stomach, desire began a slow burn in her blood.

For the first time since that horrible night when the police had come to her door and told her Beau was dead, she felt as if she was still alive. Fully, truly alive and not sleepwalking through her own life.

She felt, for the first time in a long time, like a woman again. Not a mother, teacher, daughter or friend.

A woman, someone bold enough to kiss a handsome man in the middle of a parking lot. One sexy enough, desirous enough to gain his attention. His attraction.

"You look pleased with yourself," Eddie noted.

"Do I?" She must. Satisfaction flowed through her, a smile stretched her lips. "Maybe I am. I've never done that before."

He raised his eyebrows. "You sure? You were damned good at it."

She blushed. "I meant I've never been the one to initiate a first—or, I guess in this case, second—kiss."

She'd always let the guys she'd dated set the pace, make the move.

Eddie rubbed his thumbs along her lower back, eliciting shivers of pleasure along her skin. "I'd never had a woman throw brownies at me until you."

She laughed and reluctantly pulled away. "I like that we're each other's first for something."

"Me, too." He reached past her and held the door open. She slid behind the steering wheel. "Drive safe."

He shut the door, waited as she turned on the ignition, buckled her seat belt.

When she married Beau, she'd thought her firsts were done. No more first dates or that nerve-wracking first kiss. No more first time getting naked with someone, first time having sex. No more first time saying I love you.

And that'd been more than okay with her because she'd had Beau. She didn't need the excitement and anticipation of a first time. She'd had forever.

Only forever hadn't lasted nearly long enough.

She pulled out of the parking lot, glanced in her rearview mirror to see Eddie watching her, his hands on his hips, his dark hair ruffling in the night breeze.

She turned the corner, thoughts of her husband filling her head, and the taste of another man on her lips.

EDDIE HATED SLEEPOVERS.

Not the kind he had with women. Those were excellent—and thinking about that immediately brought Harper to mind and the heart-stopping kiss she'd given him last night.

The kiss he hadn't been able to get out of his head as he'd tossed and turned alone in his bed. He wanted to make love to her, wake up with her and do it all over again.

Yeah, those kind of sleepovers were just fine with him.

The sleepovers he hated were the ones involving Max. Whenever his kid spent the night somewhere, the excitement and lack of sleep combined to make for one miserable seven-year-old the next day. But this? This was ten times worse.

When Lena had brought Max to the ice rink for his game, he'd been sullen and short-tempered, had snapped at his grandmother when she'd asked him if he wanted a sports drink for the game, pouted when Eddie refused to let him get a cookie and pushed and shoved his way to the head of the line for warm-ups.

If all of that hadn't been bad enough, he'd been a demon on the ice—and not in a good way. He'd hogged the puck, ignored his coach's instructions, yelled at his teammates and, the final straw, made a little girl on the opposite team cry when he checked her so hard, she left her feet and hit her elbow on the ice when she landed.

What had happened? Max had gone with Lena after school acting like his usual good-natured, quiet self, only to return as a miniature grizzly bear.

Damn it, Eddie should have listened to his first instinct and refused to let Max spend the night with Lena at her hotel. Now he was paying the price.

"Go to your room," Eddie told his grumpy, bratty kid as they walked into their kitchen. He set his phone and keys on the table. "And stay there until I call you down for dinner."

Max's jaw dropped. "But it's one o'clock!"

"I know what time it is," Eddie said with restrained patience, but really, his kid was getting on his last nerve. "And you're lucky you only have to spend the afternoon in your room. The way you've been acting, maybe I'll just keep you there for the rest of the weekend."

"That's not fair!"

"What's not fair is you hurting that little girl."

Max had been given a major penalty, and after that, the coach had rightfully benched him. When the game was over, Eddie had told Lena he was taking their son home and putting him in his room. She hadn't argued, something he was grateful for.

"They check in real hockey."

"You don't play real hockey." Eddie tossed his son's hockey bag on the floor. "You play in a no-check league. There are no hits. You could've hurt her and she didn't even have the puck. Go up to your room and think about what you did, and while you're thinking, write her, your coach and the opposing team's coach an apology."

"She pushed me first."

She had. Eddie had seen it, but it wasn't a no-contact league, and she hadn't done more than nudge and annoy Max. "Too bad. Just because someone does something wrong, doesn't mean you have to retaliate."

"I didn't!"

"Do you know what retaliate means?"

Max sniffed, crossed his arms, looking like a miniature Lena when she'd gotten a good mad going. "No."

"It means you don't have to do it back. Remember what we talked about last year? What I said about fighting?"

"It's not fighting. It's hockey."

"It's fighting. And you were disrespectful to your coach and your grandparents."

"I want to go to Grandma's," Max cried, tears running down his face.

"I already told you, the only place you're going is to your room." Rose had offered to take Max for the rest of the day in an effort, Eddie suspected, to save her son's sanity. But while Eddie didn't mind his parents or siblings pitching in once in a while, he preferred to handle most things on his own.

He had to make sure Max understood this kind

of behavior was unacceptable and to do that, he had to punish him.

"Go on," Eddie said. "And you know the rules. No video games so just leave your bag right here."

"I'm going to call Mommy."

It was like a knife to the heart. Max had never, not once, threatened to call Lena, had long ago stopped asking for her because what was the point? She wouldn't come. Eddie had thought his son realized that.

Except she had come, had taken Max for the night, after seeing him only two weeks ago.

"You're not calling anyone," Eddie said, fear coating his mouth. What if Max preferred Lena? What if he wanted to be with her? What if she continued to want him more often? "You're going to your room. When you come down for dinner, you can call your mom and maybe see her before she leaves."

That was reasonable. And the right thing to do.

"I want to call her now," Max said, crying full force.

"We don't always get what we want." It amazed him how he loved his kid more than anything, would lay down his own life if it meant keeping Max safe and yet, no one and nothing could make him as angry and frustrated as the little boy in front of him. "If you don't go upstairs by the time I count to three, I'm taking your video game for an entire week. One."

"No!"

"Two."

"You're mean!"

"Buddy, I've been called worse." He held Max's gaze, noted his son's defiant stare, the trembling of his lower lip. "You really want to push this all the way?"

He could almost see his son's mind working. Max knew Eddie always followed through with what he said, good or—in some cases, and no doubt in his son's opinion—bad.

"I'm gonna run away," Max said, his cheeks wet, his nose running, sweat dampening his hair.

Eddie nodded. "Drop me a line when you find work."

"I'm gonna," Max promised. "You'll see."

Some days Eddie wouldn't mind running away. "You'll have to do so without your video game," he said, pocketing the handheld game. "See you at dinner."

Eddie turned, grabbed a bottle of water from the fridge. Kept his back to his son. A minute later, Max stomped off, his feet pounding on the stairs. His bedroom door slammed. Eddie blew out a breath and took a deep drink of water.

Shit. Most of the time Max was easy to raise. But he was growing up, and the lack of sleep, plus Lena disrupting his life and schedule with her sudden reappearance, had his son acting up. It'd pass. A good, long nap would help.

Eddie threw in a load of laundry, then cleaned the

kitchen. He needed to go to Montesano Construction's shop, put some hours in on the cabinets for the Simpsons, but that could wait until tonight or tomorrow—once Max was out of trouble.

Twenty minutes later he walked upstairs, a basket of clean towels in his arms. He tiptoed up to his son's closed door, pressed his ear against the wood but couldn't make out anything. He opened the door to find his son sitting cross-legged on the bed.

"You're gonna be in trouble," Max said, glaring.

Eddie held the basket under one arm. "Why is that?"

But then he noticed his phone on the bed. Max must have taken it when he'd gone upstairs.

Narrowing his eyes, Eddie picked up his phone. "Did you call Nonna?"

Max shook his head.

Eddie dropped the basket. "Did you call—"

The doorbell rang, cutting him off.

Did you call your mother?

Max took off.

Eddie hurried down the stairs, his hands fisted, his mind racing. Damn it, Lena had no right to come here, no right to interfere in something that wasn't her concern. Yes, she was Max's mother but she had no say in how Eddie disciplined their son. Not when she was the one who'd left.

Eddie put up with her visits, but he would not put up with her interference. Fuming, trembling with his fury, he reached the entryway as Max opened the door. To find Harper standing on the porch holding a sleeping Cassidy.

Max smirked at him. "Told you you were in trouble."

HE WASN'T GLAD to see her.

Max was, but Eddie? He looked ready to slam the door in her face.

Harper considered letting him but then she glanced back down at Max, saw how miserable he was, the tear tracks on his face, his hair a mess, and she sighed.

"Hi," she said softly so as not to wake Cass.

"What are you doing here?" Eddie asked in a low growl.

She flinched. Definitely not happy to see her. Too bad. She wasn't here for him.

Max needed her.

"I called her," Max said, the lift of his chin defiant but he sidled closer to Harper.

Eddie opened his mouth but she spoke before he could. "Do you mind if we come in?" she asked, lifting Cass higher onto her shoulder.

Eddie stepped aside like a man letting in his own executioner. Harper smiled down at Max but she didn't feel all that reassuring. Not when Eddie looked angry enough to tear the door apart with his teeth, chew it up and spit out splinters.

Eddie shut the door. "This doesn't concern you."

"Probably not. But I drove all the way across town

because your son called and told me there was an emergency, so why don't you humor me?"

He led her into a messy living room. "I didn't know anyone was going to stop by."

"Please, you've seen my house. I know what it's like to have kids and a life. Do you mind if I lay her on the couch?" she asked, with a nod toward Cassidy, who was out for the count. When her kid napped, she napped hard.

He cleared a space on the couch and she laid Cass down. Eddie tucked pillows around her and moved the armchair over so Cass couldn't roll off, then he led Harper into the small kitchen, jabbed a finger at the kitchen table. "Sit."

Harper laid her hand on Max's shoulder. "Which one of us are you barking at and ordering around?"

"Both of you."

"Just wanted to be clear," she said lightly. Then, because honestly, he wasn't the boss of her, she pulled a chair out for Max and remained standing. "What's going on?" she asked the little boy.

"He's mean," Max said, his voice quivering. "And that lady who came in to talk to us said that if our parents are hurting us we needed to tell a grown-up like our teacher."

Harper glanced at Eddie, who was glowering at her. He didn't give excuses, didn't try and convince her that he hadn't hurt his child—probably because it was obvious he hadn't. Anyone who'd seen him with Max could easily see he wouldn't raise a hand to the boy, and other than being tired and angry, Max wasn't hurt.

"Uh-huh." Harper knelt and gently brushed the hair off of his forehead. "How did your dad hurt you?"

Max shrugged and averted his gaze.

"Because you know," Harper continued, "when that police officer said for you to tell a teacher if your parents are hurting you, she meant if they were being abusive. If they were hitting you or saying really mean things."

"He made me go to my room. He yelled at me."

"You think that was yelling?" Eddie asked, his eyes narrowed. "You just wait."

Harper straightened. "Okay, I think I'm beginning to see what's going on here. Max, I'm going to talk to your dad for a few minutes. Do you want him to wait here or in his room?" she asked Eddie.

He jabbed his finger at Max yet again. "Don't. Move."

Max dropped his chin to his chest, hunched his shoulders.

Harper and Eddie walked back into the living room. Cass slept soundly on her back, her arms splayed, her tiny, pudgy hands out.

"Before you lay into me," Harper said, "I want you to know I came here with good intentions."

"This isn't your concern."

"So you've said and you're right but—"

"You can stop at the part where I'm right."

"But," she repeated, stressing the word, "I get a frantic phone call from Max. He's sobbing that he's going to run away and you're being mean...well... you get the drift. The only way I could calm him down was to promise him that I'd come over. I did try to get him to put you on the phone but he can be mighty stubborn when he sets his mind to it, and I couldn't find the number for your house in the phone book."

"It's unlisted," he said, as if relenting a little. "I wrote it down as the contact number, though, when you sent home those dozens of papers at the beginning of the school year."

"Papers that are all at the school. I thought the easiest way to calm him down and to stop him from calling his uncle Leo—his next step according to what he told me—was to just come over."

"You thought I was really hurting him? Hitting him?"

"Of course not. If I'd thought that, you would've answered the door to find the cops and a social worker on your porch." She didn't hesitate when she thought one of her kids was being abused. She'd had a girl a few years ago who'd confessed to Harper that her brother "slept on top of her." Harper had told the proper officials and it'd been discovered that the precious little girl had been sexually abused.

Shady Grove was a small town. Safe. But even in small towns, bad things happened.

"I can handle this," Eddie said.

"I have no doubt about that. But something must have happened to push Max into calling me."

"He's pissed I punished him. He acted out at hockey, has been miserable ever since his mother brought him to hockey this morning."

"Lack of sleep can have that effect."

"He needs to realize there are consequences for bad behavior."

Poor Max. And poor Eddie. He looked as miserable as his son. She could only imagine how hard it must be on both of them to have Lena in and out of their lives like that. Add in a sleepover, too little sleep, probably too much excitement and junk food and things had just exploded into this mess.

Well, she was really good at cleaning up messes.

"There are definitely consequences for bad behavior," she agreed. "And Max deserves to be punished for being mouthy and disrespectful—"

"And calling you," Eddie muttered.

She grinned. "And for calling me. But why don't you hold off on that for an hour or so? Take a walk—"

"It's raining."

"Clear your head," she continued determinedly. "Go for a drive or run down to the coffee shop and grab a latte."

"I'm a man. I don't drink lattes."

"Lots of men drink lattes—" She shook her head. "Don't try to confuse me."

Max stepped into the room.

"What part of *don't move* didn't you get?" Eddie asked him.

Max started bawling and ran over to Harper, clung to her legs. "Can I go home with you? I don't want to live here anymore."

Harper patted his back. "Your daddy would be so sad if you didn't live here with him anymore. Tell you what, your dad has to run a few errands so I'll stay here with you until he comes back."

"I don't have any errands to run," Eddie said, making it sound as if he was contemplating murder. Hers.

"Find some." She led Max to a chair, sat so he could crawl into her lap. "Go on. We'll be fine."

She didn't think he was going to listen to her but he whirled on his heel and stormed out. A moment later she heard the back door shut followed by the sound of his truck pulling away. Max looked up at her, his eyes—so like Eddie's—shiny with tears. "Can I watch TV? I want to watch *SpongeBob*."

"I don't think that's a good idea. But I'll tell you what, why don't you bring me a couple of your favorite books and I'll read them to you?"

He seemed about as excited about that as if she'd suggested they pull their teeth out with rusty pliers but he sighed and dragged himself over to a built-in bookshelf in the corner. He came back with a ratty blue blanket and several books, all well-worn, which told her they were ones Eddie read to his son over and over again.

Max climbed back onto her lap, rested his head against her chest in complete trust, his body curling into hers. He was big, stocky for his age, but he was still all little boy with his round face and cartoon character T-shirt. She brushed his hair back, kissed the top of his head while he snuggled closer to her and twisted the corner of the blanket around and around his finger.

She was only human so of course, she had favorites in her classroom. Each year there was at least one kid who stole her heart, but this was different. Max hadn't stolen her heart, he simply had it.

Max had been wrong, she thought as he handed her the first book. Eddie wasn't the one in trouble here. She was.

CHAPTER FOURTEEN

"Hey," Maddie said, looking up from the board she'd run through the planer as Eddie walked into the shop. She shut off the machine. "What's up?"

"I got groceries."

At the snap in his voice, she nodded knowingly. "Yeah, buying food always pisses me off, too. Last week I paid three bucks for a tomato. One tomato."

"I didn't need groceries," he said through gritted teeth.

Now his sister frowned, put the board down and set aside her safety goggles. "Then why did you get them?"

"She kicked me out of my own house."

"She who? Mom?"

"Harper."

Maddie regarded him shrewdly. Too shrewdly, damn her. "This might be a stupid question, but why is Harper at your house and why did she kick you out?"

"Max called her. She thought I needed a break."

"Let me see if I can fill in the many, many blanks left in that explanation. Max called his teacher and invited her over?"

"He was mad at me. He called her to…I don't know. To help him. To piss me off. To save him from having to spend the day in his room."

"Yeah, he seemed like a nice long nap would do him some good."

Maddie, like the rest of his family, had been at the hockey match and witnessed Max's meltdown. Her and dozens of other people, all part of a rapt audience who'd seen how inept he'd been with his own kid.

"You would've thought I'd taken a belt to his backside the way he acted. He called Harper and she came over because he threatened to call Leo next. Probably thought he'd get through using 911."

Maddie laughed. "Bree did that once. I could've killed her. She wasn't feeling well and decided I wasn't giving her enough attention so she called and told them she was sick and her mom had left her home alone."

"You left Bree alone?"

"Of course not. I was outside. You should've seen me when the fire truck pulled up with lights and sirens going. I almost had a heart attack. Leo scolded Bree and you know he doesn't often lecture. I think that alone helped her realize what she did was wrong and made a bigger impact than anything I could've said or done. Although if you tell Leo I said that, I'll deny it."

"I remember that. It was a lot funnier at the time. And when it was your kid."

"Of course." Grinning, Maddie cocked a hip. "It

was sure nice of Harper to drop everything to help you and Max."

"I didn't ask for her help."

Maddie held up her hands. "Hey, no one said you did. Jeez, defensive much?"

"I can handle my own son. I can take care of him by myself."

"No one doubts that. You're a wonderful father. But you're not alone in this. You never were. You couldn't be, not with our family. You don't have to take it all on your shoulders. It's okay to ask for some help with the heavy lifting now and then."

"I don't remember you asking for help with Bree."

"Are you nuts? I had her when I was seventeen. Seventeen. I needed more help than even I'd realized. Mom watched Bree so I could graduate high school and after, Bree and I lived with Mom and Dad for years before being able to afford a place of my own. They helped me. Believe me, they helped me tons. Plus, Neil's parents—Gerry and Carl—pitched in, babysat when needed."

"Harper calmed him down," Eddie admitted, hating that it bothered him. Though hearing Maddie say she'd had help and had been grateful for it went a long way to easing his initial fury at letting Harper take over at his own house. "I couldn't get through to him, couldn't get my own son to listen to me, but he listened to her."

"Yeah, that sucks. But he didn't mean it. He adores

you. You're that kid's hero. But it is interesting that Harper came to your rescue like that."

"She's Max's teacher."

"A pretty devoted one, to spend her Saturday afternoon with your tired, grumpy kid."

Eddie shrugged because there was nothing else to say.

"Oh, boy," Maddie breathed. "I can't believe it. Leo was right. You've got a thing for her. I mean, I can believe you've got a thing for Harper. She's pretty and seems nice. I just really can't believe that bonehead was right. It's like the end of the world as I know it."

"I don't have a thing for anyone," he said, sounding like a middle schooler denying his crush on the teacher.

"Guess you're not quite as bright as I took you for then."

No shit.

He checked the time. He'd been gone well over an hour. Long enough for Max to have calmed down.

"I have to go." He headed toward the door, ignoring Maddie's muttered grouse about him being stubborn.

When he got home, he grabbed the grocery bags from the seat next to him. He'd picked up the makings for lasagna, Max's favorite, along with another box of brownie mix since Max had liked making them before.

He went inside, set the bags on the kitchen table,

then stepped into the living room only to slam to a stop as if someone had put up an invisible wall. Cassidy was still snoozing on the couch, her little mouth slack, her hair a tangle of blond fuzz. And on the oversized recliner Harper and Max were cuddled together, both fast asleep.

Max's head rested against the side of Harper's chest, her arm slung around his shoulders. Her head was back, her breathing deep and even, her lips parted slightly.

She stunned him. Made him want, and he didn't like wanting. It was too dangerous. When you wanted something too much, it made you reckless. Foolish. And he couldn't risk getting hurt again. Couldn't risk his son getting hurt.

Cass stirred and Eddie crossed to the couch, pulled the blanket over the little girl. She rolled onto her side, kept sleeping.

He turned to find Harper watching him, her eyes sleepy, her cheeks flushed.

She smiled.

And he knew for her, he'd be reckless. Foolish. That she'd be worth it.

Lifting her arm, she gently freed herself, lowering Max's head to the chair cushion. She covered him with the blanket he'd had since he was a baby, the one he still clung to when he was tired or sick, and gently brushed his hair from his forehead before straightening.

Eddie motioned for her to follow him into the

kitchen. "You didn't have to stay with him," he said gruffly, his resentment clear.

She yawned. "Believe me, I wish someone would've helped me last week when Cassidy had a major tantrum because I wouldn't let her watch *Baby Einstein*. She screamed so loud, I thought my ears were going to bleed. By the end of the night, we were both in tears and I was seriously considering locking her in her room while I ate a vat of ice cream. But somehow, we both persevered. And, I even shared the ice cream with her once she'd calmed down."

There was that smile again, the one asking him to join in on the joke, on her happiness. He wanted to. He'd never considered himself unhappy before, had never really thought of it one way or the other, but now he wondered: When was the last time he was happy? Truly happy?

Sure, he was content. He had a job he enjoyed and was good at, a kid he'd do anything for and a family he loved.

But was he happy?

He didn't want to dwell on it because he was afraid of what the answer to that would be.

He tugged on his ear. He felt like an idiot. Hell, he was an idiot for giving Harper a bad time, for getting pissed that she'd come to help him. For not telling her how much he appreciated what she'd done.

"Thank you." He cleared his throat. "Thank you for coming over. For staying."

"You're welcome," she said, as if she was the

grateful one, all because he'd put his thoughts into words for her.

"He was exhausted," she continued, unloading the groceries onto the table, "which I'm guessing played a big part in his meltdown. Once he calmed down enough to stop being so angry and upset, he fell asleep."

"He wasn't the only one."

"I only shut my eyes for a moment," she said without a hint of embarrassment at being caught snoozing. "Cass usually naps for at least two hours on the weekends. Sometimes I take advantage of that time to get housework done or plan my lessons for the week. Sometimes I read a book or watch a movie. And sometimes I sleep. It all balances out in the end." She held up a box of Max's favorite cereal. "Which cupboard?"

"Pantry," he said, unable to take his eyes off her, the curve of her hips, the roundness of her breasts.

He followed her into the walk-in pantry, unsure of his intentions—though by the tightening of his body, the anticipation building along his skin, he could guess. All he knew was that he had to be near her. Had to touch her. If only for a moment.

She set the cereal next to the other varieties, made sure it was neatly lined up on the shelf. He smiled at that attention to detail. Then slid the pocket door closed, encasing them in darkness.

He felt, rather than saw, her spin around. "What—"

He flipped on the overhead light. She frowned,

looked from him to the door and then to him again, her message clear.

What do you think you're doing?

She was about to find out.

The pantry was the size of a walk-in closet with shelves taking up the left and back walls. He edged forward. She retreated, her eyes wide. He continued toward her until her back pressed against the shelves. She held up her hands as if to stop him.

"Don't," he murmured, so close the tips of her breasts brushed against his chest as she inhaled sharply, close enough to see the tiny freckles dotting her nose. "Don't stop me. Not yet."

She searched his face then slowly lowered her hand, her breath washing over him on a shaky exhale.

Settling his hands on her waist, he leaned down and kissed her. Kept the kiss light. Patient. Brushed his mouth against hers again and again until she sighed, laid her hands on his shoulders like she'd done last night. And kissed him back.

He'd let her control their kiss last night and it had stretched his willpower to the limit but he understood her hesitancy. Her fears. He could only imagine how she must have felt, kissing a man who wasn't her husband. Unlike him, she hadn't chosen to end her marriage, hadn't wanted to be free from the person she'd vowed to love forever. If things had happened differently that day last November, if Beau Kavanagh had stopped at the convenience store five minutes earlier, he'd still be here. He'd be alive. He'd be with Harper.

Eddie wasn't glad Beau's life had been taken, that a good man had died too young, that Cassidy would never know her father. But he was glad that out of all the men Harper could've chosen, she was letting Eddie kiss her. Touch her.

He was glad she was with him.

He should tell her, but he'd never been good at finding the right words, had always struggled to make himself clear. He'd have to show her.

He slid his hands under her shirt, seeking her warm, soft skin. Rubbed his thumbs back and forth across the indentation of her waist, his fingers spread along her lower back. All the while he kissed her, again and again, longer, slower, deeper kisses until they were both breathing hard.

He couldn't stop from edging closer, bringing their hips together, his erection pressed against her center. She gasped into his mouth, her body going rigid, her fingers digging into his shoulders.

Keeping his touch light, soothing, he trailed his mouth across her jaw, up her neck to her ear. "That's what you do to me," he breathed. "You turn me inside out, Harper."

He went back to her mouth, that mouth he couldn't get enough of, kept his kiss undemanding until she relaxed. She slid her hands up, linking them behind his neck, her fingers brushing against the sensitive skin of his nape.

Triumph roared through him and he kissed her harder, pressing her between the shelves and his body. He rolled his hips against her, reveled in the feel of her softness, the sound of her low moan. He moved his hands up her sides, his fingers skimming the underside of her breasts.

Shoving against his chest, she broke the kiss. "The kids…"

He took a half step back, moved his hands back to her waist. "They're sleeping."

She licked her lips, looked adorably mussed and well kissed. Dazed. Aroused. His ego swelled along with his body.

"What if they wake up?"

"If they do," he whispered, "we'll hear them."

Because she didn't seem convinced, because the last thing he wanted was to stop now, he tugged aside the collar of her shirt, kissed her collarbone, then rubbed his mouth up and down the long line of her neck. Her head fell back, bumping the shelf with a soft thud.

He straightened and lifted his finger to his lip in the universal *shh* sign. Then, holding her gaze, he dragged her shirt up, inch by inch, his knuckles brushing against the silky skin of her stomach.

When he revealed her ribs, she squeezed her elbows against her sides, stopping his progress. He leaned in close and spoke directly into her ear. "Trust me."

TRUST ME.

Harper tried to swallow but her mouth was completely dry. Eddie watched her, his eyes hot with want. With desire.

For her.

Oh, dear.

She had no idea what to do, what to say. Those two simple words said in his deep, sexy voice had thrown her for a loop. His hands warm and sure on her skin, his thumbs rubbing light circles over the silky sides of her bra teased her. Tempted her.

Trust me.

Could she? Should she? Did it even matter when her body responded so heatedly, so wantonly? But even that was wrong, wasn't it? She was in a pantry, for goodness' sake, with her daughter and one of her students sleeping barely two rooms away.

Eddie leaned forward slowly—so slowly she could've evaded him at any time, could have easily stepped aside and walked away.

She didn't move. He brushed his mouth over hers then settled it there for a drugging kiss. Her eyes drifted shut and she curled her fingers into his shirt, his chest solid beneath her hands. *Trust me.*

She wasn't sure she did. But she wanted to. Or maybe she just wanted him. Too much to be rational and reasonable. Too much to feel guilty or worried. Too much.

His kiss grew hotter, hungrier and more insistent

until she clung to him, her body molded to his, her hands roaming over his biceps and chest. He caressed her stomach, traced his nails up her rib cage then slid those rough hands under her bra, cupping her breasts.

She exhaled, a cross between a shuddering breath and a sigh of pure pleasure. He kneaded her flesh gently, had her body warming, desire pooling low in her stomach and between her legs. Still kissing her he pinched her nipples lightly then rolled the tight buds between his fingers. She squirmed, her breathing harsh and ragged. An ache built at her core, her panties grew damp.

Stabbing one hand into the hair at the nape of her neck, he held her head still while he took the kiss deeper. Wetter. Hotter. His other hand skimmed her stomach and she sucked in. She wasn't skinny like his ex-wife. He was probably used to dating women with flat abs, toned bodies. Not a curved stomach and faint stretch marks marring her skin.

He broke the kiss, lifting his head, his eyes narrowed as he watched her, watched what he did to her when he touched her. She wished he'd kept the light off. She wasn't even wearing a fancy bra and underwear. Had planned on staying home today.

He undid the button of her jeans, tugged the zipper down and she stiffened. It took all her willpower not to cross her arms over herself and shove him away. She was torn between doing what she knew was right, was safe and best for her, and what her body demanded from him. But she had no idea what he wanted.

She squeezed her eyes shut. Could she do it? Could she have sex in the man's pantry while their children slept in the same house? Could she have sex with another man—quick, completely commitment-free sex—with someone who wasn't her husband? Was she ready to take this step, ready to share her body with someone else?

"Stop," Eddie said on barely a breath of a sound.

Her eyes flew open. "What?"

His lips tickled her ear as he spoke. "Stop thinking."

And then his hand was between her legs, warm and sure and insistent. It felt good. So, so good. She bit her lip to hold back a whimper. He stroked her, kept that other hand on her hair, his grip just tight enough to have a bit of bite to it, a bit of excitement. Bending his head, he took one nipple in his mouth and sucked hard. Her back arched, her hips bucked violently, urging him on, silently begging him to go faster, to touch her harder.

Her body heated as pressure built but she held it back, shook her head as if that alone could stop it. She wasn't sure why she fought it when she wanted it so badly, only that she had to, she couldn't succumb to it fully, not if she wanted to keep her self-respect. Her heart safe.

But then he tugged her head back farther and gently bit down on her nipple. The world exploded into a million pieces. Her orgasm washed over her with wave after wave of intense pleasure that rocked her to her core, leaving her breathless and boneless and shuddering with the strength of her climax.

Finally her body came down, her breathing and pulse slowed. Eddie straightened and pulled her bra back into place, his expression hard. Fierce. He tugged her shirt down and then gently, almost reverently, combed his fingers through her hair.

Tears stung her eyes and she ducked her head so he couldn't see, but she wondered if he sensed them because he backed up a step, then another. "I'll check on the kids," he said softly before slipping out and shutting the door behind him.

Harper slumped against the shelves, her hands shaking as she buttoned and zipped her jeans. She wanted to crawl next to the canned goods and hide out in here for, oh, the next few days if possible. But avoidance wasn't an option. She did wait the few minutes it took to get her heart rate and breathing back to normal before opening the door.

Eddie stood by the sink, held up a glass of water. "Kids are still sleeping."

She accepted the water and drank deeply. Avoided his eyes but she couldn't ignore what had happened, not when her body still tingled with the aftershocks of her orgasm. Not when the evidence of what they'd done—and what they hadn't—was so visible behind the zipper of his jeans.

Lowering the glass, she inhaled deeply. "Why did you do that?"

She winced. That hadn't been the exact question she'd meant to ask. She'd meant to ask if he was okay. To explain that, despite what had happened in the pantry—what she'd allowed to happen, what she'd thoroughly, obviously enjoyed—she wasn't ready to sleep with him.

"I thought you might be thirsty."

She frowned, shook her head. "No. Not that." She licked her lips. Tipped her head toward the pantry—she'd never be able to look at canned goods the same way again. "That."

He stepped closer. Lowered his voice. "Why did I touch you? Why did I kiss you? Why did I make you come?"

Hearing him say it, his words washing over her like a caress, had her body responding again. "Yes."

"I find you very attractive. I enjoy touching you. Kissing you. I want you, Harper."

Her heart soared but panic managed to find its way in and ground it again. "I'm not ready," she blurted, setting the glass down with a soft clink. "For…sex."

He nodded. "I know. I can wait."

She glanced at the proof that he hadn't been unaffected by their pantry encounter. "I'm sorry."

"I think I'll live."

And that reminder that he would, that her husband hadn't, almost knocked her to her knees. She locked them. It was just an expression, one people said every day, one she herself said. She'd only taken it that way because her feelings were messed up, her head spinning.

She tried to smile. "Good to know."

"I'll wait for you, Harper," he said, all sexy and honest and intense. Then he kissed her, a long, lingering kiss.

She couldn't help it, she threw her arms around him and hugged him tight. He returned her embrace, didn't seem to mind that she was a crazy woman—wanton and easy one minute, needy and emotional the next.

He'd wait for her. Because he was attracted to her. Because he wanted to have sex with her. She was a grown woman, had been married, had a daughter. She'd had relationships other than Beau. She understood that sometimes the physical was just that. Physical. That it was all there was for some people.

But she'd had more, so much more with Beau, and she wanted that again. When the time was right. For now, she didn't know what she wanted. So she'd do what Eddie was doing. She'd wait. She'd spend time with him and see what developed between them.

"Mommy!"

Cass's cry had Harper hurrying into the living room. Her daughter was awake, sitting on the couch, her cheeks flushed, her hair wild, tears coursing down her face.

"It's okay," Harper said, picking her up and holding her close. Rocking her back and forth. "That must've been scary, huh? Waking up in a strange place. Shh…shh…"

Cassidy's cries subsided to the occasional hiccup and she settled her head on Harper's shoulder.

"Hey, there," Eddie said to Cass in a low, soothing voice. "Want some apple juice?"

"Juice," Cass said in a sleep-roughened voice.

Eddie went back into the kitchen. When he returned he handed Cass a sippy cup. She took it and drank deeply. When she was done, she grinned at him. "I want you."

He held out his arms as if it was the most natural thing in the world to hold someone else's daughter.

A noise had them turning. Max bolted to a sitting position, his hair damp with sweat, his T-shirt wrinkled, sleep marks on his left cheek.

"You feeling better?" Eddie asked.

Max nodded, stared at his blanket. "I'm sorry I was bad. I'm sorry I said I was gonna run away."

Eddie shifted Cass to his other hip then sat next to his son. "I'm sorry I yelled."

Max slid him a sly look. "And that you made me go to my room?"

"No, but in this one case, we can forget about that. But no TV or video games for the rest of the week for taking my phone without permission and for calling Mrs. Kavanagh."

Max hung his head. "Okay."

"Is there something you want to tell Mrs. Kavanagh?"

"I'm sorry I called you and said it was an emergency," Max whispered.

"That's okay. You know I'm always here for you, Max." She was starting to become dangerously attached to him—and his father. Not a good idea considering she was Max's teacher. Quite a few of her coworkers had kids in their classrooms that they knew personally—children of friends, nieces or nephews—but Harper liked to keep her personal and professional life separate so one didn't cause problems for the other.

Looked as if it was too late for that.

"Why don't Cassidy and I get out of your way?" she said, remembering how it had felt to have Eddie's hands on her. She was confused and vulnerable, and while she didn't usually mind letting her emotions get the best of her, she had a feeling this was one of those instances where it would be better for her to keep her head. "I'm sure you have a lot you need to do."

She reached for Cassidy, who screamed and buried her face into the side of Eddie's neck, clinging to him like he was about to join the French Foreign Legion and this was their last goodbye.

"Cass, please," she muttered, "have some pride."

Eddie stood, her daughter in his arm, his free hand on his son's head. "Stay."

"Excuse me?"

"For dinner," he added. "I'm making lasagna."

Max's eyes widened. "You are?" He sent one of his shy grins at Harper. "That's my favorite."

"Brownie sundaes for dessert," Eddie said. "But we could use some help putting it all together."

He didn't, she knew that. He didn't need help with anything, didn't want to need help. But he'd asked her to stay, had asked for her assistance, and even though it was for something small like getting dinner together, it meant something to her.

"We'd love to stay," Harper said, knowing she was somehow setting herself up for a big fall, but unable to stop from making that climb anyway.

CHAPTER FIFTEEN

"I KNEW YOU and Harper knew each other," James said to Eddie the next day while they stood toward the back of Harper's living room, the football game flashing on her big-screen TV, "but I hadn't realized you had a thing."

Eddie sipped his beer. "We don't."

"No?" James asked with a raised brow. "You sure? Because it seems to me when a man and a woman—a single man and an attractive, smart, funny single woman—sit together at a hockey game and the single man shows up at the attractive, smart, funny single woman's house to watch a football game, there's something going on other than mere acquaintances."

"You're here," Eddie pointed out. "You going to tell me you and Harper have something going on?"

"I'm here because I'm with Sadie and because Sadie and Harper are cousins. Sorry, man, you have no excuse."

"I don't need one."

But he felt like he did. He felt as if everyone was watching him, wondering why he and Max were there, trying to figure out if there was something going on between him and Harper. He didn't even know the answer to that question. All he knew was that he'd had a really good time with her and Cassidy yesterday. He'd taught Harper how to make Pops's lasagna, and she and the kids had made brownies. It'd been nice. Normal. Exactly the type of situation he'd hoped for when he'd married Lena, the kind of Saturday night he'd dreamed of having with his family.

It'd taken a good hour but Harper had finally relaxed. After what had happened between them in the pantry, she'd wanted to analyze it, discuss it. Not everything needed to be spelled out, did it? He found her attractive. He wanted to touch her so he did. He'd made his intentions clear. He wanted her in his bed. He'd be patient and wait, but he hoped she didn't keep him waiting too long.

James, obviously tired of not getting a rise out of Eddie, wandered over to talk to Harper's father. Her house was packed with people. When she did a Game Day—as she called it—she did it big. Her parents, her mother-in-law, Sadie and James, Sadie's parents and younger sister, Charlotte, coworkers and friends of hers and Beau's. Eddie felt like an outsider, like all the pieces were round and he and Max were square.

This was a far cry from how he preferred to spend his weekends. He hated parties, hated trying to think of conversational topics, so he stayed in the back of the room, kept his gaze on the television screen. The Steelers got an interception and a cheer rose from the crowd. He shouldn't be here, but he hadn't been able to refuse her invitation, not after she'd reissued it again last night before she'd left his house, seeming as if she'd really wanted him there.

Now he wasn't so sure. Yeah, she'd been pleasant when they'd arrived. Pleasant. Polite. Too polite. Too distant for his taste. Not that he needed everyone to know his personal business but after she'd taken their jackets and told them to help themselves to something to eat and drink, she'd barely said two words to Eddie. Could hardly even look him in the eye.

It hadn't even been a full day since he'd had her full attention but he wanted it again.

He missed her.

It was stupid, and it pissed him off, but he wouldn't deny it.

He caught sight of her as she made her way back into the kitchen. She laughed at something someone said, stopped to speak to a middle-aged man, then continued on her way. Eddie followed, stepping into the kitchen as she put dirty dishes into the sink.

He came up behind her and pressed a kiss to the side of her neck.

Squealing, she jumped and whirled around, the silverware in her hand arcing in the air before hitting the floor with a loud clang.

"Eddie! God," she gasped, slapping her hand over her neck as if he'd been a vampire and had taken a huge, bloody bite. "You scared me."

Obviously. He shoved his hands into his pockets, viciously cursing the blush heating his cheeks. "Sorry."

She smiled but it looked pained. "No. That's okay. I guess I'm just...jumpy."

He glanced at the doorway. Still empty. "Maybe we could try that again."

He leaned down to kiss her. She leapt back. "Did you need something?"

You.

He frowned. He didn't need her. He wanted her. Big difference. Need came with strings and expectations. Expectations came with the possibility of failure.

"A beer?" she continued, already heading toward the fridge. "Or maybe something else to eat?"

He shook his head and she shut the refrigerator door.

"Where's Max?" she asked.

"Playing with Cass."

Max, like his father, preferred the known over the unknown and he wasn't friends with any of the other kids who were there.

"Good," she said. "That's...good. Are you enjoying the game?"

"No."

She frowned, chewed on her lower lip. She looked pretty today, her hair pinned back on the sides, her Steelers jersey hiding her curves. He'd come because she'd asked. He'd come because he hadn't been able to stay away, just like he'd asked her to stay for dinner last night because he hadn't wanted to let her go. Not yet. If he wasn't careful, she'd have him wrapped around her finger, doing everything she wanted, trying to be who she wanted him to be.

He was starting to wonder if that'd be a bad thing.

He moved closer so that only a foot separated them. "I didn't come for the game or the food."

"Don't tell me," she joked lightly. "You came for the free beer."

"I came for you."

Her expression softened and her lips curved into one of her real smiles, one filled with warmth. "That's—"

"The Ravens just scored," her cousin Charlotte said as she came into the kitchen carrying an empty tray. She glanced curiously between them. "And we need more nachos before things get ugly out there."

"No problem," Harper said, her voice weird. Guilty. She grabbed the tray and practically ran to the other side of the kitchen. What the hell was that about?

"You okay?" Charlotte asked. Long and lean, her bright red hair and freckles reminded Eddie of the old rag doll Maddie had as a kid.

"I'm good," Harper said. "Just…upset Baltimore has the lead back."

Sadie came in, looking like a blonde fairy playing gypsy in a long, swirling skirt and puffy shirt, followed by Joan Crosby.

A man couldn't escape people in this house. Now, because he'd wanted a few minutes alone with Harper, he was surrounded by women.

Joan smiled at Harper. "Anything I can do in here?"

"I'm just going to mix up another batch of margaritas," Harper said, setting the cheese-laden tortilla chips in the oven.

"I've got it," Sadie said, pulling ingredients from the fridge.

Harper linked her hands together at her waist. "I hope Steve's feeling better," she blurted to Joan before looking at Eddie. "Joan's husband is under the weather."

Since he had no comment about that, he kept silent.

"Can I make him up a plate for you to take home?" Harper continued.

"That's sweet, but I'm sure he'd rather just stick with his ginger ale and saltines," Joan said, not meeting Harper's eyes.

Something's going on there, Eddie thought. But it wasn't his place to point out to Harper that her mother-in-law was being less than honest.

Joan glanced at Eddie, her smile dimming. "Eddie, I hadn't realized you and Harper were friends."

"We went to school together," Harper said quickly.

"Of course. That's…nice," Joan said, making it

sound anything but. "I hope neither of you mind my saying so, but I wonder if it'd be best to keep more… distance between the two of you. At least until Max is no longer in Harper's class. I think we all know how complicated these situations can be."

"Actually," Sadie said, "Eddie and Max came with me and James."

Harper sent her cousin a grateful look. Eddie narrowed his eyes.

Son of a bitch.

This, coming here, was a mistake. She didn't want him here, didn't want anyone to know there was something going on between them. He never should have touched her yesterday. He was getting all mixed up. Confused. She was confusing him, making him think thoughts he didn't want, making him want things he'd long ago given up on.

He'd made that mistake once before, he wouldn't do it again.

"Thanks for the beer," he said, handing Harper his empty bottle before walking away.

"Max," he said, sticking his head into the playroom, "get your stuff."

Harper came up behind him. "You're leaving?" she asked. "Is something wrong?"

He wished he didn't have to look at her, that he didn't have to see her confused frown. "I have things to do."

"At least let me walk you out—"

"We know the way."

HARPER WATCHED EDDIE'S back as he walked through her living room and out the door. She was glad he was leaving—which only made her feel guilty.

Why not? She'd felt guilty all day, might as well heap some more onto what was becoming quite a large pile. She hated this. Hated feeling so torn, so sneaky, as if she didn't even have a right to invite a man to her home. As if her friends and family were watching her, judging her.

Hated that she'd done or said something that had hurt Eddie's feelings, made him feel as if he wasn't welcome there. As if she didn't want him there.

She hurried outside, caught up with him as he held the door to his truck open and Max climbed in. "Is something wrong?" she asked.

He faced her. "You tell me."

"I don't know what you mean."

He just watched her. Waiting. Patient.

He shifted. Okay, maybe not so patient.

I'll wait for you.

He'd told her that but maybe she'd taken advantage of his willingness to give her time, his understanding.

"Look," she said, "if you're mad at me—"

"I'm not," he said, flicking her a cold glance.

"You are. I'm sorry if it seemed as if I was ignoring you—"

"You're embarrassed by me."

Her head snapped back as if she'd been slapped. "That's ridiculous."

"You don't want people to know anything is going on between us."

She gripped Eddie's arm and tugged him toward the rear bumper. "This is all so new and...unexpected. And with Joan here I didn't want to do anything to hurt her. I didn't want to...throw it in her face that I'm seeing another man. And I'm not even sure if we are seeing each other," she said. "We went to dinner, and Cassidy and I hung out at your house for an evening. So who's to say what's going on? If anything," she added quickly.

"Then there's no reason for you to be embarrassed or to act weird if I go to your house. If nothing's going on between us. You could barely look at me."

"That's not true." But instead of sounding certain, her voice came out thin, as if she was lying. Oh, God, she was so lying.

He checked on his son then edged closer to Harper, lowered his voice. "I'm not a lawyer. I work with my hands. I sweat and my work is hard, sometimes dirty work but it fulfills me. I'm not comfortable around people I don't know. I can't talk someone into doing something. I'd rather keep my thoughts to myself."

"Wha...what are you trying to say?" But she was afraid she already knew.

"I'm not Beau. And that's not good enough for you."

"That," she said firmly, "is not true."

"Isn't it?"

"I just need some time. You said you'd wait."

He nodded but looked as if he regretted giving her that promise. "How about when you're ready, you just let me know. You can sneak over to my house and no one has to know what you let me do to you."

"Ouch," she whispered.

"The truth often hurts."

But that wasn't the truth.

Was it?

"This has nothing to do with my being embarrassed of you," she insisted. "It's just not anyone else's business."

"You're right. It's not. But it's nothing to be ashamed of either."

His quiet words almost undid her. He brushed past her and climbed into his truck. She stepped aside while he backed up. She wasn't ashamed of him. He may not have done well in school but he was bright and creative. He may not charm a crowd but he spoke the truth, and the words he said mattered.

And she'd somehow made him feel less than because she was afraid to move on. Afraid to admit to her feelings, to let people know that she was seeing someone else.

Was that so wrong? She could hardly spring him on everyone, let them all know that, hey, even though Beau had been dead only eleven months, she'd put her feelings for him aside and decided to move on with her life as if he'd never been her husband. As if she hadn't loved him.

It had nothing to do with Eddie. Not much to

do with him. Except he didn't understand that. He thought she considered him somehow less than Beau. She'd hurt him. She didn't want to hide him away like some dirty little secret, but that was what she'd done, she realized. That was how she'd made him feel.

And now she had to set things right.

THREE HUNDRED AND fourteen days.

"I was humiliated," Joan told Steve as she stood in their living room, her hands on her hips.

She still couldn't believe it but one day had bled into the next then into the next. Day became night, night turned to day, life went on. All around her people kept living but it was all she could do to get out of bed each morning. She hadn't lived, not truly, in almost a year.

Her husband wouldn't even look at her, which only made her angrier. She was in the right here. The least he could do was acknowledge her anger, her resentment. He could take it, absorb it into his skin. Couldn't he see that she had nothing left to give?

"Your humiliation is your own," he said, sounding like some highly enlightened individual.

"I lied for you," she said, her voice trembling with anger.

He sighed. Finally shut off the movie he'd been watching and stood, his expression serious, his eyes sad. She couldn't remember the last time she'd seen him happy but that was okay because she hadn't been happy, not really, truly happy, since the day her son had been taken from her. Why should Steve have joy in his life?

As soon as the thought occurred to her she tried to dismiss it, wanted to feel ashamed for even thinking such a horrible thought in the first place, but she couldn't. Which only made it that much worse.

"I didn't ask you to lie for me," he told her in his quiet voice. Steve never raised his voice, rarely got angry. It was those traits that had attracted her to him when they'd met all those years ago at a meeting about his son's behavior in school. Of course, his ex-wife had been there, too, but later, after she'd gone, Steve had asked for Joan's number, had been so sweet and polite, so obviously willing to do whatever he had to in order to help his son. He and his ex-wife got along well, parented together, which boded well for both of them and their children, and Joan had been attracted. Interested.

It hadn't been easy as his kids weren't thrilled with the idea of their father having a new woman in his life, especially the school's psychologist, and Joan had been gun-shy herself. Beau had welcomed Steve into their lives because, even though he was young, he could see how happy Steve made his mom.

They'd gotten through, had taken it slow and had built a life together. And now it was all falling apart, and she didn't have the strength to hold it together. She couldn't make herself care, not when it was so much easier to be numb.

"You may not have asked me to lie," she told him, "but you still forced me to. What was I supposed to say? That you couldn't attend because you were home pouting? That you were angry with me and you not accompanying me to my daughter-in-law's party was your way of punishing me?"

He flinched. "Is that what you really think? That I'm punishing you?"

"What else am I supposed to think? Just because I don't want to drop everything to attend one of your children's or grandchildren's events or have lunch with Miranda every time she asks, doesn't mean you have the right to treat me this way."

"My children? My grandchildren? We've been married for over fifteen years and now, suddenly they're my children and grandchildren? Do you even hear yourself?"

"I know what I'm saying. My child, my son is dead."

"And that's what it all boils down to. Beau is dead and you're not just grieving, you're angry and it's not getting better. You resent me because my children are alive when Beau is dead."

She wanted to deny it, but couldn't. Not when it was true. She resented him and everyone who hadn't suffered a loss like she did.

"Tell me, Joan," he continued quietly, relentlessly, "what would make it better for you? Would you feel better if one of my children were killed? If something happened to one of my grandchildren?"

"No," she breathed, appalled. "Of course not."

"And yet in your mind, I haven't suffered enough, is that it? I don't understand what you're going through, could never understand so it's okay for you to withdraw inside yourself, to keep your thoughts and feelings hidden, to walk around the house like a zombie. It's okay for you to throw away our marriage, the life we've built because you're in pain."

She started to shake, with fear and anger. She focused on the anger. It was easier to deal with, easier for her to embrace. Some days it felt as if all she had left was anger. "You have no idea what I'm going through," she said. "I need you by my side, not fighting me every step of the way."

"I've been on your side, but I refuse to stand by while you self-destruct. I won't be a part of that. This is the life you've chosen for us, you living your life, me living mine."

"What does that even mean?"

"It means I will no longer go along with this charade you've been playing, this act that we're happy. That you're healing."

Her eyes widened, tremors washed over her. "What will people think?"

She had to act strong, had to pretend that everything was all right. She had a position in this town. Her career, her sanity and self-esteem depended on everyone thinking she was in control.

But Steve, the man she'd loved for so long, the man she was losing, just shrugged. "I don't really care what they think. You're so upset that you lied for me but we both know you've been living a lie since Beau died. And I won't go along with it anymore."

He walked away, leaving her alone. He was wrong, so wrong. She wanted to fight for their marriage, for their life together.

She just didn't know how.

SOMEONE KNOCKED ON the door.

Eddie glanced at the clock. The official time for trick-or-treaters didn't start for another thirty minutes, plus he didn't have his porch light on yet. Luckily, he'd bought candy. He usually just left it in a bowl on the porch for the kids to help themselves to since he and Max made the rounds of the neighborhood.

"I'll get it," Max called, racing to the front door.

"Better take this," Eddie said, grabbing a bag of chocolate bars from the table. Max opened the door and there stood an angel.

Not a real angel but a pretty damn close facsimile.

Cass, dolled up in wings and a crooked halo, grinned. "Hi! I'm an angel."

Eddie kept his eyes on Cass, who held out her bag, her expression clearly stating that no one would dare choose trick on such an adorable child. She was probably right.

"I see that," Eddie said.

"I want candy."

"Cass, that's not what you say," Harper said from

where she stood behind her daughter. He didn't even glance her way. "You say trick or treat."

"Trick or treat," Cass said, shoving the bag at him in case he'd forgotten she held it.

Max dropped a candy bar into it.

Cass's eyes grew wide. "Look, Mama. Candy!"

Harper nodded. "Now what do you say?"

Cass turned back to Eddie. "Trick or treat."

Harper stepped forward as if unsure of her welcome. Eddie wasn't sure how he'd welcome her either so she might be smart to be cautious. "No, honey. After you get your candy you say thank you."

"Thank you."

"You're welcome," Max said. "I'm Captain America."

"Pretty," Cass said and made Max wince.

"She means you look very heroic," Harper told him.

Eddie straightened. "It's still thirty minutes until the official trick-or-treat time. What are you doing, casing the neighborhood to see who has the best candy?"

"Not exactly," Harper said, fiddling with the zipper on her jacket. "Could we come in for a minute?"

He wondered how rude it'd be to shut the door in her face. He glanced down at Cass, who'd already ripped open her candy and taken a huge bite. She smiled up at him. He sighed. Pretty rude. More rude than he could be.

Damn his mother for drilling manners into him and making sure he acted like a gentleman.

A lot of good that'd done him over the years.

He stepped aside, moved back so that Harper didn't brush against him as they entered.

"You're pretty far from home for trick or treat," he said, shutting the door.

He crossed his arms, told himself he didn't care that she looked nervous and guilty and sorry. She should be sorry. But he didn't want her apology, didn't want or need anything from her. He and Max had done just fine before Harper and Cass had invaded their lives, and they'd do just fine without them. They'd lasted the four days since her football party, hadn't they?

He'd wanted to call her at least a dozen times.

"We were actually hoping we could…that, maybe, if it's all right with you and Max…Cass and I…"

"Harper," he said quietly. He might tell himself he didn't care that she was nervous but he didn't like to see her stuttering or struggling so hard to say what was on her mind. "Spit it out."

"Can we go trick-or-treat with you?" she asked in a rush.

And that was not what he was expecting. "What?"

"We want to go with you and Max. If that's all right?"

"You want to go around our neighborhood? What? The candy in yours isn't good?"

She met his eyes, held his gaze. "We want to go with you," she repeated.

And it hit him. What she was doing, why she was there. She wanted to go with him and his son as they walked around their neighborhood, a neighborhood that would be filled with their friends and neighbors. She wanted to be with him.

She wanted people to see her with him.

And she looked so brave, as if asking him for something this simple had taken all her courage. How was he supposed to refuse her? Why would he want to?

But there was one small problem. "I don't want you falling on your sword for me."

"I'm not sure this qualifies," she said with an eye roll. She glanced over, saw Max entertaining Cass. "Look, I want to spend the evening with you. If you don't want that, too, just say so. Don't try and turn it around as you saving me from myself or some other noble act."

"That's not what this is," he insisted.

She crossed her arms, looked put out and stubborn. It was a good look on her. "No? Then what is it? Because, in case you haven't noticed, I'm trying to make a point here. Not sacrifice myself on some altar. I'm not being a martyr. I'm trying to prove that I am capable of moving forward."

"You're capable, yes," he said. "But are you ready?"

"I'm here, aren't I?" she asked softly.

So she was. "I hope you wore comfortable shoes,"

he said, "because Max likes to hit all the houses within a three-mile radius and seeing as how trick or treat is only two hours long, we tend to walk fast."

She smiled, happy and, if he wasn't mistaken, grateful. "Cass and I will do our best to keep up."

He couldn't refuse her even when self-preservation told him he should. "See that you do."

CHAPTER SIXTEEN

AN HOUR AND a half into trick-or-treating and Cass was still just as gung ho as when they'd hit the first house. Of course, it probably helped that she hopped in the stroller every few houses, letting Harper and then Eddie push her around the neighborhood like some angel queen.

It was a perfect night, though, Harper thought. Not too cool and no rain in sight. Kids and parents filled the sidewalks, the street and porch lights glowed. This was Cass's first real time trick-or-treating. Last year, Harper and Beau had dressed her in her costume—Little Mermaid—and taken her to see their parents and a few close friends and family. They'd been back at their house in time to hand out candy to all the monsters, goblins and superheroes who'd roamed their own neighborhood.

But now, tonight, she was with Eddie. She wouldn't think about Beau. It wouldn't be right.

They'd made a huge circle and were heading back to Eddie's house. At the walkway of a two-story brick home, Harper unbuckled Cassidy from her stroller, and her little girl tossed back her hair, adjusted her halo—which just became crooked again, must be someone up there trying to tell them something—and marched her little self up the walk next to Max. Max rang the bell, but it was Cass who stuck her bag out and yelled, "Trick or treat!"

"She has no fear," Harper murmured, watching her daughter hold a conversation with the elderly gentleman who'd opened the door. "Seriously. What am I supposed to do with that? I'll be nuts by the time she hits puberty."

"She's a firecracker," Eddie agreed.

"Beau loved her spirit," Harper said with a grin. "Even when she'd go on a crying jag he'd just say that she was expressing her mind and—" She snapped her lips shut. Shook her head. "Sorry."

"If you tell me you're apologizing for talking about Beau, you're going to seriously piss me off."

"I don't want you to think—"

"You don't want me to think what? That you were married to the man? That his daughter is, at this moment, heading toward us? That he wasn't a part of your life for how many years? That you don't miss him?"

"I don't want you to think that when I'm with you I'm thinking of him or wishing you were him."

"I don't think that. I think that you loved him, that you'll always love him. I don't want you to pretend he didn't exist, that he didn't matter, because he did. He still does," Eddie said, nodding at Cass as she ran down the sidewalk.

She fell and started crying. Before Harper could

even blink, Eddie was there, scooping up her little angel, holding her close, rubbing her back and murmuring to her soothingly. "I think that about wraps it up," he said to Max. "What do you think?"

Max yawned. "I'm tired."

"Let's head on home," Eddie said.

Max put his and Cass's candy in the stroller and pushed it, walking ahead of them as Harper walked next to Eddie. Cass laid her head on his shoulder, sang one of her made-up songs and twirled his hair around her finger like she did with Harper when Harper rocked her to sleep.

"I can carry her," Harper said, feeling a pang seeing him with her daughter, seeing how caring he was. How sweet.

"I've got her."

They were still two blocks from his house but people were already turning their porch lights off, the crowds thinning. She'd proved her point, she thought, as they crossed the street. They'd seen plenty of people, had stopped and chatted with more than a few either one or both of them knew. It wouldn't take long before word spread that they were out together. Before people assumed they were together.

She slid a sidelong glance at Eddie's strong profile. Were they together? She had no idea. She had no clue as to how to proceed or what came next. Were they dating? Going steady? Did anyone over the age of eighteen even go steady anymore?

Her future, the future she'd planned with Beau,

had been taken away and she missed it. Mourned its loss. But she couldn't deny that her feelings for Eddie were growing. That was what scared her.

"Beau wanted four kids," she said after they passed a family of six, the two youngest kids screaming, the two older ones fighting.

If Eddie was surprised she'd brought up her husband, he didn't show it. "That right?"

"I wanted two. He suggested we split the difference and go for three."

"Odd number. Never a good idea. Plus, if you're already outnumbered, you might as well get enough people out of it for a hockey team."

"Good point. It was important to us that Cass have siblings. Probably because we were both only children."

"He has stepbrothers, right?"

"A stepbrother and a stepsister, but his mom didn't marry Steve until Beau was older, and they spent half their time with their mother, so it wasn't quite the same as growing up with siblings."

"It's not all it's cracked up to be."

She laughed, lightly bumped him with her hip. "Come on. I've seen you and your brothers and sister together. You all are close."

That was what she'd missed growing up but luckily, she'd been a friendly child, able to make and keep friends easily so she'd never been lonely. And her parents had given her plenty of attention with-

out letting her get spoiled. She'd have to make sure
she did the same with Cass.

"We all get along most of the time," Eddie said,
shifting Cass up higher. She lifted her head long
enough to grin at him then put her face back down,
moving on to a song about candy and angels and
Cap'n 'Merica saving the world. "We have a few...
disagreements now and then. Usually with Leo but
that's only because he's an idiot."

She snorted. "Leo? Please. Remember how crazy
all the girls were about him in school?" Even though
she and Eddie were two years ahead of Leo, there
had been plenty of girls in their grade who'd crushed
on the younger, handsome Leo.

"He's pretty, I'll give him that," Eddie said.

Cassidy lifted her head again. "You pretty, too."

And she kissed his cheek. He looked stunned but
in a good way. He cleared his throat. "Not as pretty
as you, angel."

She nodded solemnly as if he spoke only the truth.
"I the prettiest."

"And so modest," Harper said dryly, reminding
herself to cut back on the compliments before her
kid got an even bigger head to go along with that
ego of hers.

"It must be hard," Eddie said, his tone sympathetic, "letting go of that dream, of having that family with Beau."

She hadn't been sure talking about her husband
was a good idea but maybe this was what she and

Eddie needed. They couldn't be together—in any capacity—by pretending the past didn't exist, that they both hadn't had relationships, children with other people.

"When the police officer came to my door that night," Harper said slowly, "when he told me Beau was dead, all I could think about was that now Cass would never be a big sister. My husband was dead and I was pissed that he'd taken that away from our child. Pretty stupid, huh?"

"You can't help what you feel in a situation like that. Seems to me there's no right or wrong way to be, to act. You were in shock."

"I was. There were times when I wished I could've stayed in shock. During the viewing and the funeral, I wanted so badly to be numb but it was as if I'd suffered some sort of steam burn. My skin hurt, just the air against it was painful. Each breath was like inhaling fire. My head ached, my heart ached. There wasn't one part of me that didn't physically hurt for him. I wanted my husband back but no amount of praying or bargaining would make it happen.

"For a week after his funeral, I could barely move, couldn't force myself to get off the couch I hurt so badly. But I had Cassidy. I had to make sure she was safe and taken care of. What kind of mother would I have been, what kind of wife if I'd let my child down during that time? So I'd force myself up and I'd feed and change her. I'd console her when she cried, live in her laughter, and at night, when she was asleep,

I'd sit on the floor in the closet with one of Beau's shirts pressed against my face and sob. Wish he was back. That he'd never been taken away from us."

"You were angry."

It wasn't a question but she treated it like one. "Angry? No," she said after a moment. "Not other than that initial reaction. I waited for the anger to come, at the shooter for taking my husband from me, for stealing my daughter's father from her but…" She followed him up the walk to his house and they sat on the porch while Max raced inside to go to the bathroom. "He was just a kid. Did you know that?"

Eddie shook his head, sat and rubbed circles over Cass's back as she twirled, twirled, twirled his hair.

"Barely seventeen," Harper said of the boy who'd been convicted of Beau's murder. "He'll spend the majority of his life in prison, if not all of it. He was caught, tried and convicted and is being punished. My being angry doesn't seem to suit much of a purpose now. I tried to be mad at Beau but other than wondering what would have happened, how my life would've been different if he'd stopped at a convenience store at another exit or if he'd filled the gas tank first before walking inside…any number of things, I couldn't even muster up a good temper. He was just getting a cup of coffee and a candy bar." She smiled. Her Beau loved his sweets. "It was a horrible thing, a tragic moment that snuffed out a promising life, that changed my life forever.

"But the hardest part wasn't the living without

him. It was realizing that I had been living without him for months just fine. Life went on, and getting up got easier, smiling and laughing and remembering him without breaking into tears became easier. I kept living."

"He would have wanted you to."

"Yes, he would have. Just like I would have wanted him to move on if something had happened to me. We weren't meant to live in the past. Humans are resilient. It's how we get through tragedies. It's what makes us strong, sympathetic and compassionate. I loved him. I loved him so much, but he's not here." Wrapping her courage around her, she took Eddie's hand. "He's not here but I am. And I'm ready to move on. With you. If…if you still want me."

EDDIE SQUEEZED HER hand, felt his heart warm. "I still want."

He wanted her. He wanted her in his bed, but more than that, more frightening than that, he wanted her around. Wanted to hear her laugh and see her smile, wanted to play with her kid and watch Harper read to his son.

It was dangerous, risky. His track record sucked, and he'd screwed up with Lena, with the whole marriage deal. But Harper wasn't asking for a commitment, not a long-term one consisting of vows, a church, a white dress and wedding bands that were like handcuffs. What they had was the here and now.

No plans for the future. She was still getting over her husband. Maybe she had no desire to remarry.

But Eddie suspected she would marry. Someone like her, she'd enjoy being part of a couple, would want that give and take, that partnership that came with marriage. With certain marriages, he amended. His parents had one of the good ones. They were each other's best friend but still had passion for each other. That was probably how Harper's marriage was, too. Not like his and Lena's where it was always strained and stressed, where there was little joy, little in common and, toward the end, more resentment than was healthy for either of them.

Yeah, Harper would find someone, some nice guy willing to take her kid as his own, to be a father to Cassidy and give her the time and attention little girls needed from their daddy. Who'd love Harper, who'd want to be tied to her for the rest of his life.

Whoever he was, Eddie knew, he was one lucky bastard.

But he wasn't cut out for marriage. He'd proven that. It was too hard, too painful and messy when it ended.

This, sitting on the porch with pretty Harper Kavanagh by his side, her daughter falling asleep in his arms, his son searching through his candy, was enough for now. It had to be.

TWO WEEKS LATER, Eddie was working at Bradford House when Harper came rushing in, still wearing what he considered her teacher clothes—pants and some sort of sweater set. Her hair was down, her shoes sensible, and she even wore a bracelet one of her kids must have given her, one made of paper chains with apples and pencils drawn on the links.

"You okay?" he asked. Though they'd been seeing each other for those two weeks, and had spent a few evenings together, along with at least one day each weekend, she'd never sought him out at work. Which was unusual as most people wanted to get a look at the goings-on at Bradford House, even if they didn't have anything to compare the renovations to, such as what the place had looked like before.

"Fine," she said but she was breathing hard, trying to catch her breath. "Sorry—" She waved her hand in front of her face. "I had to park on the road and I sort of jogged up the driveway."

Christ, but she was adorable. He felt himself grin. He was doing that a lot lately. Smiling. Being happy. "How does one sort of jog?"

"If you'd ever seen me go at anything other than a brisk walking speed, you wouldn't have to ask that question." She bent at the waist, caught her breath, then straightened and brushed back a loose piece of hair. "Wow." She did a slow turn, took in the fancy, gourmet kitchen. "Let me repeat—wow."

It was something. Marble counters from Italy, heated stone floor, the cabinets Eddie and Heath had made from the imported wood with leaded glass fronts.

"This is gorgeous," Harper said, moving around the room, her fingers trailing along the cool edge of the counter. "You made these, right?" she asked, taking in the corner hutch he'd built.

"We found some old photos of the place in the attic. There was a hutch here before so we decided to add one again."

"You do beautiful work."

He shrugged. It was what he did, what he enjoyed most. He could lay floors, put up trim, frame windows and doors—he could and did do it all. But he was happiest, most content when he was working on something that was his idea, when he made something out of nothing but boards, nails and glue.

Harper shook her head as if to clear it. "Sorry, I got so excited over how great this place looks, I forgot why I ran up that driveway in the first place." She dug something out of her huge bag and shoved it into his face, reminiscent of what Max had done when Eddie had sat in her classroom. "Look!"

He accepted the paper but it took him a moment to realize what he was seeing. He glanced at her then the paper then her again. "Is this what I think it is?"

Smiling ear to ear, she nodded. "It's a C. Plus."

Max had done it. After all his tutoring sessions, and Eddie doing the steps with him at home that Harper had suggested, after all the studying and practicing, Max had slowly progressed and had been doing better. But this, a C—a C plus—was incredible.

"Guess you were right," Harper said but she didn't

sound upset that she'd been wrong about Max's evaluation. She sounded thrilled, as happy as Eddie felt. "He just needed some help and maybe a bit of pushing."

His son was going to be okay. He wasn't going to be put into special classes or given medication to help him concentrate and stop his constant movement. He was fine. He was just fine.

"What did he say when he saw this?" Eddie wanted to know, pulling Harper aside when Art, one of the workers, came in carrying trim.

"I didn't tell him yet. I was grading papers and after I graded his…well…I sort of did a whoop, grabbed my stuff and came right over. I couldn't wait to tell you, and I thought you'd like to be the one who showed him."

He was swamped with unnamed feelings for her, feelings he didn't want to acknowledge, let alone define. "Thank you," he said, his voice gruff. "But I have a better idea. Let's tell him together."

It was a celebration to end all celebrations. Harper had left Cassidy with her parents for the night and she and Eddie had taken Max into Pittsburgh for dinner and a hockey game. Max was thrilled, his face alight as he watched the players during their warm-up skate. Maddie had asked Neil to pull some strings and he'd managed to get them seats behind the players' bench. They even got to meet some of the team afterward. Now, they drove back to Shady

Grove, Max worn out in the backseat, fast asleep in his oversize jersey.

He'd been thrilled when he'd seen his test paper. The entire day and evening had been a whirlwind. Eddie took her hand. It was always a thrill when he touched her, not that he did it much. They kept things pretty PG in front of the kids. She knew Max told some of the kids in the class that his teacher and dad spent time together but so far, she hadn't seen any problems from it. But there were times when Eddie would brush his fingers against the back of her wrist or touch the ends of her hair. Times when he'd walk her to her car and kiss her good-night.

She loved those times.

But while they'd been seeing each other, other than Halloween, they hadn't gone out of their way to announce their relationship to anyone. Joan had seemed distracted lately and Harper worried it was because she knew about her and Eddie, but Harper hadn't been brave enough to approach the subject yet. She would. Eventually. She just wanted a little more time to get her head clear, her feelings straight before trying to explain them to anyone else.

They pulled off onto the exit to Shady Grove. She'd left her car at his house so he could get Max and get ready and they'd taken off. Max had been so excited and Harper was glad they'd done this for him.

Eddie pulled into his garage and cut the engine. "I had a great time," she told him as she unbuckled her seat belt. "Thank you for including me."

"You deserved it." He played with the ends of her hair, his expression unreadable in the dimly lit garage. "Harper..." He slid his hand to her neck, cupped her head gently, then leaned forward and kissed her so warmly, so sweetly she was surprised she didn't melt into a puddle. "Thank you."

"Well, I have been told I'm an excellent kisser," she teased. "But no one's ever thanked me for it. But you're very welcome."

His grin flashed. She loved that she could make him smile, could make him laugh, this quiet, stoic man who kept so much of himself hidden. But he didn't keep everything hidden from her. He was opening up to her, slowly but surely.

"I mean thank you for what you did for Max."

"That's my job."

"Don't," he said quietly. "Don't brush aside what you do. You care about those kids. You take extra time to help them. You give up time with your own daughter and you fight for them. You make a difference in their lives."

Touched, she trailed her fingers down his cheek. "Thank you for saying that. It means a lot to me that you feel that way."

"Come inside," he whispered, kissing her again. "Let me take you to bed. Let me make love to you."

And she knew, she couldn't refuse. "Yes."

HE WAS NERVOUS.

As nervous as he'd been the night he'd lost his

virginity, Eddie realized, as he shut the door to Max's bedroom. There was a lot more at stake now than what the pretty, and yes, more experienced, Ashley White was going to say about him and his skills, or lack thereof, the next day.

He turned and found Harper standing at the end of the hall. Crossing to her, he took her hands and led her into his bedroom. She was so lovely, so bright and fun and sweet. He couldn't get enough of her time and attention, and that worried him. But not tonight. Tonight she was his and that was all that mattered.

He wrapped his arms around her and kissed her slowly, thoroughly, not wanting to rush her, to rush this. Degree by degree, she seemed to warm, to respond to him until her hands were in his hair, her body flush against his. She was all soft, sweet-smelling skin and lush curves, and he wanted, more than anything, to lose himself in that sweetness. To surround himself with her and her goodness, her patience, her sense of humor and optimism.

He slid his hands up her sides, her arms and over her shoulders so he could comb his fingers through her hair. It was like silk, fragrant and soft, and felt cool as rain. She made a humming sound that told him she liked what he was doing so he did it again, breaking the kiss so he could lean back and see the contrast of his dark hand against the pale strands of her hair.

Her lips were parted and she opened her eyes.

Smiled, but he could see the tension in her gaze, in the set of her shoulders. Damn it, he should have set the mood more. He'd asked her to come inside, to sleep with him like this had been any other night, as if she could've been any other woman. He should have waited, should have made plans for Max to stay with his grandparents, then Eddie could have made Harper dinner, one of those candlelight ones with good wine and some soft, smoky jazz tune playing.

He hadn't romanced her. Hadn't sent her flowers or cards or candy. He wasn't good at any of that. He preferred the direct route. He was attracted to her and she to him so why bother with a bunch of stuff that didn't matter. Except it did matter to some women. He hadn't given her romance, but it wasn't too late for him to seduce her.

He flipped on the lamp on the dresser. It wasn't the flickering of candlelight but it did cast the room in a soft, warm glow. Harper smiled at him almost shyly, certainly with nerves but also, he hoped, anticipation.

He kissed her again, long, slow drugging kisses. Their mouths clinging then parting, their tongues touching then retreating. He cupped her head, let his other hand rest above her breast, just over her heart. It beat, strong and a bit unsteady against his palm. He kissed her again and again until they were both breathless and then he shifted, moved his mouth across her cheek up to her closed eyes, down the bridge of her nose.

She was perfect. Lovely and sweet, and she deserved to be worshipped. He'd enjoy worshipping her. He trailed his mouth across her jaw and her head fell back, granting him access to the long line of her throat. He flicked his tongue out, tasted the saltiness of her skin.

Straightening, he undid the top button of the silky blouse she'd changed into before they'd gone out, keeping his eyes on hers. Her hands were at her sides, her fingers curled into fists. He slid his gaze down, watched as he revealed inch after inch of delicate, pale skin. Another button and he caught sight of the lace of her bra. He made quick work of the rest of them until the material fell open slightly, revealing the curve of her breasts, her belly button, hints and glimpses as tantalizing as Harper herself.

Eddie shoved the material aside, pushed it down her arms where it bunched. He took her hands, rubbed them gently until she relaxed, letting her fingers open so that the shirt fell to the floor. He undid the button of her jeans and she inhaled sharply. He tugged down the zipper, pulled the sides of her jeans down her legs, let her put her trembling hands on his shoulders while she stepped out of them. He kicked them aside. Blew out a ragged breath.

She stood before him in nothing more than a white bra and light blue panties, the lamp casting her skin in a golden glow. He swept his gaze up from her bare feet with the bright pink polish, up her curvy legs and hips, over the slight roundness of her belly to her full breasts. Her nipples were tight buds pressing against the thin material of her bra.

"You're beautiful."

And saying that to her was the easiest, the most natural thing in the world.

Now he'd show her how beautiful he found her. He kept his touch light as he skimmed her neck, her shoulders, traced the edge of her bra with his fingertip. He couldn't get enough of her, the feel of her under his hands, under his mouth. He placed hot, openmouthed kisses along her clavicle bones, dipped lower to brush across the swell of her breasts. He inhaled her fragrance, that scent he'd become so familiar with, the one that drove him mad, that would always remind him of her.

Reaching behind her, he undid her bra, tugged it off. Heat suffused him. She was perfect. He touched her breasts, lowered his head and sucked one taut peak into his mouth. Feasted on her, on her sweetness and fire. She combed her fingers through his hair, held his head still with one hand, the other clutching his shoulder as if he was her only touchstone, the only thing keeping her upright and balanced.

He flicked his tongue over her nipple then moved his head to the other breast, slid his hands between her hips and her panties, his palms cupping the curve of her waist. Shoved her underwear down, trapping her legs together as they caught at her knees. He kissed his way over the slight ridges of her ribs, across the slope of her belly. She was all lush curves, like a goddess come to life, her skin warm and so soft he couldn't stop touching her. Couldn't stop making sure she was real, that for tonight, she was his.

He fell to his knees, slid her underwear off, then trailed his hands up the backs of her legs. She shuddered. He pressed his face against her mound, inhaled her unique scent. She stiffened.

Though he wanted nothing more than to taste her, to bring her pleasure with his mouth and tongue, he wouldn't push her into something she wasn't ready for. He kissed her there, allowed himself one quick flick of his tongue, then straightened, kissing her voraciously. She returned his hunger as he walked her back toward the bed. Her gaze locked with his as she crawled, backward, onto the middle of the bed, the movements doing some really interesting things to her breasts, the roundness of her belly.

He stripped off his shirt and threw it aside, made quick work of his jeans and underwear, remembering at the last minute to grab a condom from his wallet before he joined her on the bed. He kissed her, touching her breasts, her stomach, her legs, until she writhed beneath him, her skin hot and damp with sweat. He slid his hand lower, brushed her curls. She lifted her hips and he grinned against her mouth.

Yeah, for tonight, she was all his.

CHAPTER SEVENTEEN

HARPER COULDN'T BREATHE, could barely think. Maybe that was for the best when thinking would only take her out of this moment, this surreal, wonderful moment in time. She didn't want the guilt to seep in, didn't want to hear that little voice in her head telling her it was too soon, that she shouldn't want this, shouldn't want Eddie as much as she did.

But how could she not when he touched her so gently, so reverently? When his mouth and hands were on her, bringing her body to life? Making her want him so urgently?

Still kissing her, those mind-melting kisses that made her crazy, he slid his hand lower. And lower until he cupped her. She squirmed, her hips lifting in supplication, her hands reaching for him, grabbing him for purchase, as a sign that he should keep going, to please, please keep going. As if hearing her silent plea, he flicked the pad of his finger over the sensitive bud at her core. Again. Then again.

It wasn't enough, not nearly enough, but it felt so good she couldn't complain that he was teasing her, bringing her to the brink this way. He settled his hand on her, rubbed harder. Faster. Her breathing quickened, her pulse sped. Pleasure coursed through her, spiraling higher and higher.

And when he slid one finger inside of her, that pleasure spun out of control, zipping through her with enough force to have her back arching, her hands clenching on Eddie's arms. A long, low moan ripped from her throat as her orgasm crashed through her, leaving her body sated, her muscles lax.

Eddie rolled away long enough to cover himself and then he was back, kissing her again, settling his warm, solid body on top of hers. The tip of his erection nudged her inner thigh. Hot. Hard. He gripped her butt, pulled her down and entered her smoothly, slowly. As if knowing this was a big moment for her, a huge moment, he stilled, deeply embedded inside of her, letting her body adjust to his size.

He raised up onto his arms, his hands flat on the bed by her head. "Okay?" he asked, his arms shaking with the effort to contain himself, his mouth tight, his eyes dark with want.

Tears pricked her eyes but this wasn't the time for crying. Even if those tears had been caused by him being so sweet, so concerned. She smiled up at him, touched his cheek with the back of her hand. "Much better than okay," she whispered.

He smiled and it took her breath away. Then he was kissing her again, moving inside of her, and breathing became unimportant. All that mattered was the man on top of her, inside of her. The feel of his body, the way his muscles bunched and flexed with his movements, his scent. They were what was important to think about. To try and remember. Eddie Montesano was making love to her.

And she didn't want to ever forget a single thing about this, about their first time together. Not when she knew, better than most, how fleeting these perfect, life-altering moments could be.

She had to remember as much as possible, the rasp of his tongue against hers, the light scratch of his whiskers on her skin, the taste of him. But he quickened his pace, his fingers digging into her hips, his chest rubbing against her overly sensitized nipples causing them to peak and tighten. She wanted to embed his every move into her memory but how could she when every move had desire building again, had her satisfied body craving more?

Time seemed to splinter into pieces of movement—the brush of the hair on his legs against hers, the sound of his breathing by her ear, the feel of his breath on her neck. He shifted, pulling her down on the bed even farther. She wrapped her legs around his waist, the move bringing them even closer, letting him go deeper. He pumped into her again and again. Pleasure built inside of her and she came once more, this time riding the wave of her orgasm as it washed through her.

"Eddie," she gasped, and he looked at her, startled, questioning, already slowing, but she shook her head, pumped her own hips to encourage him to keep going. She'd just wanted to say his name. For

him to know he was the only man she was thinking about, that she knew who she was with and that
she wasn't wishing he was anyone else. She held his
gaze. "Eddie."

Emotion swam in his eyes and he kissed her, his
body milking her own pleasure until he followed her
over the edge with a rough groan.

Minutes—or hours, who could tell?—later, Harper's body was cooling, her breathing returning to
normal. Eddie padded into the attached bathroom,
returning a moment later, not the least bit self-
conscious about his nudity. Then again, why should
he be? He was beautiful, his shoulders wide, the
muscles of his arms, chest and abs defined. Dark
hair covered his chest, trailed down his flat stomach.

She, unfortunately, didn't have his confidence and
ducked under the covers, pulling them up to her
chin. He climbed in next to her, gathered her in his
arms and pulled her against his side. He brushed her
hair back, kissed her temple. He tucked her head
under his chin and sighed, a sound of complete satisfaction.

Well, she had been rather amazing, if she did say
so herself.

The whole experience had been wonderful. Special and romantic and perfect.

Really, really perfect.

She pressed her face against the crook of his neck
and burst into tears.

SHIT.

Panicked, Eddie sat up and Harper's head fell back with a dull thud against the headboard. "Sorry," he muttered, frantic, as he tried to figure out what was going on. He'd just been drifting off to sleep, thinking that if round two was going to be anything like round one had been, he was one extremely lucky—and quite possibly spoiled and overindulged—man, when Harper had started crying.

He could handle crying, he assured himself. He had a younger sister, and while Maddie wasn't one for waterworks very often, she'd had her moments. He'd also been married, and Lena had used tears as a way to manipulate him into doing what she wanted—it had usually worked.

So, yeah, he had experience with women crying. He hadn't lived in a cave his entire life.

But he'd never, not once, had a woman he'd just made love to—and had thought he'd done a damned good job—cry while still in bed with him.

"Hey," he said gruffly, wanting to sound compassionate and caring, wishing like hell he knew the right thing to say. "You okay?" He winced because obviously she wasn't okay. Idiot. He laid his hand on her shoulder, relieved when she didn't turn or pull away. "Did I...did I hurt you?"

Had he been too rough? He'd thought she was right there with him but what if she hadn't been? What if she regretted what had happened between them? What if she hadn't wanted it as much as he had?

He quickly thought through everything that had happened from the moment he'd stepped into the hall and found her there waiting for him. No, he hadn't pushed her, had tried not to even rush her. He'd given her plenty of opportunities to stop him.

Still, he'd done something wrong. He'd made her cry.

Feeling inept and useless, he climbed out of bed and yanked on a pair of sweatpants lying on the chair, went into the bathroom and grabbed a box of tissues and a glass of water. When he returned, she was sitting up, his comforter clutched to her chest, her hair wild from his hands, from their lovemaking, the delicate skin along her chest and around her mouth pink from his whiskers. Her makeup smudged.

She made his heart stop, made him want to hold on to her and never let go.

He practically shoved the water at her. "Here."

She took it, her hands unsteady, and drank deeply, set the empty glass aside then plucked three tissues from the box and mopped her face, gently blew her nose. "I'm sorry. God, what a mess. Maybe it'd be better if I just went home—"

"I can't let you drive home when you're upset," he said. "Let me get Max and I'll take you."

And for some reason he'd never understand, that made her tear up again. "Sorry," she said, covering her face with a tissue. "Sorry. I don't know what's gotten into me."

"I think you do," he said softly. He waited until she met his gaze before continuing, "Tell me."

She swallowed, lowered her hands to her lap. "I'm not sure I even understand. I'm afraid if I try to explain, I'll get it all mixed up."

"You won't."

She knew how to use words, how to tell what was in her heart, what her thoughts were.

But she wouldn't even look at him now, was staring at her hands as she picked apart the tissue.

"Do you regret what just happened?" he asked, half afraid to hear her answer. Realizing he needed to know the truth even if it wasn't what he wanted to hear.

Her gaze flew to his. "No. No," she repeated firmly. "That's the problem," she said barely above a whisper.

"I don't get it."

"That's because it's crazy. Why am I crying? I mean, being with you was…well…it was great. And I don't regret it, not one bit. Because I don't, it's like I'm really ready to say goodbye to Beau and it's like I'm…"

"Losing him all over again?"

She nodded. "It's stupid. He's gone. He's not coming back and he wouldn't want me to be alone. I just can't help feeling a bit emotional, you know?"

"And guilty?"

She exhaled heavily, her shoulders falling. "Maybe a little. But it's not your fault," she assured him quickly. "I don't want you to think I'm comparing you to him or vice versa or that I was thinking of him while we...when you were..."

"I don't. I'm not." He couldn't be jealous of a dead man. Not when Harper was here with him. But he'd known she'd been truly with him, she'd said his name, had wanted him to know she knew exactly who was making love to her, and he appreciated that.

"Good. That's good."

"I'm not jealous that you loved your husband," he told her. "We'll take it slow. Maybe tonight was too much, too soon—"

"It wasn't," she said, scrambling onto her knees, grabbing the comforter at the last moment before it could slide off. She took a hold of his hand. "I thought it was perfect."

So had he. He wasn't sure if that was a good thing or not. She was so giving, so open, and he took that openness, took all she had to give without giving much back. She'd opened up to him, had shared her body and her thoughts with him. She trusted him.

The least he could do was trust her in return.

"Lena didn't want any kids," he heard himself say.

Harper frowned. "Excuse me?"

"On Halloween, when we were walking home you told me Beau wanted four kids. Lena hadn't wanted any."

"So Max was unplanned?"

"Not quite." He knew he'd have to start at the beginning, would have to share the story of his marriage, his greatest mistakes and failures. "Lena and I dated for only six months before we decided to get married. I wanted to settle down, and we loved each other and couldn't figure out any reason to wait."

"You can know a lot about a person in six months," Harper said.

"We were okay for a while. The first year was great but by the second we were arguing more and more. Lena started bringing up divorce but I didn't want that failure. I figured if we both tried harder, we could force it to work."

"Sometimes that's what it takes," Harper said, as always compassionate and trying to see all sides of an issue. "I hadn't realized how hard it was to live with another human being until I got married. Sharing every part of your life, compromising on so many things…it takes a lot of work each and every day."

"I was willing to work at it. Lena went along with it. Things still didn't get better, and even though I knew at that point I didn't love her anymore, that maybe I never had, I brought up the idea of having a baby, a way to bring us closer. I thought if we had a child together, that bond would strengthen our marriage and we'd be this instant family and everything would be okay. I'm still not sure why Lena went along with it but two years into our marriage, we had Max. Lena tried, but she didn't know much about kids. She missed her family, her friends in Chicago, and wanted the opportunities for her career she could have there. When she told me she was leaving, that she wasn't cut out for marriage or motherhood, that she wanted to focus on her career, I was relieved she was leaving but I still felt like I'd failed my son because I hadn't been able to keep my family together."

"That is such bull," Harper said with enough venom, Eddie raised his eyebrows. "Max's family is intact and right here. You are his family. Your parents and your grandfather and your brothers and sister. That little boy has more family than he knows what to do with. He's lucky. Lena is the one who's missing out."

He was grateful she thought so. "I'd like to believe Lena realizes what she gave up, but I'm afraid something else pushed her into wanting to spend more time with Max. At the beginning of the year, she was diagnosed with ovarian cancer."

"That's horrible. But she's okay now?"

He nodded. "Max doesn't know. Lena didn't want to worry him and I…I don't want him to know it took a life-threatening illness to make her realize she wants to be a bigger part of his life. I just can't bring myself to ask her how big of a part. I'm afraid she'll want shared or even full custody."

"You need to find out so you can face it. Your marriage failed, Eddie. Not you. Or at least, not just you. You made a mistake and you can't keep punishing yourself for it. You're a wonderful father and you give Max love, support and discipline. He's a very lucky little boy."

Her words were a comfort, a balm. "Stay with me tonight."

She smiled. "No."

"No?"

"No." She stood, kept the blanket wrapped around her. "There's no way I'm spending the night at the house of one of my students."

Of course not. "You're right. Sorry. That was—"

"If you say stupid, I will hit you."

He couldn't help it. He grinned. "Stupid."

She swatted his arm and he took the opportunity to grab her and pull her onto his lap. He kissed her deeply, wanted to make love to her again, but she was right. They had to think of their kids and her career and reputation.

"Stay," he murmured. "Just for a little while longer."

She wrapped her arms around his neck. "I'm not saying yes, but I will give you a chance to convince me."

So he set about doing just that.

JOAN SWITCHED THE plate of cookies to her other hand and knocked on Harper's door. The moon glowed in the sky but snowflakes fell softly to the ground, melted on the roads and sidewalks, clung to the grass. She hoped she caught Cassidy before her bath.

She loved giving her granddaughter a bath, loved seeing her laugh and play in the water, loved wrapping her in a towel and holding her little body close while she inhaled the clean scent of her grandbaby.

Beau had loved his bath time until he'd reached the age of eight, Joan remembered with a fond smile, and then it was as if he'd suddenly become violently allergic to water. Until he'd hit puberty and he'd started taking long showers at all times of the day.

Harper must have company as there was a Montesano Construction truck in the driveway. Harper's cousin lived with one of the Montesano boys so maybe they were over. Harper loved to entertain. Joan felt guilty for not seeing Harper or Cass much lately but she'd been so confused, so conflicted about Steve's attitude toward her that she'd known the best way to keep up the pretense that she was fine was to limit how much time she spent with others.

Still, she hadn't been able to stay away another day, not when she'd realized she hadn't seen her granddaughter in a week, that she missed talking with her daughter-in-law. Plus, Steve barely spoke to her anymore, seemed so resentful and angry. She couldn't fix that, couldn't fix him.

The door opened and Harper looked surprised— and not completely happy to find Joan on her doorstep.

Joan smiled. "Hello. I hope Cass isn't asleep because I brought her favorite cookies." She held up the plate of sugar cookies. Beau had loved her sugar cookies, too, but just the sight, the smell of them made Joan's stomach turn.

Since Harper was just staring at her, Joan brushed past her, stepped inside. Looked around. It smelled as if Harper had cooked beef for dinner. Joan glanced into the kitchen, noticed it was clean but empty, the living room, too. Usually when her granddaughter heard her, she came running.

She handed the plate to Harper, started taking off her coat. "Where's Cassidy?"

Then she heard the unmistakable sound of her granddaughter's laugh coming from the playroom. Without waiting for Harper, Joan kicked off her shoes and walked across the living room.

"Cassidy," she called, stepping into the room. "Guess what Grandma brought you?"

Joan stopped in the doorway. Blinked.

"Hi, Nana," Cassidy said, smiling from her spot in Eddie Montesano's arms.

"Hey, punkin," Joan said, trying to smile. What were Eddie Montesano and his son doing here? Why was he on the floor holding her granddaughter? Why did Harper look so guilty?

Harper stepped into the room, still holding the cookies. "Uh, Max and Eddie came over for dinner."

"Oh. How…nice." Joan kept her smile firmly in place even as it felt as if she'd just been kicked in the chest.

Harper was seeing Eddie.

How could she betray Beau that way?

"We were just leaving," Eddie said. His voice was deep and he was nothing like her blond, blue-eyed boy. Beau had been charming, talkative and full of joy while Eddie was dark and quiet.

What did Harper see in him?

"Oh," Harper said as Eddie got to his feet and Max cleaned up the toys they were playing with. "Okay. Well, thanks for coming."

"Thanks for having us," he said. He touched his son's shoulder.

"Thanks for dinner," Max told Harper, giving her a hug.

"You're welcome."

"No," Cassidy said, her little forehead crinkling into a scowl. "You stay," she told Eddie.

"Cass," Harper said, sounding overly cheerful, "Eddie and Max need to go home now. Besides, it's time for your bath. Want Nana to give it to you?"

Cass shook her head and grabbed ahold of Eddie's pant leg. "I want Deddie to give me a bath."

Joan went cold all over. "Daddy?"

"Deddie," Harper said quickly.

But all Joan could think was that her son's child was calling someone else daddy. Cass started screaming, crying that she wanted *Deddie,* and Eddie picked her up, rubbed her back as Cass laid her head on his shoulder.

It was like a knife to the heart.

It should be her son holding Cassidy. Beau should be the one giving her comfort, murmuring to her and calming her down. Beau should be the one playing with her on a snowy, Sunday evening, the one who got to put her to bed, not some stranger.

Furious, heartbroken, Joan whirled on her heel and stormed through the house toward the front door.

"Joan," Harper called, chasing after her. "Joan, please." She caught up with her by the door, stopped her from leaving by slipping in front of her. "I'm sorry. I'm so sorry you had to find out this way."

"Find out what?" Joan snapped. "That you're sleeping with that man. That you don't even have the decency, the respect to tell me you're involved with another man less than a year after you buried your husband?"

Harper flinched and Joan felt triumphant, gratified that she'd been able to cause someone else's pain when pain was all she felt anymore. "I didn't mean for it to happen," Harper said, holding out a hand beseechingly. "I wasn't looking for any type of relationship but Eddie and I got to know each other and…"

"And you're having sex with him. Fine. But why let him around Cassidy? It's too confusing for her to have another man in her life so soon after losing her father."

"She's two," Harper said gently. "She doesn't remember Beau."

"Only because you've already moved on." She couldn't believe this. Out of all the people in the world, she'd thought she could trust Harper to understand, to respect Beau's memory as she did. Instead, she'd turned her back on them both. "She needs to know how much her father loved her, how nobody can ever replace him."

"She will know that. I promise."

"Your promises don't mean much to me," Joan said, pushing Harper aside and opening the door. "Not anymore. I never would have thought you were the type of woman who'd betray my son the way you did, who wouldn't have the common decency, the courtesy to let a proper amount of time pass before you blithely went on with your life."

"Is that what you think? You think it's been easy for me? I've suffered with guilt and doubts every day. Do you think I wanted this? I didn't go searching for Eddie, I didn't go out trying to find a man to take care of me. I wasn't looking to have feelings for another man."

"Feelings for him? Well, why not? My son's been dead almost a year. Time to move on, right? I can't believe I was so wrong about you. I didn't know the real you at all."

"That makes two of us," Harper whispered, then she quietly shut the door in her mother-in-law's face. Leaving Joan out in the cold. Alone.

WELL, HARPER THOUGHT the next morning, that had been a rotten night.

She walked into her dark classroom, flipped on the lights. She'd come to school early to get caught up on some work but she had only a few hours before her students started arriving. She'd had a restless, sleepless night and it was catching up to her.

Eddie had apologized but Harper knew that she was the reason Joan was upset with her. It was her own fault for not letting her mother-in-law know she and Eddie were seeing each other.

She hadn't wanted to upset Joan. Guess that hadn't worked out quite so well.

Harper walked to the break room and went through the motions of making a pot of coffee. After Eddie and Max had left last night, she'd given a very cranky and miserable Cass a bath. The only person her daughter wanted, it seemed, was Eddie.

It hadn't bothered Harper before; she'd actually found it endearing how good Eddie was with her baby, how much Cass adored Eddie and Max, but now, with Joan's words echoing in her head, she couldn't help but wonder if she'd been wrong to encourage a relationship between them. Not only was she Max's teacher, but she had no idea where her relationship with Eddie was going—if it was going anywhere.

Things were confusing, getting more and more complicated and now she could add upsetting her mother-in-law to the mix.

The coffee done, Harper filled her large mug three-quarters full, added a hefty dose of cream and walked down the quiet, empty hallway to her room, crossing to her desk. It had taken longer than

sual to get Cass settled down and into bed. She'd
een upset about Eddie leaving and had no trou-
le showing it in the form of a tantrum the likes of
/hich made Harper want to rip her own ears off to
ave herself the pain of listening to her daughter's
ngry screams.

Cass had finally calmed down enough to let
Iarper read to her in the rocking chair. By the time
ney'd gotten a few pages into the book, Cass had
een asleep. Harper had sat there holding her baby,
ninking about Beau and Eddie, how different they
vere.

How could she love them both?

Yes, she thought, dropping her head into her
ands. She was in love with Eddie Montesano. How
ould she be? She'd loved her husband, still did, and
iow, after barely a year of him being gone, she'd
;iven her heart to another man. No wonder Joan
vas furious. But Harper couldn't help how she felt.
5he could, however, control what she did about those
eelings.

She was keeping them to herself.

Eddie wasn't exactly a big proponent of marriage.
At least not for himself. He took great pride in tak-
ng care of Max on his own, in not needing anyone.
He cared about her and Cassidy, of that Harper had
10 doubt. But she didn't know if he'd be willing to
rust Harper with his heart.

And she wouldn't settle for anything less than the
ype of commitment she'd had with Beau.

She tipped her head back and blew out a heavy breath. No sense worrying about it now. Not when she had so many other things to worry about such as mending the rift with her mother-in-law, figuring out a way to tell Sam McNamara that she was involved with the parent of one of her students. Oh, yes, and getting these damn papers graded.

Sipping her coffee, she opened her bag, took out the thick pile of papers. She'd left school Friday halfway through grading the rest of the tests so she still had marking to do, plus she needed to work on her lesson plan for the week. She'd meant to work on them at home over the weekend but she'd been too wrapped up in celebrating Max's good grade, and in her feelings for Eddie and their first time together to get anything done. She laid the papers on her desk, smiled at Max's which sat on top. She'd gotten a few others done before that so she set those aside, took another sip of coffee and picked up the next paper on the pile.

Red pencil in one hand, she scanned the answers to the test, comparing them to her answer key. Paper after paper she marked, checking off a wrong answer, writing notes in the margin, letting students know they'd done a good job and to keep up the excellent work, adding smiley faces where appropriate.

She picked up the next paper. Checked a wrong answer. Then another. Frowned as she reached the bottom and realized that something seemed amiss. That the paper she'd just graded seemed very familiar.

Too familiar.

Her heart sinking, she quickly leafed through the graded papers. *Please, please, let me be wrong. Please.*

Finding the one she'd been searching for she laid next to the one she'd just graded. They were the same. Same right answers. Same wrong answers. Even the misspelled words were spelled exactly the same.

They'd cheated, obviously. One of them had copied off the other. She'd bet her life on it.

She wanted to bang her head against her desk, wanted to pound her fists against the wall. She wanted to lay her head down and cry.

Oh, Max. What did you do?

CHAPTER EIGHTEEN

EDDIE STOOD IN the school's main office trying not to fidget. He'd been sent to the principal's office plenty of times during his student days, had been called down there for Max as well last year when Max was fighting in the playground. But he had no idea why he'd been called in today. The lady who ran the school's office had called him at work and told him there was a problem with Max and Eddie needed to come in right away.

A pair of cherubic girls entered the office and almost barreled into him. He shifted, giving them space, stared at the clock on the wall.

"Mr. Montesano?" Mr. McNamara, the principal, said as he let another couple and a little boy out of his office. "Please come in."

Eddie nodded at the couple. Their son, one of Max's classmates—Joshua or Jacob—was crying.

This couldn't be good.

Why hadn't Harper called him herself? Why did they have to meet here instead of the classroom?

Eddie stepped into the office, saw Max sitting with his head down, Harper talking to him quietly. "Is there a problem?"

At the sound of Eddie's voice, Max's shoulders hunched even more if that was possible.

"Thank you for coming in," Mr. McNamara said. "Please have a seat."

Eddie sat on Max's other side, looked at Harper but he couldn't read much in her expression.

The principal sat behind his desk. "Mr. Montesano, it has come to our attention that Max cheated on a test."

Eddie's head whipped around to Max. "What?"

Mr. McNamara slid two papers forward, one Max's test, which he'd done so well on, the other with the name Joshua written on the top. "As you can see, the answers are identical on both papers. We just spoke with the Chalkes and Josh admitted that Max asked if he could copy his paper during the test and Josh agreed."

Eddie stared at his son. "Max. Is this true?"

Max shrugged.

Eddie leaned forward to look at Harper. "Did you know about this?"

"I just discovered it this morning."

"And you didn't tell me?"

"It's school policy," Mr. McNamara interrupted, "for teachers to inform me of any cheating or violent behavior. Mrs. Kavanagh thought it was in everyone's best interest, considering your personal relationship with her, if I were involved."

Eddie narrowed his eyes. When the hell had their private relationship become public? And why didn't

Harper handle this on her own in the classroom instead of involving her superior? Not that Eddie thought Max shouldn't be punished, but certain things needed to stay within the family.

But that was it, wasn't it? He and Harper weren't family. He wasn't sure what they were and he couldn't worry about it now.

"Max, look at me," he said and waited until his son met his eyes. The guilt and regret there about did Eddie in. "Why did you copy that boy's answers?"

Another shrug.

He wanted to shake an answer out of his son but knew nothing would get Max to talk when he didn't want to.

Mr. McNamara looked at Max. "Max, you will stay inside with me during recess for one week. Now, could you please wait outside with Miss Brown while I talk with your father?"

Without raising his head, Max walked out, shut the door quietly behind him.

Eddie nodded, put his hands on his knees. "Thank you for letting me know," he said. "I can guarantee that Max will be punished at home for this, as well."

"I'm glad you understand how serious this is."

Eddie bit his tongue as he didn't quite agree with his assessment. It was wrong of Max to cheat, to copy answers, but it's not like he broke a law.

The principal rose and crossed to the front of the desk to lean against it. "Mrs. Kavanagh has informed me that she suspects Max cheated to over-

ome or hide the problems he's been having with
his schoolwork."

Eddie sent Harper a narrow look. "He's been
doing better. Harper...Mrs. Kavanagh...has been
tutoring him."

"I'm aware of that but unfortunately he's not making the progress any of us had hoped he'd be making
at this time. In my opinion, it would be in Max's best
interest to put him in remedial classes—"

"No," Eddie said, standing.

"Surely you can see that this is what's best for
Max and his future. His self-esteem will suffer if he
continues to struggle. We want all our children to
succeed on their own terms and in their own ways."

"Max will succeed. He'll be fine. I'll hire a tutor
to help him."

Harper sighed as she stood. "I'm still willing to
tutor him—"

"I don't think that's a good idea," he said stiffly.

Her eyes narrowed. "Are you serious?"

In answer, he walked out. "Come on," he told
Max, who was sitting on a chair next to the wall,
"we're leaving." He gripped his son's hand and
tugged him out of the room.

Harper caught up with them in the hallway. "Oh,
no," she said, her quiet tone not softening the edge
to her voice, "you don't get to walk away from this,
Eddie. We need to discuss this."

He kept walking. "There's nothing to discuss."

She followed him, the wind lifting her hair, snow dotting her shoulders. "We need to hash this out."

He didn't want to hash anything out. "I'll hire a tutor since it's obvious our personal relationship is causing problems for your career." At his truck, he unlocked the door and urged Max to get in. Eddie started it and turned on the heater then faced Harper. "You should have just told me when you found out he'd cheated," he said, trying not to soften at how pretty she looked with snow melting on her hair, her cheeks pink. "Did you really have to get your supervisors involved?"

"Of course I did! How would it look if I hadn't? I have a job here, Eddie. A career I love and a reputation I take great pride in. We're all trying to help Max but you're too stubborn and full of pride to realize it."

When he remained silent, she sent him a disappointed look as if he was the one in the wrong. As if he didn't want to help his own son. As if he was messing everything up.

Then she walked away.

Leaving Eddie to wonder, to worry that she might be right.

EDDIE ANSWERED THE door ready to lay into whoever was knocking at ten o'clock at night only to blink in surprise. "Lena. What are you doing here?"

He told himself he was disappointed only because it was never good to find his ex-wife standing on his porch, especially this late on a weeknight. He wasn't disappointed that it wasn't Harper standing there. He didn't want to talk to her, didn't want to see her. Not yet. Not until he'd thought things through a little bit.

"Where's Max?" Lena asked, pushing past Eddie as she stepped inside, her clothes wrinkled, her face pale. "Is he okay?"

"He's sleeping." What time did she think little boys went to sleep on school nights? "What are you even doing in town?"

Now she frowned, played with the strap of her purse. "Max called me. He said he needed me."

It was like a knife to the gut, the pain sharp and unexpected. "He called you?" Eddie patted his pockets, felt the familiar shape of his wallet but no phone. Damn it, he needed to keep that thing under lock and key. "So instead of phoning me to ask what was going on, you flew across three states and showed up here unexpected?"

Unwanted.

"I wanted to be here for him." Her chin lifted despite the flush staining her cheeks. "To prove I'll be here when he needs me. And I knew if I called you, you'd brush whatever happened aside. You'd brush me and my concerns aside like you always do."

"You left." Eddie kept his voice low and controlled so as not to wake Max but the effort cost him, had his throat raw. "No one pushed you out that door."

Her mouth pinched. "Is he all right? What happened?"

Eddie didn't want to tell her but if he didn't, he'd

never get rid of her. He shut the door and crossed his arms. "He's fine. He got into a little trouble at school—"

"What kind of trouble?"

"He got caught cheating on a test," Eddie admitted reluctantly.

"Cheating? Why would he cheat? That doesn't sound like Max."

Eddie wanted to tell her she didn't know their son, not like he did, but he bit back the words. "He's having some issues with his schoolwork but it's nothing I can't handle."

"What about getting him some extra help?"

Did she think he was an idiot? "He's being tutored." *Was* being tutored. But now that Harper had proven she put her job ahead of what was best for Max, Eddie would have to find someone else.

"If he's struggling," Lena said, "maybe we should consider putting him in special classes."

He bristled, went so rigid he was surprised he didn't simply break in two. "No."

"But if we don't get him the help he needs, he'll have a harder time."

"He doesn't need to be taken out of his regular class. I'll figure it out." He always figured it out. On his own.

Lena switched her bag from one shoulder to the other. "I don't want to argue or fight with you on this. I just want what's best for Max. I want to help him." She met his gaze, held it. "I want you to let me help him. And you."

Harper's face flashed in his thoughts, her voice teasing him about not needing any help.

He pushed them both aside.

"Why?" he asked.

Lena's eyebrows—thinner than they were before her chemo treatments—drew together. "Why what?"

"Why do you want to help? Why do you want to be a part of Max's life now? Do you..." He swallowed, forced the words past the lump in his throat. "Do you want more time with him? Are you going to ask for shared custody?"

Her expression softened and for a moment, he remembered how he'd once loved her, how she'd once loved him. "I do want more time with him, but I'd never take him away from you, Eddie. He belongs here. I just...I want to be a part of his life. A real part."

The worry he'd carried with him for months eased. "I haven't stopped you from seeing him more."

"No, but you haven't let me in, either. Not fully. You don't ask my opinion on anything, you don't tell me when he's hurt or having problems in school. We should be partners in raising him, but you shut me out."

"I'm the one who took care of him, of all his needs—emotional, physical, financially—all these years. And now, just because you've had something life-changing happen doesn't mean you get to change the rules, rules you set in place."

"I love him," she said, her voice shaking. "I may not be a perfect mother and maybe I didn't realize how precious each and every moment is until I got sick, but I've always loved Max. Always wanted what's best for him." She opened the door, her hand trembling on the handle. "Which was why I didn't want him shuttled back and forth between here and Chicago. Between us. I knew—I *know*—he's better off with you. He needs you. Are you ever going to realize that maybe, just maybe, he needs me, too?"

She walked out, her quiet words echoing in Eddie's mind long after she shut the door.

JOAN'S ENTIRE BODY hurt. Her head ached, her muscles were sore as if she'd run a marathon. Turning, she thought about reaching for Steve, but she hadn't done that in so long, she was afraid she'd be rejected. He'd been cold toward her, hadn't once touched her, not in weeks. Even now he was up before her, his side of the bed empty.

She let her hand travel over the space, the sheets soft and cool against her fingers. She curled her fingers into her palms. Tears stung her eyes but she blinked them back. She had to be strong. There was no room for weakness. It would break her. Kill her.

She rose and pulled on a robe. She hadn't slept well, had replayed her argument with Harper again and again. Just thinking of the horrible things she'd said to her daughter-in-law, to the mother of her grandchild, to the woman her son had loved so fiercely made her sick to her stomach.

But she'd been in the right. Hadn't she? She'd had to tell Harper how wrong she was to get involved with Eddie, with any man. She shouldn't be over Beau so soon, shouldn't have those feelings for another man.

Harper shouldn't be happy, shouldn't be living again when Beau was dead.

Joan went into the kitchen, her heart doing a little flip at the sight of her handsome husband drinking coffee as he stared out the window at the softly falling snow. In the past, she would have gone up behind him, wrapped her arms around his waist, laid her head on his back. He'd turn and they'd embrace. Kiss. Share coffee and breakfast and conversation.

Now she didn't even know how to approach him, couldn't even say good morning because how could it be good when she had so much pain bottled up?

She went to the coffeepot, poured herself a cup and added cream. When she turned, Steve was watching her. Something in his eyes, in his expression gave her pause, had panic coating her throat.

"I'm leaving," he said.

Her shoulders relaxed. She tried to smile but it seemed like such a huge effort, too big to pull off even for her husband. "Early day at work?"

"No." He set his coffee down. Held her gaze. "Joan, I'm leaving you."

Everything inside of her went still. "I don't understand."

"Yes, you do. Our marriage is over. It ended the day Beau died."

Her hands trembled so she sat and tucked them in her lap. "You can't leave me. What will people think?"

"They'll think we drifted apart. That we weren't strong enough to survive the loss of our child."

"He was my child. Mine."

Instead of getting angry, Steve looked defeated. "Right. Your child. Never mind that I'd known him since he was ten years old or that I loved him as much as I love my own children. Never mind that I was here for him every day since we got married, that I stood up for him as best man at his wedding, that he looked to me like a father." His voice broke and his eyes welled with tears. "Never mind that when he died it sure as hell felt like I'd lost a son. That I love him and miss him every single day."

Joan was shaken. She didn't like to think of other people grieving Beau's death, could only concentrate on her own pain. "We can work it out—"

"I don't want to work it out," he said softly. "I'm tired of trying to be close to you when all you do is turn away from me."

That wasn't fair. "I've never denied you."

"Not physically, no. You lie there, doing your

wifely duty, gritting your teeth and bearing it while I feel like some goddamned rapist because I want to make love to my wife. Do you have any idea how it makes me feel when I touch you and you get that blank look in your eyes? To make love to you knowing you've gone somewhere inside yourself where I can't reach you."

She hadn't considered it. But what did he want from her? "I give you all I can. All I have to give."

"I believe that, and it breaks my heart that you won't let any of us help you through this grief, help you move on with your life. That you have so much anger and resentment inside that you'd turn away my children and grandchildren, children and grandchildren who have loved you and respected you all these years. But mostly, it breaks my heart because while I believe you are doing your best, that you're giving me all you can, it's not enough. Not for me. Not anymore."

He stood in front of her. "I love you, Joan. I'll always love you. But I can't live with you. I can't stand by while you slowly die inside, not letting me help you. I'll pack a bag now, get a hotel room until I can figure something else out. I'll come back later for the rest of my things."

And as her husband walked away from her to pack, to leave her, Joan bent at the waist, her arms wrapped around herself, as pain suffused her, had her gasping to catch her breath. She'd been wrong. She wasn't numb inside after all.

HARPER SHIFTED CASSIDY higher on her hip, adjusted her purse which had fallen to hang on her elbow and then knocked on Eddie's door. They hadn't spoken since he'd left the school yesterday and she'd been too upset over everything—his reaction and her continued rift with Joan—to call him last night. But today she was ready to face down Eddie and get things resolved between them.

She knocked again. If he ever answered his freaking door.

Finally, the door opened and there he stood, all scowly and hard-looking.

"Hi," she said, trying to hold on to Cass as she went wild, calling Eddie's name, reaching for him. "Can we come in?"

He looked like he'd rather give her the boot but he finally stepped aside, taking Cass from her before her kid did a nosedive onto the floor trying to get to him. "Do you have a minute to talk?" she asked, shutting the door behind her and setting her purse and Cass's bag on the table.

"Does it matter? You're here, so obviously there's something on your mind."

She pressed her lips together. Oh, there was something on her mind. Giving him a swift kick in the shin being at the top of the list. "I know Max is at hockey practice so I thought now would be a good time to discuss what happened yesterday."

"You went behind my back," he said, setting Cass down when she squirmed. He gave her a Barbie to play with, and she plopped on the floor, began tearing off her doll's clothes. "That's what happened."

"I did no such thing. Look, I know it's not easy for you to consider this but Max needs extra help. All Mr. McNamara was trying to do is what's best for Max."

"I'll decide what's best for my son."

Stubborn, stubborn, stubborn man. "I know this is hard for you, but you can't keep denying what's in front of your face." She softened her words by keeping her tone gentle, laid her hand on his arm. "You're a wonderful father and I know you'll make the right decision."

"You mean the decision you want me to make," he said, backing up.

Her hand fell to her side. She tried to ignore the panic skittering up her spine, how hurt she was by his dismissive attitude.

"I'll do whatever it takes to help you." She had to keep talking, to convince him to let her fix this for him. To at least let her be a part of it with him. "We'll sit down, make some decisions about Max's placement in school."

"You're not putting him in some special class or medicating him for being a boy. I don't want him ostracized."

"He won't be. Things aren't like they used to be. Kids are all integrated into the same classrooms. He'd still be in my class, he'd just go to a different room for the subjects he's struggling with. He'd have work that reflects the level of where he's at. I know once you see how well he can do, how happy he is to have success on his own, you'll see what a good idea this is, how it can only benefit Max."

"I don't want or need your help with my son. Don't you get it? We don't need you to save us."

Her head whipped back as if she'd been slapped. Her fingers went numb. "That's it, isn't it? You don't need me. You don't need my advice as Max's teacher. You don't want my help as someone who cares about you and Max. You don't want me in your life at all."

She held her breath, waiting, hoping he'd deny it but his expression remained closed off. "I think it might be better if we didn't see each other anymore outside of the classroom."

While her daughter played happily at their feet, Harper could only stare at the man in front of her. "So that's it?" she whispered. "I don't agree with you on something and you're just going to toss me aside?"

"It has nothing to do with you agreeing or disagreeing with me. You want to fix me and Max and we're not interested in having you save us."

"Is that what you think? God, maybe you really are stupid." His eyes flashed, his nostrils flared but she was too worked up to care about hurting his feelings or making him angry. He should be hurt after the way he'd hurt her. "I don't want to save you. I want to be a part of your lives."

"Max and I are better off on our own."

"Well, look at you, two rock walls. God, I am so tired of you trying to control everything, including our relationship. This whole time I've let you set the rules, the boundaries, but no longer. I won't be satisfied to sit back while you decide where our relationship will go based on how much of yourself you're willing to give. I'm sick and tired of giving everything I have, my thoughts and emotions and my heart, and waiting to see if it's enough for you. I was so stupid to settle after having a man who loved me unconditionally. I won't make that mistake again."

With her heart breaking, her eyes stinging, she picked up her baby, grabbed their stuff and ran out.

CHAPTER NINETEEN

"HOW WAS PRACTICE?" Eddie asked Max after he'd been dropped off an hour after Harper and Cassidy had left.

Max shrugged.

He'd been quieter than usual following the cheating scandal. On one hand, Eddie wanted to press his kid to talk to him, to tell him what was on his mind. On the other hand, he understood, better than most, that sometimes a guy just wanted to keep his thoughts, his feelings to himself.

Harper hadn't understood that, had accused him of trying to control things. Maybe he had. What was wrong with that? He had to watch out for his heart and, more importantly, he had to watch out for his kid, make sure no one hurt him.

"You want a snack?" he asked Max, opening the pantry door only to be blindsided by memories of him and Harper in there, the feel of her skin, how she'd sounded when she came.

Shit.

He needed to get her out of his head, keep her out. Their being apart was better for all involved. She had to see that, to realize it. He wasn't for her. He was the complete opposite of the man she'd married and he wasn't about to change, not for anyone.

"Max?" he prodded when he realized his son hadn't answered him. "Do you want a snack?"

"No."

Eddie sighed. "Sit down," he said, motioning to the kitchen table.

When Max sat, Eddie took the chair across from him. He remembered having talks with his parents at the kitchen table in the exact same way. They'd always been a unit. Partners.

We should be partners in raising him, but you shut me out.

And damn Lena for sneaking her way into his head.

He didn't need her, he'd do this alone.

Max, his hair sweaty from practice, his cheeks still red, stared at his lap. Eddie struggled to find the right words and decided there might not be right words. He'd just have to go with the truth.

"Did I ever tell you about the time I cheated on a math test?" he asked.

Max's head came up, his eyes huge. "You cheated?" he asked in an awed, scandalized whisper.

"Once." The memory of it still made him feel itchy inside. "I was around Bree's age, maybe a year older, and I was failing math. I was worried if I didn't get at least a C on the next test, Papa and Nonnie wouldn't let me go to basketball camp so I copied the answers of a buddy of mine."

"Did you get in trouble?"

"Not at school. The teacher didn't seem to notice but when I brought home an A, Papa and Nonnie thought it very suspicious that I'd gone from barely passing to getting such a good grade. So, they decided to see if I'd really learned what I needed to in order to pass that test. They got another test from one of the teachers at school and made me take it at home. I didn't do so well and I had to admit to them that I'd cheated."

"Did they take away your video games?"

"They grounded me which meant I couldn't go anywhere or do anything for two weeks. Including basketball camp." It'd been the most miserable two weeks of his life. "I learned that no matter how much I want something, I can't take the easy way. If I wanted a good grade, I'd have to earn it."

Max's head hung so low, his chin hit his chest. "I can't."

"You can't what?"

"I can't get good grades. I try, I try real hard to listen and to understand but things get mixed up in my head and then I forget what Mrs. Kavanagh said and I can't remember how to spell the words and which letters are which." He started crying softly. "Everyone else in class gets good grades. They get stars and happy faces, and it's easy for them but not for me. I'm the dumbest kid in my class."

"Hey, you are not dumb," he said firmly. He stood and gathered his little boy in his arms, sat with him on his lap. "You are bright and creative. Some kids just learn differently than others. It's like not everyone can draw and paint as well as you do."

Max laid his head against Eddie's shoulder like he used to when he was little. "I just wanted to be one of those kids who got a good grade for once."

Harper's words about Max finding success floated through his mind. She was right. He really had been an idiot not to see what his son needed, to let his pride and fears keep him from doing what was best for Max.

"I didn't do very well in school either," Eddie told Max. "But I had help and I'll get you help, too, as much as you need. All I want is for you to do the best you can. It doesn't matter what grades anyone else is getting, you hear me? All that matters is that you're trying your hardest."

Max turned and hugged him, and Eddie knew he'd finally done the right thing. Luckily, it wasn't too late for him to give his son what he needed. He just hoped he wasn't too late to fix things with Harper, either.

"I THOUGHT ABOUT what you said," Eddie told Harper the moment she opened the door.

He stepped forward but she shut the door so that only her body was visible, her message clear. He wasn't welcome in her home.

She didn't want him there.

How dare he show up all glowering and intense

and act as if she should welcome him with open arms? Did he really think she was just going to forget everything he'd said—or, better yet, all the things he'd never said?

"Your thoughts are your own," she said, proud that she sounded so strong and snippy, "and none of my business. You've made that perfectly clear."

He blushed but she didn't feel the least bit remorseful. "I'd like to talk to you."

"So talk."

"Are you going to let me in?"

"No."

That seemed to take him aback. Good. Seemed she could keep him on his toes, off balance like he'd done to her all these weeks. "You were right," he ground out.

"About?"

"Max. He needs help. Lena and I discussed it—"

"You spoke with your ex-wife about this?" There went his lone wolf status.

"We decided this is the best course of action for our son. I'll sign whatever you want, do whatever you need to help him. Including putting him in special classes."

At least that was something. She wondered why he'd changed his mind but she wasn't about to ask. She was done begging him for scraps of information, for his thoughts and feelings. "Good. I'll set things up when I go into school in the morning. Good night."

And she shut the door.

He knocked—make that hammered—on the wood.

She wrenched it open. "Could you keep it down?" she asked quietly. "Cass is in bed."

And the last thing Harper wanted was her daughter hearing Eddie's voice, not when it was such a chore just getting the baby away from him.

"We need to talk," he said, hunching his shoulders. Well, it was cold and windy outside. "About us."

"There is no us. Again, something you've made perfectly clear."

"I want there to be."

Her heart went pitty-pat with joy. She ruthlessly squashed the feeling. "Why?"

He glared. "We're good together."

"You mean the sex was good," she said, beyond disappointed that she'd allowed herself to hope he'd open up to her. Disappointed he didn't care enough about her to do so. "I'm pretty sure both of us can find that with a number of other willing partners."

That idea didn't seem to set too well with him. Too bad.

"I think we should give it a try," he insisted stubbornly. "You and me. For real. A...a..."

"God, you can't even say it."

"A relationship." He stepped forward, lowered his

voice so that it was husky, sexy and intimate. "Let me in so I can convince you."

He could. She had no doubt about that. But she needed more than just sex, wanted more from the man in her life.

She deserved more.

She shook her head, held on to the door, making it clear she wasn't going to budge. Not physically or emotionally. "It's too late. I was going to give you everything I am, everything I have. I would have shared my daughter with you, my heart, my life. But you have nothing to give. Not your heart. Not your thoughts or words. And I realized after I left your house the other night, I want them. I want the man I'm with to have enough respect for me, to care enough about me to give all of that to me and more."

"You want to change me, for me to be someone I'm not," he said, sounding angry and resentful.

"No," she said softly. "I wanted you to share yourself with me fully. But you couldn't even trust me when it came to your son, couldn't trust my opinion. I never wanted you to be anyone other than who you were. I just wanted you to share that person with me. It's partly my fault for expecting so little of you. I thought it would be enough."

"You thought what would be enough?"

She met his eyes and gave him all she had. "Loving you. I thought loving you would be enough but it's not. I need you to love me, too."

I THOUGHT LOVING YOU would be enough but it's not. I need you to love me, too.

Harper's quiet words echoed in his head. Panic slid up Eddie's spine, spiraled through him. He wanted to shout at her that she didn't mean it. She couldn't love him. Love was too big, too powerful. There were too many expectations.

He'd failed at it once.

He wanted to insist she take the words back but he couldn't get anything out past the tightness of his throat. She looked so sad, so disappointed but resolved, too, as if nothing he did could change her mind.

As if nothing he did could win her back.

"Goodbye, Eddie," she said, and shut the door, leaving him out in the cold.

He raised his fist, would have pounded on the door but he remembered at the last moment that Cass was sleeping. Cass. He'd lost her, too. The little girl who'd stolen his heart.

He'd never told her, he realized, his entire body going numb. He'd never told Cass how amazing she was, how smart. He'd never told Cass how much she meant to him. That he'd do anything to keep her safe. That he'd protect her always.

That he loved her.

He'd never told Harper any of that either. He'd never given her the words she needed to hear.

And he'd lost her. Forever.

JOAN SHIVERED IN the cold, almost turned around and went back to her car but she couldn't run now. She knocked on the hotel door.

It'd been two days since Steve left her. Two days she'd lain in bed, the blinds drawn. She hadn't eaten or showered, hadn't brushed her teeth. Hadn't cared what she looked like or what people might think if they knew she was so overcome with grief, with pain, she couldn't even get out of bed.

She'd never been more alone.

Even now she looked a fright—her hair a mess, her complexion wan. She'd forced herself to bathe, to get dressed but she'd only pulled a comb through her shampooed hair, hadn't bothered to style it or put on makeup. She wore sweatpants and one of Steve's old sweatshirts that still smelled of him. She looked like death warmed over and she didn't care.

The door opened and Steve frowned at her. "Joan?" He scanned her from head to toe. "Are you all right?"

She must have been asked that question a hundred times since Beau died, and each time she'd force a smile and say she was fine, that she was getting through it, taking it one day at a time and it was easier each day. But hearing it in Steve's lovely deep voice, seeing the concern and surprise in his eyes undid her.

Tears coursed down her cheeks. "No. I'm not all right. I haven't been all right in so long, and there are days when I don't think I'll ever be all right again."

Steve ushered her inside his room, led her to the bed and helped her sit. She couldn't stop crying, couldn't stop shaking. He got a bottle of water from the mini fridge, opened it and handed it to her. She sipped, spilling it on her pants.

He took the bottle from her, sat next to her, their legs touching. "What are you doing here?" he asked, not unkindly.

"I miss you," she whispered.

He nodded, stared at his hands. "I miss you, too. I've been missing you for over a year."

"I wanted so badly to be strong," she admitted. "I was terrified if I broke down I'd never be able to put myself back together again. It was easier to be numb, to remain that way. But I miss him." Her voice broke on a sob. "I miss my boy so much. Some days it's as if I can't even breathe. And I'm angry. I'm so angry that he was taken away from us, that he won't get to see Cass grow up, won't get to drop her off for her first day of kindergarten or see her graduate from high school, won't get to walk her down the aisle. I'm furious that kid took my child's life, that he pulled the trigger and that I can't forgive him for it. And I'm so resentful of everyone who still has their children, who get to see them, talk to them, hug them and tell them how much they love them. It's not fair. It's just not fair."

He held her, smoothed her hair back. "No, it's not fair. But you're not the only one who loved him. The only one who misses him. Who mourns him."

She lifted her head, looked up at her husband through vision blurred with tears. "No, I'm not and I couldn't see that before and I'm sorry. I'm so sorry I hurt you, that I shut you out. I need you, Steve. I need our family. I can't get through this alone."

He kissed her temple. "You're not alone," he said gruffly. "You'll never be alone."

She held him tight and cried, and when she was done, they lay down on the bed side by side, hands entwined, and talked about Beau, remembered her son. And she knew she'd never get over losing her child, but she would go on.

She would heal.

"Uh, you're not planning my violent and gruesome death, are you?" Sadie asked Harper.

Harper, cutting squares of brownies, frowned at her cousin. "Why would I? And doesn't violent death indicate a gruesome one?"

"To answer your second question, I'm not sure. To answer your first…well…here," she said, plucking the knife from Harper's hand. "Let me take this just to be on the safe side. And maybe you should step away from the forks. They look awful pointy."

"They're forks," Harper said. "If they weren't pointy, they'd be spoons. Now what is it?"

Sadie inhaled deeply and on the exhale said in a rush, "Eddie's here."

Harper couldn't stop herself from glancing over Sadie's shoulder into the great room and, of course,

her gaze immediately zoomed in on Eddie. He stared
right back at her.

Harper had debated about accepting Sadie and
James's invitation to their Christmas party, but ultimately had decided she wasn't going to let her fear
of running into Eddie stop her from doing something
she wanted to do.

"I'm sorry," Sadie continued. "I really didn't think
he'd show. James said he avoids all social gather-
ings that aren't mandatory—meaning ones his mom
and sister throw—and he never actually said he was
coming—"

"It's fine," Harper said, deliberately averting her
gaze. "We run in the same circles—sort of. It's only
natural that we're going to see each other from time
to time. Besides, his son is still in my class and
Shady Grove is a small town."

Small but big enough that she hadn't seen Eddie
in weeks. She'd survived without him. Had gotten
through Thanksgiving and Beau's birthday. The anniversary of Beau's death. It hadn't been easy, but
she'd managed. And she and Joan were working on
repairing their relationship, trying to get back to
where they were.

Harper was surprised Eddie hadn't asked to have
Max switched to another teacher. She was glad. She
loved that little boy and would've been heartbroken
if he'd left her class.

She smiled at Sadie, who knew the whole story
about what had happened between her and Eddie.

"Don't look so upset. It's fine," she said again, giving her a hug. "I promise not to make a scene at your party."

"But I love a good scene," Sadie said.

Harper laughed. "Maybe your mom will drink too many fuzzy navels and get tipsy. That's always fun."

"We can hope," Sadie said, taking a tray of food into the other room.

Harper shut her eyes briefly. She could do this. She could do this. All she had to do was ignore him. It wasn't all that big of a house but there was still plenty enough room—and more than enough people—for her to avoid being around Eddie or talking to him.

"Hi."

Shoot.

She opened her eyes. "Hello."

Eddie stood before her, a grinning Cassidy in his arms.

Harper smiled tightly. "Looks like someone found her favorite guy."

"Deddie's here, Mommy," Cass said, patting Eddie's cheek and gazing at him adoringly. "See?"

"Yes, Cass, I see."

Harper wanted to rip her baby from his arms but that would be cruel as both Eddie and Cass looked pleased as punch to be back together.

"You look pretty," Eddie said, his gaze intense, his mouth solemn.

Her stomach fluttered. She stopped herself from

moothing a hand down the front of her dress. 'Thank you."

Cassidy took his face in both her hands so that he looked at her. "I pretty, too."

He nodded. Kissed her nose, which made her smile. "You're pretty, too."

And while Harper wished she could stand there and try to make idle chitchat with him, she couldn't. Not when it was so hard seeing him, hearing his voice. Not when he was being so sweet to her daughter.

"Come on, Cass," she said, knowing there was only one way she was going to get her daughter away from Eddie without a full-blown tantrum, "I think I hear Santa Claus."

James and Sadie had hired a Santa for the kids.

Her daughter wiggled so that Eddie set her down. "Santa!" she screamed and ran off into the other room.

"Thrown over for a fat, bearded man," Eddie said.

"Yes, well, we women can be quite fickle," Harper said, forcing a lightness she didn't feel. "I'd better go check on her before she gets into the presents under the tree again."

"Harper," he said, reaching for her but she just shook her head and walked away.

She congratulated herself on being so calm, so poised with him as she went into the great room. Sure, her knees were weak and her palms sweaty but Eddie didn't know any of that.

"O Holy Night" played in the background an people milled about, eating, drinking and bein merry. It was her kind of scene. Christmas, bein around people.

She wanted to go home.

Figuring she could slip away in fifteen minute or so, she checked on Cass, who was with Harper' parents. She crossed the room toward them.

"Harper."

She froze. Not because someone had said he name but because Eddie had said her name.

More like bellowed it.

At least it seemed that way coming from the quie Eddie. She slowly turned, her eyes widening to se him standing in the middle of the room, the conver sations around them dying down.

What on earth was he doing?

Her heart sped as he walked purposely towar her. She told herself she didn't like that glint in hi eyes but secretly, she did.

"I miss you," he said, loud and clear. Loud an clear enough for everyone in the room to hear.

She glanced around, lowered her voice. "Wha are you doing?"

"I miss you and Cassidy. Max does, too." He glanced at his son, who nodded shyly then pressed against his grandfather's leg. Eddie faced her again "You're beautiful. I didn't tell you that enough. I think you're the most beautiful woman in the world. You make me laugh. You make me a better man."

His gaze held hers as he closed the distance between them. "I need you. I need you so much. Please be in my life. Please be a part of Max's and my family. Let us be a part of yours. Share your daughter with me, your life."

"I can't," she whispered shakily. "It's too late."

"It's not. Give me your heart and I promise I'll do everything in my power not to hurt you again. I love you. I will always love you. Just…please…say you still love me. That you'll give me another chance."

The entire room seemed to be holding its breath. Harper's heart soared. She was scared, yes, but life didn't come with guarantees. You had to take your happiness wherever and however you could. "Wow, that was quite a speech. How can I possibly say no?"

Eddie kissed her and the room erupted into cheers. He wrapped his arms around her, lifting her and holding her so tightly, she could barely breathe.

Then again, who needed breathing?

When he broke the kiss, he continued to hold her and whispered in her ear, "Tell me you love me. I need to hear it."

She cupped his face in her hands as her daughter had done. "I love you, Eddie. I love you and I will share my daughter, my life and my heart with you. We might not have forever—I've learned it's not a guarantee—but I'll take as many days, hours and minutes with you as I can get."

Eddie grinned and kissed her again as their friends

and family applauded, and Harper knew that it might
not have been the right time for her to fall in love
again, but it was definitely with the right man.

* * * * *

Want more of the Montesano family?
Look for the next IN SHADY GROVE *novel*
by Beth Andrews.
Available in 2014
from Harlequin Superromance.
And be sure to check out
the first two books in the series,
TALK OF THE TOWN
and WHAT HAPPENS BETWEEN FRIENDS.

LARGER-PRINT BOOKS!
GET 2 FREE LARGER-PRINT NOVELS PLUS
2 FREE GIFTS!

HARLEQUIN®

super romance®

More Story...More Romance

REQUEST YOUR FREE BOOKS!
2 FREE WHOLESOME ROMANCE NOVELS IN LARGER PRINT
PLUS 2
FREE
MYSTERY GIFTS

٭٭٭٭٭٭٭٭٭٭٭٭٭٭٭٭٭٭٭٭٭٭٭٭

HEARTWARMING™
٭٭٭٭٭٭٭٭٭٭٭٭٭٭٭٭٭٭٭٭٭٭٭٭

Wholesome, tender romances

YES! Please send me 2 FREE Harlequin® Heartwarming Larger-Print novels and my 2 FREE mystery gifts (gifts worth about $10). After receiving them, if I don't wish to receive any more books, I can return the shipping statement marked "cancel." If I don't cancel, I will receive 4 brand-new larger-print novels every month and be billed just $4.99 per book in the U.S. or $5.74 per book in Canada. That's a savings of at least 23% off the cover price. It's quite a bargain! Shipping and handling is just 50¢ per book in the U.S. and 75¢ per book in Canada.* I understand that accepting the 2 free books and gifts places me under no obligation to buy anything. I can always return a shipment and cancel at any time. Even if I never buy another book, the two free books and gifts are mine to keep forever.

161/361 IDN F47N

Name	(PLEASE PRINT)	
Address		Apt. #
City	State/Prov.	Zip/Postal Code

Signature (if under 18, a parent or guardian must sign)

Mail to the **Harlequin® Reader Service:**
IN U.S.A.: P.O. Box 1867, Buffalo, NY 14240-1867
IN CANADA: P.O. Box 609, Fort Erie, Ontario L2A 5X3

* Terms and prices subject to change without notice. Prices do not include applicable taxes. Sales tax applicable in N.Y. Canadian residents will be charged applicable taxes. Offer not valid in Quebec. This offer is limited to one order per household. Not valid for current subscribers to Harlequin Heartwarming larger-print books. All orders subject to credit approval. Credit or debit balances in a customer's account(s) may be offset by any other outstanding balance owed by or to the customer. Please allow 4 to 6 weeks for delivery. Offer available while quantities last.

Your Privacy—The Harlequin® Reader Service is committed to protecting your privacy. Our Privacy Policy is available online at www.ReaderService.com or upon request from the Harlequin Reader Service.

We make a portion of our mailing list available to reputable third parties that offer products we believe may interest you. If you prefer that we not exchange your name with third parties, or if you wish to clarify or modify your communication preferences, please visit us at www.ReaderService.com/consumerschoice or write to us at Harlequin Reader Service Preference Service, P.O. Box 9062, Buffalo, NY 14269. Include your complete name and address.

ReaderService.com

Manage your account online!

- Review your order history
- Manage your payments
- Update your address

---

*We've designed
the Harlequin® Reader Service
website just for you.*

Enjoy all the features!

- Reader excerpts from any series
- Respond to mailings and
  special monthly offers
- Discover new series available to you
- Browse the Bonus Bucks catalog
- Share your feedback

Visit us at:
ReaderService.com

RS13